# Marry a lady,
# Tom Dilhorne thought.

Well, Hester Waring was a lady. But no lady of the first light would marry him. She was a sensible little thing—clever, too, by the ingenious way in which she answered him when he teased her. Yes, she'd make an excellent housekeeper, and a wife who would know what's what, the right fork to use and what to say and do.

But the idea of getting into bed with any man, especially him, would no doubt send her scurrying away like a hare. She'd nearly run away when she'd seen him that day, for all her brave face. Her dreadful father might have made her frightened of him, but, judging by the way she looked at them, he'd made her scared of any man she met.

Well, Tom knew a trick or two that might bring a smile to Hester's face!

# Paula Marshall

# HESTER WARING'S MARRIAGE

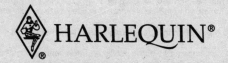

TORONTO • NEW YORK • LONDON
AMSTERDAM • PARIS • SYDNEY • HAMBURG
STOCKHOLM • ATHENS • TOKYO • MILAN • MADRID
PRAGUE • WARSAW • BUDAPEST • AUCKLAND

ISBN 0-373-30456-0

HESTER WARING'S MARRIAGE

First North American Publication 2004

Copyright © 2000 by Paula Marshall

This edition published by arrangement with Harlequin Books S.A.

® and TM are trademarks of the publisher. Trademarks indicated with ® are registered in the United States Patent and Trademark Office, the Canadian Trade Marks Office and in other countries.

www.eHarlequin.com

**Printed in U.S.A.**

## PAULA MARSHALL,

married with three children, has had a varied life. She
began her career in a large library and ended it as a
senior academic in charge of history in a polytechnic.
She has traveled widely, has been a swimming coach
and has appeared on *University Challenge* and *Master-
mind*. She has always wanted to write, and likes her
novels to be full of adventure and humor. She derives
great pleasure from writing historical romances, where
she can use her wide historical knowledge.

# Chapter One

*Sydney, New South Wales, 1812*

'Oh, but,' said Tom Dilhorne, his face alight with amusement, 'one thing is certain. No one is going to accuse me of furthering my own wicked ends if I promote the claims of Hester Waring to be the new teacher for Governor Macquarie's little school. Have you seen her lately? Robert Jardine pointed her out to me yesterday. A more downtrodden grey mouse you never saw. She looks like a lost soul.'

'Oh, we all know your tastes run to buxom blondes, Tom,' said Dr Alan Kerr with a sideways grin directed at his redheaded wife, Sarah, 'and Hester Waring's far from that.'

They had just enjoyed their weekly dinner together at the Kerrs' splendid new villa overlooking the Harbour, and Tom was, as usual, asking their advice on a matter which exercised him.

'The trouble is,' he went on, 'that although she's the only applicant, no one on the Board really wants to appoint her.'

'No one but you, I suppose,' said Sarah, handing him Sydney's newest citizen, Master John Kerr, to hold.

'True,' said Tom, manoeuvring the little bundle gently to avoid damaging his beautiful broadcloth coat—he had lately taken to respectability, and no longer wore the rough clothes of an Emancipist. Emancipists were so called because they were ex-felons, transported from Britain, who had served their time. Those who had arrived in New South Wales as free men and women were commonly spoken of as Exclusives. They were the Government officers, soldiers, sailors and those men and women who had, for one reason or another, emigrated willingly to Britain's newest colony.

Exclusives despised and ignored Emancipists and did not recognise them socially. Governor Macquarie was currently annoying them by attempting to bring Emancipists into the official life of the colony. Tom might be the richest man in Sydney, but he remained a social outcast despite Macquarie's having appointed him to the School Board. The divisions between the two groups ran deep. It might be true to say that Tom's success increased the resentment against him.

Hester Waring continued to dominate the conversation.

'She must really need the post,' said Sarah reflectively. 'Her father, Fred, thought himself one of the foremost Exclusives by reason of his gentle birth, even whilst he was drinking and gambling himself to death. Did he leave her anything, do you know?'

'Nothing but debts,' said Tom shortly, using his spotless handkerchief to mop up his godson's milky bubbles: a sight which caused both Kerrs great amusement.

'Oh, you may laugh,' he told them, grinning himself, 'but a man of parts should be able to manage anything, even a leaky baby,' he added ruefully as John successfully marked out his territory on Tom's new trousers.

In the hubbub which followed Hester was temporarily forgotten, and only after Sarah had taken John off to bed did normal conversation resume again. This time the talk was of something else which would have been an impossibility a few years earlier.

Tom had finished sponging his damaged trousers, commenting that one of the advantages of his former ruffian's clothing was that it did not matter what sins were committed in or on them.

'Pity, when you looked so fine today,' said Alan.

'Yes,' replied Tom. 'I'm practising.'

'For what?' asked Alan, who sometimes liked to be as brief as Tom often was.

'Now that he's put me on the School Board,' Tom said, taking up the wine Alan had poured for him, 'he's thinking of making me a magistrate. You, too,' he added, waving at Alan. 'He asked me to speak to you of it.'

'Oh, how splendid,' Sarah exclaimed. 'You'll be Sydney's first Emancipist Justices.'

'Aye, that's the trouble. There are those who think ex-felons like Alan and me have no right to be on the Bench.'

'Well, if the Governor wants us to be magistrates, then magistrates we shall surely be—in the long run, if not the short.'

Alan was referring to the fact that the Governor's powers were boundless by reason of his distance from England and Government. True, the Government could overturn his edicts, but only after many months had passed.

'It's too soon,' Tom said. 'I've enough to do with the School Board. Let me do well there before moving on to the next hurdle. The long run will be better than the short.'

'Fred Waring must be turning in his grave at the idea of you being a magistrate,' said Sarah, laughing.

'Aye, and that brings me to his daughter again. I trust you, Sarah, to tell me what talents I should look for in a teacher of small children.'

'Patience,' said Sarah with a smile. 'The ability to teach them their ABCs, a little simple figuring, and some history, perhaps, to introduce them to old England.'

'Aye. I thought so. If she can do all that then she should be mistress—if only the Board gives her a fair chance— but Fred made so many enemies.'

'Not her fault, poor girl,' said Sarah and Alan together.

'She probably needs the money, too,' added Sarah. 'Why don't they want her—apart from Fred, that is?'

'Too ladylike and too retiring. Not strong enough to do the post justice. I don't want to condemn the poor thing out of hand, regardless of Fred's dislike of me.'

Hate would have been a better word, Alan thought.

Tom ploughed doggedly on, thinking aloud. 'The thing is, Jardine told me in confidence that she's far worse than respectably poor. He says she can barely afford a square meal and is as proud as the devil, although living on the edge of starvation and penury. Fred left her nothing.'

'As bad as that?'

Both Kerrs looked at one another and then at Tom. 'So you want to make sure they appoint her?'

Tom nodded. Alan thought, not for the first time, what a deceptive creature his friend was. Despite his mild, almost handsome appearance with his sandy-blond hair and his brilliant blue eyes, Tom was quite one of the most dangerous men Alan had ever known, certainly the cleverest and the most devious.

'There's another problem for you, Tom. I suppose that

Miss Waring will be fearful when she sees that you are on the Board.'

'Surely not,' said Tom, his intuition letting him down for once. He never bore minor grudges, they didn't pay, and he had never seen Fred as more than an ineffectual irritant. He had simply been a junior Government clerk who had lost his place in good society through his own folly and who had had no more sense than to cross verbal swords with a master like Tom—and lose.

'I'm afraid that Fred told Hester repeatedly what an ogre you are, Tom,' Sarah said. 'You know what an inflated idea he had of himself—and he really did come from a very good family. Poor Hester was brought up as a lady, even though, once Fred was ruined, they had no money to sustain her in that role. I do hope that you can help her.'

'Oh, aye, but it may be difficult. Depends a little on Hester, too, you know. It's hard to do the right thing for those who won't, or can't, help themselves. But I don't like to think of the lass starving.'

And that was that. All three of them, having eaten well, and sitting in comfort, if not to say luxury, felt a little guilty at the thought of poor, half-starved Hester Waring. They agreed in hoping that Tom might be able to help her before, inevitably, they passed on to other things.

It was the following Sunday, the one day of the week in which Sydney lay quiet under a mid-October sun already beginning to take on summer's heat.

On one side of the town was the boundless sea across which every British inhabitant had come, either willingly or unwillingly. On the other side lay miles of bush; vegetation as far as the eye could see, most of it uncrossed and unexplored by whites, still the home of those aborigines who had not come to Sydney to live naked in its streets, beggars in the land which had once been theirs. They existed only as objects of passing interest, barely more than the wild animals, kangaroos and wallabies which also wandered around the town.

To look upwards was to see the Blue Mountains, vague in the distance, cutting the colony off from the rest of the vast continent. Convict legend held that freedom—and China—lay beyond them. Whether anyone really believed in the China part was dubious. As for freedom, no one who had ever escaped from Sydney and fled towards them had returned to tell whether freedom, or anything else of value, was to be found there.

Hester Waring, unaware that she was the subject of interest among what passed for the great and powerful in Sydney, as well as the notorious, walked out of St Philip's church after attending morning service.

For Hester, it was one of the few times when she enjoyed the society of which she had once been a part. Joining in the service, she could forget for a short time her unfortunate situation, and the hunger which gripped her permanently these days.

Today she had offered God, or whatever power there might be which ruled this cruel world, a small prayer that the letter which she had sent to Robert Jardine, Clerk to the School, and half a dozen other Boards, would bring her some relief from hardship.

She had met him in York Street the day before and he had been kind to her in his stiff, formal way. He had offered her a little, a very little, hope. She clutched that hope fiercely to her, had tried not to show him how much she depended on it, and had walked away, her head high, even if her stomach was empty.

She had not deceived Jardine, who had stared after her gallant, if pathetic, figure. It was painfully obvious to him that she was not eating properly. He was trying to influence Godfrey Burrell in her favour, but he dare not press him too hard—Godfrey would simply fly off in the opposite direction and damn the girl forever.

He had also informed Hester that Tom Dilhorne would be a member of the Board which would interview her. He did not share Fred Waring's view of Dilhorne and, to re-assure her, told her that Tom, unlike others, had torn up Fred's debts when he had died, rather than dun his penniless daughter.

Hester had stared coldly at him. 'The man is detestable,' she had said. 'He did everything in his power to hurt my father. Father told me that no man was safe from his machinations, and no woman, either.'

Jardine had shrugged his shoulders before he left her. There was no point in telling her that she was wrong about Dilhorne's behaviour towards her father—or to women. She wouldn't believe him. He had to trust that, for her own sake, she would not let it ruin her performance before the Board.

Hester left church, hoping against hope that her prayer would be answered. Outside in the brilliant sunlight she made her quiet way through the chattering worshippers, bowing slightly to the odd acquaintance who was prepared to acknowledge that she still lived.

Her old friend Mrs Lucy Wright came up to her when she reached the church gate.

'Oh, Hester, there you are,' she exclaimed. 'I missed you last Sunday. Are you well? You don't look very well,' she finished doubtfully.

Hester resisted the temptation to say, truthfully and savagely, 'Of course I'm not well. I would have thought that plain to the merest idiot and, whatever else, you are certainly not that.' Instead she replied quietly, 'I had an ague last week which prevented me from attending.'

'Oh, I'm so sorry, Hester. You are quite recovered now, I trust?'

Lucy herself looked very well, her whole charming ensemble serving only to make Hester look even more pinched and shabby than she already was.

'Yes, I am quite recovered now,' Hester said, adding nothing further about her ailment or her reduced condition. She was sure that Lucy, for all her easy kindness, did not really want to hear about either of them. She was also acutely aware that Lucy's husband, Lieutenant Frank Wright, had pulled out his watch in an impatiently pointed manner in order to hint to Lucy that she had spoken to Hester for quite long enough.

Well, she, Hester, was not going to take any notice of Frank. Lucy rarely did, going her own way in her cheerfully spoiled fashion, secure in his admiration even if she occasionally exasperated him.

'How is baby, Lucy?' she asked. 'I hope she is still in health.' Her interest was quite genuine. Hester loved babies.

There, that would serve to restore Lucy's wandering attention. Her face had lit up. The way to her affections was through her two-month-old baby girl. She began to talk eagerly of her charms, of how forward she was—there had never been a baby like her. At the same time she was trying to avoid looking too hard at Hester, for the more she saw of her the worse she thought she looked.

Why in the world was she wearing such an out-of-date black dress, which appeared to have been made over rather amateurishly from one of the late Mrs Waring's old gowns? Surely Hester possessed something more suitable to attend church in! It was too bad that she had let herself go completely since her father had died. A reasonable marriage was all that was left to Hester, but who would want to marry such a scarecrow?

Lucy debated handing out some useful advice to her friend about buying a better gown, for instance, or a more becoming bonnet—the one she was wearing was deplorable—but she decided against it. She could almost feel Frank's impatience with her for talking to Hester at all. He was not an unkind man, but he did not approve of his wife's friendship with the late Fred Waring's unattractive daughter who had neither looks, presence, nor money to recommend her.

Beside him, Captain Jack Cameron, who had, for once, attended a church service as other than a duty to his men in the 73rd Highland Regiment, was also growing increasingly impatient. He really had better things to do than stand about waiting while Lucy Wright patronised Hester Waring, whom even the shortage of marriageable women in the colony could not make attractive to Jack—or anyone else's—eyes. Bad enough to endure the Parson's whinings without doin' the charity round afterwards!

Frank's patience finally ran out just as Lucy was on the point of asking Hester to dinner—she thought some company might cheer her up.

He walked over, took his wife by the arm and gave Hester a cursory nod. 'Come, my dear,' he said to his wife, 'dinner will be growing cold and Jack and I are on duty this afternoon. You will excuse us, Miss Warin', I'm sure.'

His look for Hester was so casually indifferent that she timidly dropped her eyes to avoid it. She was only glad that his fellow officer, Captain Parker, for whom she had long nursed a *tendre*, was not there to see her in her present forlorn state.

She put out a hand to touch Lucy's for a moment before

she left, grateful for even this poor contact with the life she had once known. Not for the world would she have told Lucy of her true condition, how much she needed a good meal, how desperate she was for company. She had developed in her poverty a fierce pride which, in happier times, she had not known that she possessed.

'Kiss baby for me,' she said in her quiet, ladylike voice, no guide at all these days to her true feelings. 'I must go, too, my own dinner will be growing cold.' Oh, dear, what a dreadful lie that was! She seemed to be telling more and more of them these days, but to let Lucy know the truth of what was waiting for her was impossible. Lying was inevitable.

The pang which she felt on seeing Frank and Lucy move away to rejoin the others was made all the more sharp when she heard, floating through the clear spring air, Jack Cameron's unkind comment, 'Thought you was stuck for ever with Fred Waring's plain piece, Luce. Haw! Haw!'

Fred Waring's plain piece! Hester's ears burned at the horrid sound, but her fierce pride kept her tears from falling. Better to be alone than be exposed to such insults. She quickened her pace to get away from them all—even going in the opposite direction from her own poor lodgings so that she might avoid their pity and their derision.

Mrs Cooke's house where Hester lodged was of two-storied brick and stood in a lane off Bridge Street which was still unpaved. Like most houses in Sydney it boasted a veranda, and hanging in it a cage containing Mrs Cooke's brilliantly feathered red-and-yellow parrot. It was larger and noisier than most.

Hester could hear it squawking as she neared home. Her father had rented the top floor from Mrs Cooke, an army widow who preferred to remain in New South Wales rather than return home to England.

After his death, Hester, burdened with her father's debts, had asked to keep only one room and to feed herself. She had a little ready money, most of which she had realised from selling the last of the few bits of her mother's jewellery which had escaped Fred Waring's greedy fingers. He had parted with everything he possessed in order to continue drinking and gambling in the vain hope that he might recoup his lost fortune.

Hester was thinking of her father when she mounted the steps to the veranda and stopped to pet the bird which seemed to be as rapacious as most of the parrots in Sydney. At least, she thought, handing the noisy creature a large nut, parrots were properly fed.

She pushed the front door open to find that the house was full of the pleasant smells of a good dinner. She tried not to let her mouth water, only to find her thoughts wandering again. If she were a parrot, she presumably would not want stew, but would prefer nuts. Did nuts smell sweet to parrots?

'Oh, there you are, Miss Waring,' said Mrs Cooke, coming out of her small kitchen. 'I thought as how I heard you. Was there many at church today?'

'Yes,' replied Hester, removing her bonnet. 'Mrs Wright was there. She said that her baby was well.' She made for the stairs, hoping that Mrs Cooke would not offer her any stew. In her present famished state she did not think that she could refuse it, but she would not take charity from Mrs Cooke, no, never!

With a sigh Mrs Cooke, who had already decided to offer Hester some stew, watched her whisk away to her room. Miss Waring looked right poorly these days, which was no surprise seeing that she was not getting enough to eat. Pity that all her fine friends never thought to offer her dinner, or even a little something.

Sitting on her bed in her room, Hester was wondering what she would have said to Lucy if she *had* asked her to dinner. She thought that for one moment Lucy had been on the verge of doing so, but Frank had soon put paid to that.

Well, she hadn't, and Hester had learned not to waste time thinking about remote possibilities, particularly those which were never going to happen. Her dinner would be the heel of a loaf of bread scraped with some rancid butter which the grocer at Tom's Emporium had let her buy cheap, and a withered apple which had just managed to survive to spring. Her drink would be water.

She had just finished buttering the bread when Mrs Cooke put her head around the door.

'I've made some stew today, Miss Waring. I was a-wondering if you might like to help me out by eating it up for me.'

'Oh, dear...' Hester was as pleasant as she could be, hiding the bread and the apple under an old towel '...I'm afraid I've already eaten, but it was kind of you to think of me. Another time, perhaps.'

Mrs Cooke walked downstairs, thinking glumly that there was nothing you could do to please some people. She had been sure, knowing perfectly well how meagre Hester's dinner was likely to be, that she would not be able to refuse such a tempting offer.

Hester, however, felt that she had no alternative. More than her pride was at stake. Once she had accepted Mrs Cooke's charity, where would it end? There had been others who had offered charity to the Warings, but their patience had always run out in the face of her parents' ingratitude—Mrs Waring had been as proud and thankless as her husband. Hester had no wish to find herself bitterly resented, perhaps ultimately turned away, by Mrs Cooke.

If she did both Mrs Cooke and herself an injustice by thinking this, she was not to know and preferred not to find out.

Her meal over, she lay on her bed and—tired to the bone—tried to sleep. Instead she remembered her past; usually she tried to forget it, preferring not to remember why and how the Warings had been exiled from England so that she had ended up, alone and penniless, lost on the frontier of Britain's newest empire.

Her father had ruined himself by drinking, gambling and making unwise investments. Everything had gone: his estate and the house which the Waring family had owned for over three hundred years.

His only comment to his wife and daughter—his son Rowland had died in the Peninsular War—on the new life his relatives had arranged for him, as a remittance man in a penal colony so far away from all he had known, was typical of him in its feckless optimism: 'A new start, my dears, in a new country. We shall make our fortune yet!'

The harsh realities of life in New South Wales and Sydney, which he found when he reached there, drove him immediately back to the bottle which became his constant companion, even in death. Hester had found him at the bottom of Mrs Cooke's stairs one morning, stiff and cold, an empty brandy bottle clutched in his hand.

Mrs Waring had died shortly after settling in Sydney and, once she was gone, no one was ever to know of Hester's suffering during the last years of Fred's life while he declined slowly to the grave.

The worst of it, as Hester painfully remembered, was that Fred had still kept his pride of birth despite the loss of everything which went with it. He, the poor clerk, dismissed for incompetence from the government post his relatives had found for him, but who had once been a country gentleman, had particularly resented the rich and successful Emancipists who flaunted the wealth which he felt was rightfully his.

He had hated Tom Dilhorne most of all because he was the most successful. Going one day to the committee meeting of a small club to which he belonged, he was surprised to find Tom coolly sitting there among his betters. This was before Tom had reformed his dress and he was garbed in what Fred Waring called his felon's rags.

'What is that convict doing here?' he demanded.

The chairman, Godfrey Burrell, a fellow Exclusive of Fred's who was a grazier and entrepreneur of some wealth—and a desire to become even wealthier—closed his eyes at the sight of Fred's red, belligerent face. He was, as usual, barely sober. Tom settled back in his chair and looked Fred straight in the eye with what Fred could only deem was confounded insolence.

'*Mr* Dilhorne is here at the committee's invitation,' Burrell said, stiffly. 'He is a man of substance, a friend of Governor Macquarie and, as such, we have invited him to join the club.'

He might more truthfully have added that in this club, where no women were ever admitted, and would therefore not be offended by having to associate with an ex-felon, they were prepared to tolerate Dilhorne in the hope that they might share in his rapidly growing wealth. A pity to cut one's self off from profit, after all.

Fred was unwise. 'You have invited this…felon…to join the club! Pray, why was my opinion not asked?' There was an unpleasant silence since no one cared to answer him. Fred was tolerated these days, not liked. He flushed angrily.

'I don't care to sit down with transported scum who arrived here in chains,' he said at last, 'however rich he might be, and however much some of you may wish to make money out of him. I tell you, either he goes, or I go.'

Tom leaned even farther back in his chair. He was always impervious to insult. He looked at Burrell, then at Fred, and murmured, 'I have no intention of leaving.'

Burrell's response was to stare coldly at poor Fred. 'And I have no intention of asking Mr Dilhorne to leave, and I believe the committee is of the same opinion. He is here at our invitation. I ask you to change your mind, Waring, and be civil to him. Otherwise, it is you who must leave.'

Fred's pallor was extreme. He had put himself into a position from which there was no retreat. In his early days in the colony he had been a great friend of Burrell's and several other members of the club. But his drinking, his losses at cards, his inability to pay what he had lost, coupled with his own descent into a barely clean raffishness, and his open sexual looseness, had lost him most of the friends whom he had once possessed.

He rose unsteadily to his feet. 'I told you I'd not sit down with Dilhorne,' he replied, 'and I meant it.'

He staggered from the room, ending up at Madame Phoebe's gaming hell and night house, and was later deposited, dead drunk, on Mrs Cooke's doorstep for Hester to haul him painfully upstairs, to clean him up as best she could, and somehow get him into bed.

Later he told her, in detail, of how Dilhorne had done for him at the club, as in business. He had lost his clerkship because of his inattention to his duties, but chose to blame Tom rather than his own carelessness. He never entered the club again: it was his last link with respectability and his own folly had severed it.

Then there were his gambling debts. He borrowed from a friend who sold his IOUs to Tom. Another friend's debts went the same way. Fred found himself owing money to the man he detested most in the world.

Even before his quarrel with the committee over Tom, he had pointed him out to Hester as the author of his misfortunes in language so lurid that Hester had shuddered at it, as well as at her father's persecutor. His subsequent descent into ruin he firmly and unjustly blamed on the man he saw as its author, and he taught Hester to hate and fear him.

Hester rose and looked out the window at the garden below where Kate Smith, the little daughter of Mrs Cooke's neighbour, was playing.

Her memories of her father were always of what he had become in the colony. She could hardly remember what he had been like before he reached Sydney. Dimly she seemed to recall a big, jolly man who had been idly kind to her, although his true affections were always centred on her brother.

And her mother? Somehow she had never seemed to have had a mother at all, and once they had reached Sydney, Mrs Waring had taken one look at it, and gone straight into a decline which ended in her early death.

To be fair to her mother, the town which they had reached nearly eight years ago after a long and miserable sea journey was very little like the town which Governor Macquarie was now so urgently building. Most of the houses had been wooden shacks; to land here must have seemed to her mother like arriving in a wilderness peopled with convicts, strange animals and savages, particularly after her previous life in their beautiful country house in Kent.

She had written to her uncle, Sir John Saville, telling

him of her father and mother's deaths, but she had heard nothing from him. It was all too painfully evident that Sir John had washed his hands not only of his brother-in-law, but of his brother-in-law's child. She was obviously settled in Sydney for life—but what sort of life? What would she do when the last of her pathetic store of money ran out if she failed to be appointed to teach at the new school?

The scene before her disappeared. She closed her eyes, and began to shiver at the mere possibility. If she did not gain this poor post, she knew that there was only one destination left for her. It was one that the penniless daughters of the lesser gentry and poor clergymen had often taken before her, and that was the streets, to sell the one thing which she still possessed—her body.

How much would anyone pay her for *that*? Hester had no illusions about herself or her possible fate. Such a poor creature as she was would command only pennies from private soldiers, grateful for anything so long as it was a woman and available. Unless Madame Phoebe thought that she might make something of her and took her into her brothel.

She must not think of the past. Common sense said think only of the present. It also said that she must sit down and plan what to say to the School Board in order to persuade the gentlemen on it not to listen to Tom Dilhorne so that he might not ruin her as he had ruined her father.

'Dilhorne! Hey, Dilhorne, come here, damn you!'

Tom Dilhorne sauntering, apparently idly, along under the hot midday sun of a busy weekday—although nothing Tom did was ever genuinely idle—ignored the contemptuous cry behind him and strolled on.

The man who had called after him was Jack Cameron, Hester's recent tormentor, who was one of a group of officers of the 73rd Highland Regiment, part of the garrison which guarded Sydney and its surrounding districts in New South Wales in 1812. Several of the officers laughed openly at his anger. It was not that they liked Dilhorne, but Jack was far from popular with his fellow officers.

Jack, aware of their barely concealed amusement, swore beneath his breath, started forward, caught Tom by the shoulder and tried to swing him around. This was a little difficult as he was shorter and slighter than Tom, who was one of the largest men in the colony.

'Damme, Dilhorne. Can't you answer when a gentleman speaks to you?'

'A gentleman, is it? So that's what you are,' muttered Tom, pulling away from the detaining hand, bending his head to look down at Jack from his greater height.

His barely masked insolence was not lost on Jack, who had missed Tom's exact words but had caught his intent. His dark face darkened even further. No damned ex-convict was going to speak to him in such a fashion.

'Goddammit, you felon! If it ain't bad enough to be sent to the ends of the earth, but we have to endure the insolence of the rogues we're sent to guard as well!'

His eyes raked Tom's appearance dismissively. He added, after further looking him up and down as though he were something vile laid out for a gentleman to sneer at, 'Even if you are tricked out to ape your betters these days, Dilhorne, you still look like the scum you are!'

Tom's face remained impassive under these insults.

'You wished to speak to me?' he drawled. He managed, without trying, to sound vaguely menacing.

Jack exclaimed roughly, 'They tell me that you have a hoss for sale. How much d'you want for it? And no tricking me, mind.'

'Shouldn't dream of it,' murmured Tom, bright blue

eyes hard on Jack's black ones. 'If I had one to sell, that is. Only, I ain't.' He brushed the dark blue shoulder of his fashionable coat where Jack had held it, almost absent-mindedly, but the hint of danger which always hung about him was in that, as in everything else he did.

His answer was a lie and the man opposite to him knew it was. True, Tom had had a horse for sale, but the moment Jack had enquired about it, Tom had withdrawn it from the market. He knew of Jack's reputation with dogs, horses and women, and had no intention of allowing his good black to be mistreated by such a creature. Would keep it rather.

Jack's anger mounted. 'You know damned well you have a hoss for sale, Dilhorne. Ramsey here told me of it, didn't you, Ramsey?'

Captain Patrick Ramsey, who didn't know which of the two men he liked less, Jack or Dilhorne—the one being a cad and the other beneath a gentleman's consideration—shrugged his shoulders, and offered carelessly, 'So I thought I heard.'

'There, you see,' said Tom equably, 'A rumour. I'm sorry you were deceived by it, Captain...Cameron...ain't it?'

'You know damned well who I am,' roared the enraged Jack.

'Seeing that we've not been introduced...' Tom began.

This outrageous statement amused all the officers but Jack. Tom thought that, with luck, he might begin to gibber if he baited him much more. The mere idea of a Highland officer and gentleman being introduced to such as Tom Dilhorne...

'If that is all, Cameron—' Tom was now politeness itself '—you will allow me to take my leave.' His manner was so coolly courteous that it added fuel to Jack's anger.

'Sir to me, Dilhorne,' he shrieked, only to find Tom bowing slightly to him and his fellow officers.

'Good day to you, Captain Cameron, gentlemen.' And his bow encompassed the other officers before he turned to saunter away.

Jack began to follow him—only to be pulled back by Pat Ramsey.

'No,' said Ramsey, sharply. 'Dammit, Jack, why give him the opportunity to roast you? Whatever else, he has the wit of the devil. You should know that by now.'

'Take your hands off me, Ramsey,' Jack snarled. 'You know damn well that he has a hoss for sale. He's insulting me by refusing to sell it to me. You know that.'

'It's his horse to do as he pleases with,' said Pat reasonably. 'Why give him the pleasure of taking you down?'

'Because these…Emancipists…and Dilhorne in particular, are getting too big for their boots since Macquarie became Governor here. Who'd have thought that he, of all people, would be sweet on felons? Push them up to be the equal of gentlemen. He'll be making magistrates of them yet. Dilhorne and that low creature, Will French—you'll see.'

'Doing it too brown, Jack,' said Pat easily. He was always one of life's observers. 'Not even Macquarie would make a magistrate of Dilhorne.'

There were times when Pat felt a grudging admiration for the man. Until recently Dilhorne had worn the clothes of an ex-felon. These clothes, loose black or grey trousers and jacket, battered felt hat and a red-and-white spotted neckerchief, were almost a uniform and it was doubtless their lack which had enraged Jack. He resented the sight of an ex-felon losing his outward and visible brand and pretending to be a gentleman by wearing a gentleman's clothes. Only trouble was, rumour said that Dilhorne had made himself the richest man in the colony.

Pat shrugged. That was Dilhorne's business, not his. Stupid of Jack to let the man rile him so, but then, Jack had always been a hot-headed fool unable to control his temper.

To placate Jack he said lightly, 'How about a drink? Wash away the taste of this place a little. Forget we're here when we're in the mess. Imagine we're back home.'

'You're right. At least once we're there we don't have to talk to scum such as Dilhorne and his kind. My dream is to see that impudent dog writhing beneath the lash again before we leave Sydney.'

He called back to the others, 'Come on, let's go in out of the damned sun and pretend that we're anywhere but here, being insulted by felons!'

Tom emerged from his livery stable driving his gig. He looked up and down the road and watched the officers disappearing in the direction of the Barracks. Well, at least they were not there to see the direction in which *he* was travelling. That would merely have served to give Cameron another attack of the dismals so severe it might have caused him an apoplexy.

He laughed to himself, flicked his whip lightly on his horse's flanks and drove in the direction of Government House to visit Governor Macquarie. Passing a chain gang, he raised his whip in reply to a hoarse cry of 'Mornin', Tom,' from one of them, saluting them more courteously than he had done Jack Cameron.

He had been such a labourer once himself, and, if chance now saw him rich, well-dressed and behind a prime piece of horseflesh, he did not allow that to make him forget what he had once been.

Fleetingly, and for no reason at all, he found himself thinking of Hester Waring and the School Board which was meeting on the morrow. He wondered briefly how she was faring before the world of business claimed him again.

# Chapter Two

Hester Waring was painfully trying to make ends meet in the last few days before the School Board met to decide her fate.

Mrs Cooke, taking pity on her, had agreed to Hester's request that she help her in her little business as a sempstress. She was supplementing her late husband's tiny pension by making shirts, dresses and underclothing for men and women, and she was beginning to acquire more orders than she could cope with.

Once she understood that Miss Waring's request for employment was serious, she passed on the less fine work, and also instructed her in the more elaborate sewing. What Hester earned was enough to pay the rent for her room and leave enough over to shield her from total ruin.

Mrs Cooke was beginning to worry about her lodger, who resolutely refused to accept any form of charity from her. She would have been even more distressed if she had known what was beginning to happen to Hester in the false euphoria that near starvation was bringing on.

Ever since reaching Sydney, Hester had acquired an internal voice which said irreverent and dreadful things to her and informed her of people's real motives rather than

their spoken ones. Lately it had developed the unpleasant
habit of using the most unsuitable language which it had
apparently picked up from Fred Waring when he was in
drink, or in the grog shop from which Hester had often
rescued him.

Hester herself never used such language aloud, did not
know where the cynical knowledge about her fellows came
from and was alternately amused and appalled by her Mentor, as she came to call the voice: it so often advised her
what to do. At first she tried to suppress it, but (correctly)
came to understand that, far from driving her mad, it was
saving her sanity.

Her Mentor was now nastily informing her that if she
could not pay her rent or her bills, even Mrs Cooke's kindness would have its limits. No, her only salvation was the
School Board meeting and she would think of that and not
beyond it.

Even so it might not be wise, she thought, to arrive at
the interview in a state of near collapse, so she accepted
Mrs Cooke's offer of tea on the evening before it: it would
be churlish to refuse everything. She happily ate a large
slice of fruit cake, having been slyly informed by Mrs
Cooke that she had made it a few days ago and Hester
would do her a favour by eating it.

Nevertheless, she woke the next morning feeling sick
with fear. She broke her fast with a piece of dry bread and
some butter which Mrs Cooke had given her on the pretext
that it was going off and shouldn't be wasted.

'Surely, Miss Waring, you could find a use for it,' she
said. She knew how important this post was to Hester, and
she handed her a tankard of ale, saying, 'You really ought
to have a little something inside to warm you, Miss Waring, before you go.'

Perhaps the ale was a mistake. True, it had warmed Hester at first, but had also served to increase the strange state of light-headed giddiness which seemed to have overpowered her lately. Hester was not informed enough to know that she was suffering from near starvation and was beginning to display many of its symptoms.

She could not but own, as she examined herself in her cracked looking-glass, that even her best dress was dismal enough and hardly served to improve an already dragged-down appearance. Nevertheless, she did what she could to try to give the impression of eager liveliness which she thought might impress the Board.

All except that monstrous ogre, Dilhorne, damn him—nothing which she did would impress *him*. Hester's Mentor seemed even more disastrously vulgar and outspoken than ever this morning. It was greatly at odds with her downtrodden and demure appearance. Oh, boo to all geese! she thought as she stepped out into one of Sydney's few light drizzles with only a shawl to protect her.

The rain scarcely improved her appearance. Her hair became stuck to her face and attempts to dry it with an inadequate pocket-handkerchief didn't help much.

Jardine, the Board's clerk, raised his eyes to heaven when she came in through the back door, as instructed. He wondered why the girl hadn't taken a little more trouble over her toilette. Besides she didn't look strong enough to do anything at all which required exertion. Even caring for small children seemed beyond her.

'Ah, Miss Waring. Early, I see. Good, good, punctuality is everything,' he said smoothly, carefully concealing his dismay. A kind man, he wished that he had offered her some advice. He knew that she was poor, but even Jardine did not know of the depths into which Fred Waring's daughter had sunk, and how little use his advice would have been since Hester had no means of carrying it out.

He courteously bowed her into an ante-room panelled in cedar. The Board's offices were part of a building given over to minor Government departments and the ante-room was sufficiently large and well appointed to allow Hester to wait in comfort. She saw none of the Board's members. They were obviously using another door. Probably the big one with a huge brass ring in the middle which opened into George Street.

Despite Jardine's approving comment, she soon concluded that being early was a mistake, for once Jardine had taken himself away, murmuring kindly, 'My best wishes for your success go with you, Miss Waring,' she had far too much time to agonise over what was about to happen.

She had just reached the point when she thought that her application was so hopeless that she might as well go home and spare herself humiliation, when Jardine put his head around the door and said that the Board was now in session and would see her.

She found herself in a big room with an oak table facing the door. The Board sat along one side of it. Godfrey Burrell as Chairman was in the middle. There was one empty seat which she quickly realised, on looking around, was the odious Dilhorne's. He had not come after all! She felt so giddy with joy at this reprieve that she hardly heard Jardine ask her for her name.

As though they don't know me already! For she was well aware that all of Sydney knew drunken Fred Waring's unfortunate daughter.

She had just managed to stammer it out and Jardine was writing it down, after Godfrey Burrell had solemnly said,

'The clerk will duly note that in the book,' when a door behind the Board opened, and a man came in.

Hester did not immediately recognise him. The newcomer was a picture of sartorial elegance. It was not only his beautifully cut suit—Hester remembered seeing such in the Warings' better days—but he wore an embroidered waistcoat of a magnificence which she had seldom seen before. Pinky-mauve Chinese peonies rioted delicately across it. Its silver buttons were set with minute diamonds: yes, diamonds, her dazzled eyes told her, and he was carrying a beaver hat in the new style, and an ebony cane topped by a Chinese idol carved from ivory.

He sat down and said in an elegant drawl, 'Your pardon, Miss Waring, fellow Board members and Mr Jardine, but I was detained by the Governor, who asked me to send you his apologies for keeping me. But the matter discussed was urgent.'

It was only when he turned his brilliant blue eyes full on her that Hester realised that this stunning vision, who was also the Governor's friend, was her father's ogre, Tom Dilhorne!

She was so overset by this that she lost track of everything and sat, a picture of confusion, her mouth slightly open. It struck her that the reason she had seen so little of him in Sydney's streets recently was not that he was missing from them, but that she had been looking for someone entirely unlike the man he now was.

Tom, looking down on at her from his seat next to the Chairman, was seized with an enormous pity. If this was the best that she could do for such an important occasion, then she must be at an even lower ebb than Jardine had privately informed him. He also thought that he knew why she had gone such a hectic red, and then an ugly white when he came in, and he damned the dead Fred Waring, something which he was to do with increasing frequency in the coming months.

Dismally aware that her performance, never very brilliant, was rapidly deteriorating into incoherence, Hester pulled back her shoulders and tried to recover herself. Godfrey Burrell asked her, foolishly, she thought, 'And pray, Miss Waring, what are your scholastic attainments—I mean, in the more serious areas of learning?'

As though, she thought disdainfully, I am going to be teaching the little ones Caesar and Livy, but her answer was polite. 'I was taught by my brother's tutor and I have a tolerable command of Latin and some Greek.'

This statement, coolly made, seemed to impress all the Board except the ogre, who leaned forward and asked, 'So you think that a knowledge of the classics will be useful to the youth of Sydney, Miss Waring?'

'That is the Board's decision, not mine, Mr Dilhorne,' she retorted. 'Should they wish me to ground them in *amo, amas*, so be it!'

This show of spirit appeared to amuse the monster. 'And figuring, Miss Waring? How do you stand on figuring?'

'I can calculate a percentage as well as any, Mr Dilhorne.'

'Ah, you would make a useful addition to my counting-house, then, Miss Waring,' he returned smoothly. 'Some of my clerks seem a little unsure about percentages.'

'I thought that I was being hired to teach small children, not your clerks,' was Hester's mutinous—and spirited—response to this sally.

'Indeed, but one likes to learn of competence, wherever one finds it, Miss Waring.'

This exchange of discourtesies would have gone on longer had not Godfrey Burrell glared at them both and in the tone of one calling the meeting to order announced repressively, 'About small children, Miss Waring, I hope that you believe in the old maxim, "Spare the rod and spoil the child".'

Before she could stop herself, Hester, whose face had become increasingly animated as she sparred with the ogre, came out with what she immediately knew was the wrong answer. 'Indeed, I do not believe in the rod, Mr Burrell. I am of the opinion that more is achieved by affection than by severity.'

For some reason which she could not understand, the damnable Dilhorne seemed to find this answer amusing—if the smile he gave her was any indication of his true thoughts. God sink him—a favourite oath of her father's—and his fine clothes, too, was her Mentor's nasty reaction.

In an effort to mend fences which now seemed broken beyond belief, if Robert Jardine's expression was anything to go by, she added, 'But, of course, I should hope to be able to control the children with, or without, the rod.'

Tom would have liked to say bravo to this display of spirit; etiquette demanded that he restrain himself, but it could not prevent him from inwardly noting that there was a great deal more to Miss Waring than her unpromising exterior would allow.

The interview continued. Hester felt that she was hardly covering herself with glory. She was again rude to Godfrey Burrell when he announced patronisingly that he did not expect the girls to be brought along at the same pace as the boys. She next reprimanded the infernal Dilhorne when he asked a perfectly reasonable question about methods of teaching a group of children of different ages and accomplishments.

She was painfully aware that her manner veered between the spiritlessly servile and the unpleasantly rude—the latter whenever she caught Tom Dilhorne's sardonic blue eyes on her. After she had made her unlucky statement about sparing the rod, it was plain that the majority were not happy about her ability to control children, either.

The ogre had thrown his sandy head back and was contemplating the ceiling. She hoped he liked it. He suddenly dropped his head, saw her staring at him and for one dreadful moment she thought that he was about to wink at her. She must be going mad! She put her trembling hands together, and as she did so Tom winced at the sight, so red raw were they.

The interview was at last drawing to an end and she feared by Jardine's expression, the amusement of the ogre—what could he be smiling at?—and the nature of the Board's response to her later answers, that she had thrown away her one chance of avoiding starvation.

What was worse, she also feared that if they did not end the interview soon she would faint before them all. The pangs of hunger, which had grown very strong of late, were beginning to trouble her so much that they were almost unbearable.

Hester would have been greatly surprised to know that there was one member of the Board who was well aware of what was wrong with her, and that was the man whom she so bitterly resented. He was cloaking his pity, which he instinctively knew she would fiercely reject, beneath a mask of amused indifference.

Besides, it would not do to let his fellow Board members know of his sympathy. He must push them gently towards hiring her if he were to take them with him. He had no doubt of her competence: it shone through her weariness and misery.

Presently it was over. Hester, her heart hovering somewhere above her shabby shoes, rose and bowed before leaving the Board to their deliberations. Tom had one last

memory of her at the end of the interview. She was sitting
forlornly before them, head bowed, red hands in her lap.
If he had never seen quiet desperation before, he saw it
then. He listened to his fellow Board members talking and
it was plain that they did not know what was wrong with
Hester.

Burrell's comment was that he found Miss Waring's
manner unpleasant.

'No common sense,' said Fitzgerald sharply. 'She'd not
even be able to control small children. And a plain piece,
too,' he added.

Tom, while agreeing with him about Hester's looks, was
not quite sure what they had to do with schoolteaching.
Some, he knew, might consider her plainness an advantage.

'She's starving,' he offered bluntly. 'That's why she's
so plain and skinny and has such a bad colour.'

They stared at him. But Tom had seen hunger and its
consequences in his London days and he recognised them
in Hester. The sticklike arms, the hollow cheeks and throat,
with the bones sharp against the skin, the face all eyes,
and the eyes dull and sunk into the head, the sallow complexion and the lustreless hair. By her appearance she had
not enjoyed a good meal for years. His dislike for his fellows, always great, grew. Well fed, hard drinkers all, they
would not know a starving creature if it dropped dead before them.

He judged it time to intervene on her side by saying,
'Fred Waring's money, such as it was, went on drink for
himself and, now that he's dead, God knows what she's
living on. What's more important, though, is that I think
she could control the children—there's spirit there—and
she has the knowledge to teach them effectively. She spoke

to me sharply enough and once or twice when speaking to you, Burrell, what she said was very much to the point.'

Godfrey Burrell announced pompously, 'I sense that the feeling of the meeting is against you, Dilhorne.'

Tom grinned—he was suddenly a blunt Yorkshireman again. 'Aye, well, it wouldn't be for the first time, would it? But if you turn her down, think on. What do you propose to do? Who will fill the post? She was the only applicant. Do we have to wait for another ship from England to dock—and find that there's no one suitable on it? What then?'

'There's that,' Burrell conceded.

They contemplated their lack of options gloomily. It was clear that none of them wanted Hester, and that for all the wrong reasons. Most would sooner delay opening the school rather than employ her, despite the Governor's wish for an early start.

Fred Waring's ghost had risen from its grave to haunt his unfortunate daughter. Lack of imagination also meant that they could not understand the consequences for the girl if they failed to appoint her.

Tom did not push Hester's claims further. To do so might antagonise them. With his usual grasp of possibilities he saw a way out. 'Let's compromise,' he offered. 'Put her on probation. See how she does. If she don't suit, then out she goes. We might find someone else by then.'

They wrangled a little more but, as was becoming increasingly common in their meetings, they ended by accepting his suggestion. Miss Waring should be given three months' trial and count herself lucky she got it.

Tom leaned back in his chair, content that he had had his way, content that the Board were hiring a worthy teacher, and also content that plain Miss Waring would not need to walk the streets to find employment. Though a man would have to be desperate to buy her for his bed in her present state.

Hester, waiting in the ante-room, felt each minute that ticked by was another blow to her hopes. She was sure that she would fail, and that Tom Dilhorne would be the author of her failure. Perhaps if he had not been on the Board she might have succeeded. He was bound to dislike promoting the claims of a Waring after his clashes with her father.

She did not care for the way in which he had looked at her. Her father had often said that he was a womaniser—but it could not be that. Common sense—and her glass—had told her clearly of her own lack of attractions. A man as rich and as unscrupulous as he was could have his pick of women, both respectable and from Madame Phoebe's.

Mrs Cooke had told her once, after her father's death, that Tom Dilhorne didn't chase women. 'It's just that he's not the marrying kind,' she had finished. 'He keeps the Widow Mahoney, who's been my friend for years, and leaves it at that.'

Well, marrying man or not, she had never thought that her fate would depend on a Board with Tom Dilhorne on it. Were her father alive, he would have had her out of the room in an instant—once he had recovered from the shock of seeing an ex-felon enshrined in state, that was. Just as well, perhaps, that he was not alive.

She had to acknowledge, however, that the wretch was a lot better looking than she had expected, quite handsome in an odd way—though he did not attract *her*, by no means. But she had to admit that he was very well turned out, particularly his waistcoat. *That* was very fine.

At this point Hester twisted her hands in her lap. If the Board did not return soon with their verdict, she feared that she might faint before them from a mixture of fear and hunger.

She sat up smartly. Oh, no, I won't, she thought, and if they turn me down I won't cry or have hysterics, although God knows what I shall do if they don't appoint me. Her mind went round and round until she felt dizzy, so that when the door opened and Robert Jardine beckoned her in she gave a great jump and turned a white scared face towards him.

'The Board will give you their decision now, Miss Waring,' and he held the door open for her.

She walked in, her head high, a little colour staining her thin cheeks. She tried to keep her hands still as she bowed to them, and waited for the Chairman to speak. Her father had been a friend of Godfrey Burrell's before drink had destroyed him. Once, when she was a little girl, he had given her a paper of sweets—but that was long ago.

He began in his usual pompous style. 'Miss Waring, the Board is prepared to offer you the post, provided that you understand that you must serve a probationary period of three months to determine your suitability. If, at the end of that time, your performance is not satisfactory, you will be dismissed forthwith. Mr Jardine, the clerk, has so minuted. Do you understand me?'

'Perfectly,' said Hester shortly, staring blindly in the direction of Tom who shifted uncomfortably in his chair at the sight of her evident distress.

Godfrey Burrell felt impelled to make Hester fully aware of the precarious nature of her appointment. 'I feel bound to tell you, Miss Waring, that the Board has made you this offer with some reluctance. There are those among us who fear that you will not be up to the task. It is to be hoped that you will prove them wrong.'

I was right, thought Hester. It's Tom Dilhorne, still trying to get back at Father. Well, damn him, I'll prove him wrong. I'll have to prove him wrong. It was impossible for her to imagine the truth: that only her father's ogre had saved her.

'I will do my best to give you satisfaction,' she added steadily.

'Good, good.' Burrell was in haste to go to his dinner. Something about Hester disturbed him. Probably Dilhorne was right again, damn him. As he looked at her, it seemed possible that she was not getting enough to eat.

He had a sudden flash of memory of the pretty little girl she had been when the Warings had first arrived in Sydney. He shifted uncomfortably in his chair. Well, they had given her a chance, which was more than many got. He indicated the clerk, standing by the table, head bent.

'Jardine will give you the particulars of your post and he will be in charge of your remuneration. He will give you a small advance to tide you over until pay-day. If you wish to communicate with the Board, you will do so through him. So far as monitoring your performance is concerned, I am proposing that Mr Dilhorne shall oversee you for the next three months.'

What the devil does he know about education, or teaching, for that matter? thought Hester's Mentor nastily. I'll see him and the rest of you in Hell before I give you the satisfaction of dismissing me.

Hester's expression was so demure that the only person who could detect the seething rage behind her subservient mask was Tom himself. He had seen her eyes change while Burrell was speaking, and he knew dumb insolence when he met it. His almost-feminine intuition told him that there was more to her than met the eye.

Plenty of time to find out, though. The Board's remit meant that he would have the opportunity to discover exactly what poor plain Hester Waring was made of!

# Chapter Three

Lachlan Macquarie was reading the brief report sent to him by Jardine concerning the School Board's decision to appoint Hester Waring on probation, thinking to himself that he saw the Machiavellian hand of Tom Dilhorne in its form, when Lieutenant Munro put his head around the door to inform him that Colonel O'Connell, his successor as Lieutenant Colonel of the 73rd Foot, had arrived and was waiting to see him.

He sighed and put the report down. O'Connell's visits these days were not usually pleasant ones. He disliked intensely many of the measures which Macquarie was introducing, seeing them as pandering to the convict population. He wondered what it was that O'Connell wanted to complain about this time.

'Send him in,' he ordered wearily.

O'Connell was a big man, running to fat in the peace of Britain's southernmost frontier.

'Good to see you,' said the Governor after the formalities had been dispensed with.

O'Connell grunted, and said coolly, 'You might not be so happy when you've heard what I have to say.'

'No?' said Macquarie. 'What is it this time, Jock?'

'Dilhorne,' returned O'Connell heavily. 'There's a rumour goin' around—I don't know whether there's any truth in it, mind, since it seems to have started with Jack Cameron…and you know how unreliable *he* is—that you intend to make a magistrate out of Tom Dilhorne of all people. The man came here in chains, he's still as artful as the devil, has taken over everything in sight—they say that somehow he's even persuaded the Yankees to let him in on their whaling business.

'You know as well as I do that he owns a controlling interest in the brickfields—I curse him every time the wind blows from that direction and covers us all in red dust—he monopolises haulage, is probably the man behind Dempster's woollen mill, is fighting Will French for control of quarrying, and on top of that, is almost certainly the money man behind the building contractor who is changing Sydney for you…'

He ran out of breath before he had finished detailing the whole of Tom's empire in the colony. After all, Macquarie knew its scope as well as he did.

'All of that,' returned Macquarie coolly, 'would justify me in making such a man of substance a magistrate rather than not.'

'Goddammit,' roared O'Connell violently, 'the man's a felon! And how did he gain such a control of everything so quickly, tell me that?'

'Ex-felon,' said Macquarie, determined not to be ruffled. 'He has served his term, and I have no reason to believe that he has been criminal in acquiring his wealth. He's known, in fact, for being a man of his word. All the more credit to him when you realise that he arrived here as a very young man with absolutely nothing. I consider that such a career deserves to be rewarded, not punished. The colony needs such people.'

'Needs such people!' howled O'Connell, fascinated. 'What in God's name has happened to you, Lachlan, since you became Governor here? I never thought that you, of all people, would be soft on criminal scum. What a cake you're making of yourself.'

'Tom Dilhorne is a talented man,' said Macquarie steadily. 'He is bound to stay here, he cannot ever return to England, and the colony needs men of intelligence and vision whose allegiance is to Sydney and to New South Wales and not to some imagined home months away in the Northern Hemisphere. I have no doubt that he will make an excellent magistrate, not least because he understands the mentality of the people who will be brought before him.'

'Dammit!' O'Connell was beside himself. 'Of course he'll understand them! That's the rub. He's one of them. Sophistry, Lachlan, sophistry. I didn't believe Jack Cameron when he prophesied this, but even he seems to have more sense than you. Where will it all end, eh? Tell me that?'

'I can't agree with you. I had better tell you now that I also wish to make Dr Alan Kerr a magistrate, too. But until Dilhorne agrees to be one, I shall not invite him. I want to appoint them together.'

'Make Kerr, a traitor and a mutineer, a magistrate! Wait until Dilhorne agrees! D'you tell me that he has had the infernal gall to refuse you? Or can it be that he has more sense than you?'

'Dilhorne is a wary man, as I suppose even you might grant,' replied Macquarie severely. 'And he is as eager as I am that we do not go too fast. He is already on the School Board and has shown himself most helpful and useful there.'

'Oh, appoint him Deputy-Governor and have done,'

snarled O'Connell nastily. 'Really, Lachlan, all this comes from your nonsensical notion that this hell-hole surrounded by impenetrable bush will become a great capital city to rival those of Europe! Imagine it, peopled by convicts and light skirts, the dregs of Britain!

'As well make legislators and magistrates of kangaroos, wallabies and aborigines as put Tom Dilhorne on the Bench. And as for Kerr... He may once have been a gentleman, but he's as bad as Dilhorne. He wants convicts' food improved, and demands better housing for them. What next, I ask you?'

He had almost choked himself to a stop. He started again. 'Face it, Lachlan, this place has no future except as a useful penal settlement and, by your conduct, you ain't even allowing it to be that.'

Macquarie's whole body was stiff with anger. He was visibly controlling himself as he replied to the infuriated O'Connell.

'I can't agree. But I can see why you think as you do, because you are only looking at the short term, which really is not surprising, because the short term is all that you and the 73rd have. Give Dilhorne the benefit of the doubt. Some of the Exclusives, like Godfrey Burrell, are already doing so.'

'I'd give him a cat-o'-nine-tails for his back, rather,' replied O'Connell, rising and jamming his shako on his head. 'No point in talking to you these days, Lachlan. But I warn you that my officers are most disturbed by what you are doing, proposing to entertain such as Dilhorne and Kerr at Government House, having them to dinner with officers and gentlemen and gentlewomen of good family. You are storing up trouble for yourself.'

'But that will not prevent me from doing my duty, and

if I see that my duty lies in making Dilhorne a magistrate, then that is what I shall do.'

O'Connell's only response was to bang uncivilly out of the room, leaving the Governor to sigh at a world in which he found himself more sympathetic to an ex-felon than to his old comrade-in-arms and friend. Given time, Dilhorne, and men like him, could create the kind of society in New South Wales which Macquarie wanted to see.

Tom Dilhorne was not thinking either of Governor Macquarie or of Hester Waring. It was his own changing life to which he was giving his mind and to its effect on his long-term mistress, Mary Mahoney.

She had always said that she did not wish to marry him, but recently he had become aware that as she grew older she was changing her mind about marriage. In consequence he had to face a truth about himself and her. He might wish to marry, but if he did, he would not want Mary Mahoney for a wife, nor did he think that she would be happy with him for a husband.

Only long-term loyalty and a sense of decency kept him with her. He could see no way of ending their liaison without hurting her, so he was tied to her, and that, as he often said to himself, was that.

He was handed his freedom in the most unexpected manner, one which made him laugh at his own conceit in thinking that he was the only one of them who was dissatisfied.

On paying his weekly visit to her she told him quite coolly, even if with some regret, that their relationship was at an end.

'A good man wishes to marry me, Tom,' she said, 'and you never will. Besides, I'm not the wife for you now. You're not the man you were, you've changed, and what once might have worked now will not. You'll be wanting a fine lady for a wife, Tom, someone like Sarah Kerr, someone to whom you can talk, who will live easy in your grand new house as I never would, or could. I could never entertain the nobs, nor do I want to.'

He said nothing—and that, too, she understood.

'It's been over for you for some time, but for all your reputation you're a good man, and you wouldn't turn me away after so long. No, don't deny it.'

'You're sure you want this, Mary?'

'Quite sure—and you want it, too.'

He could not deny what she had said so simply.

Instead he said, 'I'll see you right, Mary. You may have this cottage, and a little income.'

When she would have refused him, he insisted. 'Who knows,' he told her, 'what you might need in future?'

At length she agreed with him, and they parted in friendship, without bitterness.

'Find that grand wife, my love, and find her soon,' she bade him as she kissed him goodbye.


Tom had said he'd keep an eye on Hester and he always carried out his promises. Strolling by her school, which was in one room of a converted warehouse in York Street, on a bright and shining morning not long after Mary Mahoney had given him his *congé*, he heard the sound of childish laughter coming from the schoolroom. He rejected the idea of peering through an open window to find out what was happening—too undignified—instead he entered through the front door. The classroom door was ajar, and he stood quietly outside so that he could not be seen.

That was undignified, too, but he did not want Hester to know that he was there. His presence would distract her, she would behave unnaturally, and for some reason he

wanted to find out what she was like when she was unaware of being watched.

She was sitting before a group of little children, a smiling baby girl on her knee, reading to them from a children's book which was one of the few relics of her old
life in England. Behind her were two small groups of boys
and girls painstakingly copying pot-hooks on to their slates
from two larger slates which she had propped up before
them.

Her face was alight with mischief. She was still painfully thin and starved-looking, her clothing was shabby
and old, but her expression and demeanour were so different from those he remembered from the interview that
he drew in his breath a little at the sight. There was no
doubt that she was in full control of the class and that
she—and they—were happy.

He listened to her amused voice and watched her absent-
mindedly hug the little one to her. She was not only
starved of food, he thought suddenly, she was starved of
affection. The story over, she put the child down with
some reluctance.

Tom judged that this was the moment when he could
show himself. He made a great noise of coming in so that
she might not know of his earlier presence. He entered the
schoolroom to find that her face was shuttered again. The
liveliness in it was gone, and the old look of barely suppressed fear was present at the sight of him.

In God's name, what had that drivelling fool Fred Waring told her of him to frighten her so? Or was she like this
with all men?

Hester gazed dumbly at him in his gentlemanly finery.
Why was he here? Had he come to torment her? She had
been so happy a few minutes ago. She watched him walk
across to the group of very young children to whom she

had been reading. He put his hand in his pocket to do something which he had seen his old friend Dr Alan Kerr do many times to disarm little ones.

'I've a paper of comfits here, my dears. Do you think that your teacher will allow you to share them?'

Hester looked at him stonily. Then, to her dismay, she heard her voice come out in a squeak. 'Of course.'

Tom handed her the packet, and she divided the sweets among the children while he watched.

'I thought that I'd come to see you without warning,' he drawled. 'Better for you and the children, too. I told the Board that I would check your progress regularly.'

Damn him, thought Hester, dismally aware that her Mentor's language deteriorated even more than usual in his presence. What does Dilhorne know about anything that gives him the right to check on me? But meekly, head bent, she explained what she was doing in a defeated manner which contrasted so strongly with her behaviour when she had thought that she was alone that it was almost as though he had imagined what he had previously seen.

Tom grinned inwardly. He decided to see how Miss Waring's defeated manner would stand up to a little teasing provocation. When she had finished he looked at her earnestly, and drawled, 'The Latin, Miss Waring? When do you get to the Latin?'

She stared at him. What could he be talking about?

'The Latin which you promised the Board. Or was it Greek? *Amo*, I believe you said. What exactly does that mean?'

'I love,' she replied, before she could stop herself, her expression stupefied and her Mentor screaming, Is the man mad?

'You love.' His expression was as grave as a parson's.

'When do you begin to teach the little ones this important discipline?'

'I shall not teach them Latin,' returned Hester repressively. 'The mere idea is ridiculous.'

The lunatic ruffian appeared to consider this.

'If you say so,' he remarked dubiously.

'I do say so!' Hester was more firmly repressive than ever.

'Then Greek, perhaps?' The air with which Tom offered this might almost have been described as helpful.

Could the man be serious? There was not the ghost of a smile on his face.

'I shall not teach them Greek, Mr Dilhorne. Mother Goose is quite sufficient for them at this age.'

How can I be having such a ridiculous conversation with a man who, whatever his other faults, is supposed to be inconveniently clever?

'You relieve my mind, Miss Waring. The mere idea of a roomful of youthful prodigies was beginning to worry me.'

Madder still. Hester had an insane desire to laugh. Indeed, her voice wobbled a little with amusement as she answered him. 'I have no intention of creating prodigies, Mr Dilhorne.'

'Splendidly said, Miss Waring. Nursery rhymes and easy sums are the thing, I see. You have set my mind at rest. I shall not be haunted by thoughts of overset children.'

Hester gritted her teeth to prevent the giggles from escaping. 'You may rest easy, Mr Dilhorne. I have no intention of oversetting them. Neither do I intend to teach them percentages or the rudiments of Hebrew.'

Her whole face, her body, her speech had changed. She was warm and living where previously she had been cold and inanimate. She was now twitting him with the memory of the foolish questions of Godfrey Burrell. Defeated Miss Waring had flown away, to be replaced by a lively girl who possessed a sharp wit and was not afraid to use it to try to set Mr Tom Dilhorne down. He decided to reward her immediately.

'Excellent. I am glad to hear it. I shall be exceeding happy to report to the Board that I find your performance most satisfactory, Miss Waring.'

'Thank you, Mr Dilhorne. I should not like to think of you being haunted, either by overset children—or anything else.'

Bravo, Miss Waring, was his internal response. His provocation had brought colour to her cheeks, a sparkle to her eye and her whole body vibrated with a combination of amusement and indignation. Judging by her expression, her opinion of Mr Tom Dilhorne would have been interesting if made aloud.

He bowed to her, she bowed back and ordered the little boys to bow to him, and the little girls to curtsy.

'Splendid, very well done,' was his comment to this. 'You are obviously teaching them their manners as well as Mother Goose. I regret that I must leave you after so short a time, Miss Waring, but I have, alas, a meeting to attend. I remain your most humble and obedient servant,' and he bowed elaborately on the last word.

You were never my servant and you may go to the devil for all I care, thought Hester, flashing him her most demure smile while she bowed to him. But he had seen the look in her eye and he knew what it meant: Miss Hester Waring was inwardly roasting Mr Tom Dilhorne again!

'What are you doing here, Tom Dilhorne?' asked Madame Phoebe, née Fanny Dawkins, who ran a most respectable gaming hell and brothel in one of Sydney's new-est streets, most such houses being found in less reputable quarters like The Rocks. Only the rich, the outwardly re-spectable and the officers from the garrison patronised Phoebe's, particularly since you could get a good meal there, although how she managed that, Sydney always be-ing short of good food, was a mystery known only to her-self and Tom Dilhorne. Better than that, she ran an honest house and provided clean girls, so authority winked at her presence in a respectable suburb.

Tom, who had changed into his working clothes after leaving Hester, said nothing. He had been helping to un-load cargo on the docks since he never refused even man-ual labour when the need arose, one of the reasons why those who worked for him were loyal. He rarely explained himself, and did not care to tell Phoebe that he was at a loose end since he and Mary had parted company.

In his earlier, wilder days he had been a constant cus-tomer at Phoebe's, in her first house on the edge of The Rocks, not for the girls, but to use it as a meeting place for business and to play at cards—but never at dice.

Boredom had brought him back after a long absence. He knew that the officers of the garrison and the richer Exclusives and Emancipists would be there and it would be an opportunity to discover whether his old skills had grown rusty. The mixture of intuition and sheer cold cal-culation which made him such a formidable businessman was equally as formidable when applied to cards—which was why he never became involved with dice. Games of pure chance held little appeal: there was nothing for him to control.

In the past his presence at the table had deterred some, but was a challenge to others. To say that you had beaten

Tom Dilhorne was almost an accolade and one that was but rarely earned.

'It's his memory, isn't it?' said green young Ensign Osborne to Captain Pat Ramsey, as they watched Tom who, before playing, was drinking with Madame Phoebe. She was known to have a soft spot for him. There were those who would not have believed the truth that they had never been lovers.

'I never get into bed with anyone I'm going to do business with,' Tom had once said, years earlier, to an impertinent question about his relationship with her.

'Parker says that he seems to remember every card he plays—and yours as well. I've always wanted to see him in action, but he's not been here for some time. What brings him here tonight, I wonder?'

'His memory, is it?' said Pat, who had lost to Tom more than once. 'I doubt if it's as simple as that. He knows the odds, does Tom, and he knows men, and it's something you can't teach anyone. I shouldn't get into a game with him, if I were you, Osborne. Depend upon it, he'd fleece you.'

'He wouldn't fleece me,' sneered Jack Cameron, who had come up as Pat was speaking. Cameron's own bad temper and rather surprising good luck seemed to go together.

'No?' Pat shrugged. 'You've not played against him, have you? Is it because he's an Emancipist?' For Jack, who had little beyond his pay, had become even more fierce in his condemnation of Emancipists since Dilhorne had refused to sell him his horse.

'Damn him, no,' snarled Jack, flinging himself into a chair. 'His money is as good as anyone else's, ain't it? It's chance I've not met him on the tables. He gave up coming here before I arrived from home. We'll see how good he is tonight. I've a mind for a game with a so-called master.'

He looked around for those he considered easy marks to make up a table. 'I can see Parker, but where's young Wright these days? I thought he'd be here tonight.'

'Oh, Frank.' Pat yawned. 'He's a dull dog since he married Lucy Middleton. She won't let him play often. He rarely visits Phoebe's now.'

'Damme if I'd let any skirt, wife or not, keep me from play,' said Jack contemptuously. He swung around in his chair and shouted rudely across the room to Tom.

'Hey, Dilhorne, they tell me you're a master. Why not take a hand with us and let me find out? Be a pleasure to take an Emancipist down.'

Tom regarded Cameron mildly. He was drinking brandy and water and, since he had come to play, his glass contained a great deal of water and very little brandy. While other men drank deep while they played, Tom only seemed to. More than one of the glasses of rum, brandy and fierce rot-gut whisky which he appeared to swallow had ended up watering Madame Phoebe's potted palms or the floor.

'Happen I will,' he drawled, and made his way over to the table.

Tom knew full well that Jack Cameron's reputation as a gambler, both on the tables and at other games of chance, was suspect. However, to accuse a man of cheating at cards was something few cared to do.

There was a code of honour about these things and Jack's cheating would have had to be sufficiently marked for anything to be said or done. A false accusation, or one which could not be sustained, would ruin the accuser, instead of the accused. Those caught cheating at cards or dice became pariahs. Honour demanded that they resign from the army and decent society.

Tom knew of, but cared little about, codes of honour. Gentlemen invented them to pass the time. The only code for which he cared was that governing survival. To survive you did anything, played any trick, destroyed enemies, defended friends fiercely, although if you were sensible you didn't have too many of them. You kept your given word, but only if others kept theirs, and avoided stupidity—such as cheating at cards.

Above all, you watched your back. Honour was keeping to your own rules, not some imaginary niceties which merely served to perpetuate social differences.

So he began to play against Jack, using his excellent memory as the young officer had said, calculating the odds, and finally employing his intuition which rarely failed him at cards, as in life.

He soon knew that Jack was cheating, and that most of the other players were too green, or too drunk, to care. Too drunk to notice that the brandy in the bottle before Tom, its level dropping, was not going down his throat. He thought, too, that Jack also was not as drunk as he appeared to be, and slowly he and Tom were the only consistent winners.

Tom's success in life was partly based on his knowledge of how far to go in any enterprise. His cold eyes on Jack, he rapidly came to the conclusion that he was going to come off second best in any game he played against a man whose skill was nearly equal to his own, but who had the advantage of misusing the cards by false deals and shuffles and sheer sleight of hand. The deck had probably been marked, but Tom had no interest in how that had been done.

He had no objection to losing in fair play, but he had also no intention of enriching the grinning sharper opposite to him. Neither did he want the trouble of exposing him,

and to cheat him back—using his own conjuring skills—
would be to invite trouble for himself, the criminal out-
sider.

After a decent interval he stood up. His winnings had
diminished in the last few hands. He scooped up his remaining counters, staggered realistically, yawned and said,
'I've had enough. Time for bed.'

Jack leaned forward, sneering. 'Scared, Dilhorne?
Frightened of losing? Take another hand. Let's see who's
master.'

Tom was all drunken charm. 'Oh, you're master, right
enough—but of what, I'd not like to say.'

He staggered again, picked up the brandy bottle and in
his turn grinned at Jack in the deathly silence which had
followed his last words.

Jack, his face now purple, glared furiously at him.
'What's that, Dilhorne? What's that? I'll not have an ex-
felon impugn my honour.'

Tom swayed, held on to the table to steady himself,
waved the brandy bottle and took a long pull at it, a genuine one, this time. 'Impugn your honour, is it? I was
merely wondering what you were best at. Picquet or Ha-
zard, which would you say?'

His speech was slurred but his eyes were impudent. The
watching men, who ranged from the officers of the garrison through moneyed settlers down to a few who had come
to see the fun rather than play, like Jack had the choice of
taking his words at their face value, or of seeing them as
a veiled accusation of cheating—which both Tom and Jack
knew that they were.

'Put up, or shut up,' Jack roared. 'Dam' well say what
you mean!'

Tom sat down with a crash clutching the brandy bottle
to his chest. 'What I mean is, Cameron, I'll not play with

you again. Not tonight, not tomorrow, or ever. You're too purely skilful for a poor ex-felon.'

His last words came out in a clear, though mumbled, drawl, and after he had finished speaking he fell headlong under the table, still clutching his bottle. He lay quite still while the remaining liquor in it ran along the floor to soak his shirt and breeches.

Pat Ramsey, who had left the game a loser, much earlier, began to laugh. Like many of his fellow officers, he had long had his suspicions of Jack. He had neither dared to voice them nor stop playing with him, which would have been tantamount to an accusation.

But in a few well-chosen words the master of deviousness who lay prone under the table, had said what everyone in the room thought—and there was nothing Jack could do about it. To go on insisting that Tom had accused him of cheating would have been to protest too much. If there were those who suspected that Tom's drunkenness was a masterly ploy, there were none who cared to test it.

What was worse, the accusation, however cloaked, had been made, and there were those around the room who would now use Tom's words as an excuse not to play with Jack—he was a master. It would be a folly to throw money away playing against him.

Lying under the table, eyes closed, Tom laughed to himself at the altercation which followed. Jack loudly expressed his intention to pull Tom up, and deal with him. He was told not to be a fool.

'When a man is incapable through drink,' drawled Pat Ramsey, delighted to see Jack put down for once, 'you can't attack him for no reason at all.'

He smiled sweetly in Jack's enraged face. 'He's just complimented you. What's wrong with you, man?'

There was a lot wrong with Jack, but one thing he knew.

Somehow he would get even with that damned felon Dilhorne before he left this benighted hole to which he and the 73rd had been consigned.

I'm happy down here, thought Tom, not so uncomfortable that I can't sleep. Which he did, tired by the day's exertions, his last memory, unaccountably, being of Hester Waring mocking him that morning, until, as dawn approached, Madame Phoebe arrived, stared at the recumbent bodies littering the floor, and took the trouble to prod Tom awake and push him to her room.

'Don't try to tell me you were drunk, Tom Dilhorne, I know better.'

About the time that Tom was having his fun with Jack Cameron, Hester heard that Tom and Mary Mahoney had parted—and was childishly pleased at the news.

Sydney thought that it was Tom who had thrown Mary out, particularly when she and Jem Wilkinson began to show signs of setting up in marriage. The breach was put down to Tom's jealousy. No one knew the truth, nor that Tom had settled money on Mary.

Now the monster knows what it's like to suffer a bit, Hester's Mentor said uncharitably. Having an unfaithful mistress will be a good lesson for him. Teach him he can't have his own way all his life. She sang around the house that afternoon to Mrs Cooke's surprise and pleasure.

Mrs Cooke was, however, unpleasantly surprised to see that, despite her new salary, Hester's living standards did not improve. She was not to know that Larkin, who had bought up all Fred's remaining debts, had upped the rate of interest and consequently the quarterly amount to be paid, after he had heard the news of her appointment. Hester found that she was not much better off than before she had begun to teach at the school.

But she liked her work there, though, and this, together with the good news about Tom Dilhorne and Mary Mahoney, put a slight spring in her step. She even accepted Mrs Cooke's invitation to take tea with her and her neighbour, Mrs Smith, and Mrs Smith's little daughter, Kate.

Kate was a pretty child and she and Hester got on famously. After tea, Mrs Cooke, knowing this and wanting to have a good gossip with Mrs Smith about matters not fit for a single young woman's ears, suggested to Hester that she take Kate into the backyard to show her the latest batch of newly hatched chicks.

She and Mrs Smith had just settled down to a comfortable chat when there was a knock on the door. Mrs Cooke's surprise on seeing who her visitor was could hardly have been greater.

'Why, Master Dilhorne, whatever can you want with me?'

He was as spruce as usual, but had left his cane behind and was carrying a small parcel of books under his arm. His bow to her was as punctilious as though she were the Governor's wife.

'Not with you, Mrs Cooke. I wonder if you would allow me to come in to speak to Miss Waring?'

Mrs Cooke smoothed down her apron. Overwhelmed by his magnificence, she wished that she had put on her best black dress.

'Come in, come in,' and she held her front door open.

Tom entered her small parlour and bowed to a curtsying Mrs Smith, also dazzled by his sartorial splendours. Putting his parcel on the table, he looked around for Hester.

'Miss Waring is outside,' said Mrs Cooke. 'I'll fetch her in for you.'

'No need,' replied Tom, 'I'll speak to her there—no need to interrupt your tea party.'

He walked through the lean-to kitchen and stopped at the door to the yard.

Hester Waring was on her hands and knees on the hard ground among a brood of chickens. Sitting by her was a small girl and, while he watched, Hester carefully picked up one of the fluffy yellow balls and placed it gently in the little girl's hands. She then rose, took the child in her arms and sat on the low brick wall at the end of the yard. She kissed the child's soft cheek as she did so.

Tom moved forward and Hester became suddenly aware of his presence. She grew quite still, like a frightened animal, ready to fly, and her grasp of the child tightened involuntarily. The liveliness of a moment ago which had transformed her face, had disappeared, as it had done when he had caught her by chance in the schoolroom.

'Mr Dilhorne?' she said, her voice quite composed, whatever her inward fears.

Tom walked carefully towards her, being careful not to tread on the little balls of fluff while he did so. Hester could not suppress a smile at the sight of the big man in his finery treading so daintily.

'You may laugh, Miss Waring, but I have no desire to slaughter any of Mrs Cooke's flock.'

'I was not laughing, Mr Dilhorne,' Hester informed him primly.

'Pray do not tell me that, Miss Waring. You were distinctly about to laugh. You are smiling now.'

Hester put on her most serious face. 'I am not smiling now, Mr Dilhorne. I advise you to stand where you are. The chickens will be safer.'

'Excellent advice, Miss Waring. I can see that your appointment was a wise one. You are able to instruct the older among us, as well as the children.'

'You have a reason to speak to me, Mr Dilhorne?'

'Even better, Miss Waring. You remind me that I am being remiss, and also inform me that my presence in Mrs Cooke's yard can only be because I wish to speak to you, and not herd newly hatched chicks.'

Hester could not prevent herself from laughing aloud at his bland impudence, which served to exorcise her fear of him and silence her inward Mentor who saw him as a ruffian and a monster.

'I fear that we never seem to engage in a proper conversation, Mr Dilhorne.'

'I see nothing improper about this one, Miss Waring. I have merely called to bring you the reading primers which Jardine told me that you needed.'

Hester wondered briefly why it had not been left to Jardine to give them to her, and why it was necessary for the great Mr Tom Dilhorne to act as an errand boy. She decided that this was not a profitable line to follow with him, given his ability to turn conversation on its head.

Their meeting followed a more normal pattern thereafter. Tom asked to sit by her on the wall. He petted the little girl while he questioned Hester idly about her work with the children. Except that somehow, in the middle of this, she absent-mindedly handed him Kate and the chicken to hold without so much as asking him if she might.

Or was it he who relieved her of Kate, saying mildly, 'I fear the child is a little heavy for you, Miss Waring.'

Odd things seemed to happen to her perception of reality whenever Mr Tom Dilhorne walked over her horizon. Oddest of all was that she spoke to him so freely and boldly—she who had blanched and stuttered whenever the officers of the garrison had tried to talk to her.

Tom declined Mrs Cooke's offer of a cup of freshly brewed tea, pleading another engagement, and took himself and his magnificence away. Hester really could not accommodate herself to the sight of his splendid clothes.

'Well!' exclaimed Mrs Cooke, when he had gone and Hester was examining the books which he had brought. 'What was all that about, Miss Waring?'

But Miss Waring could not tell her.

Tom walked home with the memory of Hester kneeling among the chickens—home, because despite what he had said to her, he had no other engagement, deviousness being as natural to him as breathing. A monstrous idea was beginning to take shape in his brain. It was an idea born of his loss of Mary Mahoney and the news that very day that his housekeeper was giving him notice.

He saw Hester with the child again, and remembered her evident affection for the little ones she had been teaching when he had seen her in the classroom. He remembered also the sudden bright eye which she had turned on him in the middle of their ridiculous conversation, which she had obviously enjoyed as much as he had. The desire to provoke her, to see her spring to life, to hear her ripostes to the nonsense he so gravely treated her to, grew on him each time that he met her. Only her thin, pinched face still troubled him—for surely she could afford good food now.

That's it! I do believe that the poor creature would be quite pretty if she got some good food down her, was given a little affection and some new clothes. She's already beginning to display much more spirit since she became a schoolteacher. She's not my style, of course, being little and dark instead of big and fair like Mary Mahoney and the others. But what of that? I'm not in any danger of losing my heart to her.

What was it Mary had said to him before they parted? Marry a lady. Well, Hester Waring's a lady, though she won't be if she falls any further. But no lady of the first flight would marry me. She's a sensible little thing, clever, too, by the ingenious way in which she answers me when I tease her. I thought that she was capable when we interviewed her. Yes, she'd make an excellent housekeeper, and a wife who would know what's what, the right fork to use and what to say and do. There's a thought!

But the idea of getting into bed with any man, especially me, would send her scurrying away like a hare. She nearly turned and ran when she saw me today, for all her brave face. Her dreadful father might have made her frightened of me, but, judging by the way she looks at them, he's made her scared witless of any man she meets.

A slow grin spread over his face. Well, I know a trick or two, and one of them might bring Hester Waring to a place she might not have fancied originally!

# Chapter Four

'I want a word with you, Jardine.'

Jardine rose and bowed as Tom entered. He was a conscientious man of indeterminate age, not an ex-felon, who held a number of small appointments under the Governor.

All of these offices brought him into contact with a large number of people in Sydney and Tom found it useful to talk to him when there was anyone or anything about whom he thought that he needed information. He was careful not to appear to bribe him, but Jardine had more sense than to enquire who it was who left the occasional bag of groceries or the odd bottle of whisky propped up against his back door.

Jardine had grown used to Tom's ways, and he wondered what information he needed now. He was surprised when, after nodding his assent to Tom's request, Tom said brusquely, 'Hester Waring. I take it that her salary is being paid promptly?'

Jardine knew better than to bridle. 'Of course—why do you ask?'

'Because the girl looks more thin and harried than ever. She's still not getting enough to eat. I should have thought she'd be plumper by now on what we're giving her.

Where's the money going? I know it's not going to Mrs Cooke. She's getting that room for a peppercorn's rent.'

So here was something Tom Dilhorne did not know. Probably because he had never cared enough before what Hester Waring was doing.

'There's a perfectly reasonable explanation,' Jardine began.

'There is?' Tom was satiric. 'I should like to know what it is.'

'You are aware that Jem Larkin does a little business in buying up debts—' He got no further. Tom was there before him.

'By God, you're telling me that Larkin is dunning her to pay her father's debts—and she's fool enough to pay them.'

'Exactly, and Larkin's upped the interest since we appointed her—or so I've heard.'

Tom felt an anger which he could not explain. How had Hester Waring's plight come to affect him so deeply?

'Why was I not told of this?'

Jardine thought that his superior's concern was excessive for a man whose own moneylending activities, on a scale much larger than Larkin's, were notorious.

'I had no notion that it would be of interest to you.'

'Everything interests me,' said Tom shortly. 'Particularly this. So that's why she still looks as though she's not had anything decent to eat in years. We'll see about that.'

Robert Jardine was to claim afterwards that he was the first person in Sydney to become aware that Tom Dilhorne was taking a shine to Hester Waring—how else could this untypical behaviour be explained? And he knew what Tom was going to do. Buy up Fred Waring's debts and then cancel them.

'It's the Board's Christmas Party next week, for all the

teachers in the different schools. You can make sure that she has something to eat there,' Jardine offered.

'So it is,' said Tom, struck. He would not normally have chosen to take part in such innocent junketing but, what with being lonely since Mary's departure from his life, he really needed some other interests.

It's nothing to do with Miss Waring herself, he told himself untruthfully. Yes, he would go along to see that she had enough to eat for once. He might also try to provoke her into the charming liveliness which she had displayed among the chickens, and he would also pursue his monstrous idea—which became less and less monstrous every time that he thought about it.

First he would buy Fred's debts from Larkin. He was not to tell Hester who had bought them, and Tom intended to destroy them in front of Larkin, so that Larkin should not think that he, Tom Dilhorne, was reduced to screwing widows and orphans, particularly half-starved mice like Hester Waring.

Jardine watched him stride off in some amusement. Really, the man was unpredictable. First he bullied the Board into employing the girl, then he hung around the schoolroom being snubbed by her, then he took the books to her himself, instead of leaving it for him to do. Next he complained that she wasn't getting enough to eat, and now he was off to pay her father's debts, and finally, having already informed Jardine that he was giving the Christmas Party a miss, he was going to turn up to see that she had enough to eat there!

If it had been any other than cold-hearted Tom Dilhorne, he would have said that he was sweet on the girl. Which, thinking of what she looked like and Tom's previous taste in women—Mary Mahoney had been a luscious blonde piece—was more than improbable, it was total nonsense.

Well, he, Jardine, might stir the pot a little if he got the chance. Poor Miss Waring deserved some excitement in her drab life. The right word in her ear and anything might happen.

Parties were rare enough in Hester Waring's drab life that the prospect of attending the one which the School Board gave each year on Christmas Eve could not but command her whole attention.

Money still being short, she turned to one of her mother's old black dresses, went to Lucy Wright for help and trimmed it with some rather nice lace which Lucy, taking one look at Hester and the dress, mendaciously said that she had no use for and helped Hester to sew it on.

Her husband came in while they were so engaged and gave poor Hester what her Mentor called 'his look'. Why are you such a persistent hanger-on of my over-generous wife? it said. He was undoubtedly responsible for Hester seeing so little of Lucy these days.

Captain Parker was with him and he was his usual kind self. This normally threw Hester into a fluster. She had always found his fresh good looks, blond hair and strong athletic body disturbing, particularly since she knew with some despair that he was kind to her only because he was sorry for her.

Today, however, she found him as handsome as ever, but very young and slightly gauche. His conversation was really rather dull and uninspired, no ridiculous jokes delivered in a way which brought on the giggles. This revision of her opinion of him came as a great surprise to her—ever since she had first met him he had been her masculine *beau ideal*.

Perhaps it was meeting older men like…well…like Tom Dilhorne. Not that *he* was her masculine *beau ideal*, far from it, but there was no doubt that his impudently cool manner made Captain Parker seem rather callow.

Consequently, her awe of him gone, she was more forthcoming with him than usual, if not to say vivacious, when he asked what was occupying the two girls so much after looking dubiously at Hester's drab gown with which she and Lucy were struggling.

She stared him straight in the eye for once and said airily, 'Oh, Captain Parker, I am going to the most important party of the festive season and Lucy is helping me to trim my splendid new dress.'

He looked rather surprised and asked her, 'What party is that, Hester?'

'Oh, it's much too important for you and Frank to be invited,' she replied giddily and untruthfully. 'It's the one which the School Board gives to all the teachers, and only really tremendous swells like Mr Tom Dilhorne get invited to it.'

It occurred to her that Tom seemed to be getting into her thoughts and her conversation a lot lately, and she watched Frank's look of distaste at her presence, and her light-minded conversation, grow deeper at the sound of his name.

'Are you sure you ought to go, Hester?' he said. 'I know you work for them, but from what you say the people whom you will be going to meet there are not quite the thing.'

Hester became totally reckless. 'Well, you see, Frank, as I'm sure you appreciate, and Stephen, too—' this was the first time she had ever used Captain Parker's Christian name '—I am really not quite the thing, either, these days. And they do say that the food they give us is really rather good, and I don't want to miss that. People who are quite the thing don't seem to offer me very much to eat!'

There was a ghastly silence after this home truth was shot at them with such panache.

What can be the matter with me? Hester thought, surprised by her own daring. Where am I getting this dreadful impulse from to say these terrible things aloud to everyone instead of just thinking them?

Now I find myself doing it all the time. I must go before Lucy throws me over completely. As it is, Frank will be telling her not to have me again. Not that she'll take much notice of *that*. He's properly under her thumb, if I don't mistake. And why on earth did I ever think so much of Captain Parker? He's just an ordinary, nice, kind…boy. It must be talking to Tom Dilhorne that's making me so awful. I seem to start thinking dreadful things like this after every meeting with him. There must be something catching about his constant teasing.

All the time that this was running through Hester's fevered brain, she was saying goodbye to Lucy, picking up the horrible gown, paying impudent farewells to Frank and Stephen, who stared at her, aghast, and taking herself out the front door.

There was a moment's silence before all three began talking at once. 'Well,' from Lucy, 'Oh dear,' from Captain Parker, who had been flattered by Hester's timid adoration, so markedly missing today, and 'Good God!' from Frank. 'She's plainer than ever and cheeky with it. I shan't have her visiting you again, Luce.'

'Oh, yes, you will,' said Lucy. 'She's no one else, poor thing.'

She paused, suddenly inspired. 'You don't think she's really hungry, do you? Perhaps that's what's wrong with her. Delirious from hunger. I should have offered her something. I never thought to wonder what she is living on now that Fred is dead. Oh, dear!'

'No, Luce, it's all those commoners she's mixing with,' said Stephen dismally. 'She used to be such a biddable little thing, if plain. Now she's plainer than ever and a bit of a shrew as well.'

He was relieved that his pity had never taken him so far as to say anything which could have been construed as an offer of marriage.


Hester walked home in an ecstasy of liberated wickedness. For the moment she had no regrets. They would probably come later. All her past life she had been a timid child who had barely raised her voice. Everyone had made it quite clear to her that what she might have to say was of little interest or consequence.

Her mother's most common expression when she had looked at her at all had been one of distaste. Fred, her father, had treated her as merely a convenient servant, very convenient, since even a servant would not have stood for the treatment which he had meted out to Hester.

Well, she had raised her voice today, and made her presence felt, too. She was so taken with her own naughtiness that, when she turned the corner into the lane where she lived, she bumped into Tom Dilhorne before she knew that he was there.

He stepped back with some surprise and a little amusement as he registered her defiant air.

'Good afternoon, Miss Waring.'

'Good afternoon, Mr Dilhorne,' she almost carolled at him.

He looked gravely at the disgraceful gown which she was clutching to herself.

'Busy, Miss Waring?'

The giddiness which had overtaken her at Lucy's overwhelmed her again. She stared rudely at her tormentor.

Well, her inward voice was right. The ogre was a man who made Captain Parker look juvenile and unformed, but he was an ogre, nonetheless.

'Yes, you might say that, Mr Dilhorne. I have been trimming this extravagant dress for the Board's party.'

'You intend going there, then,' he said, his mouth twitching. The moment she showed spirit she was transformed. He was right. There was some real, red-hot passion roiling around there beneath the sober exterior.

'Yes, you might say that I intend to favour it with my presence.'

'Very gratifying, Miss Waring. I look forward to seeing you there.'

'Do you, Mr Dilhorne? You surprise me. I thought you more used to less, shall we say, decorous gatherings!'

Hester unfurled this piece of insolence at him as though she were setting up a banner. Let him make what he would of that!

He was gravity itself. 'On the contrary, Miss Waring. I shall attend tomorrow with the keenest interest.'

He bowed. She bowed back. Damn his impudence for looking at her dreadful gown with such a satirical eye. Well, she would wear it tomorrow, and she would try to show a little more decorum than she had exhibited today. One might almost think that she had been drinking.

Tom knew that she had not been drinking, and he knew the delirium of despair and starvation when he saw it. And she's growing up, he thought. I wonder if she realised how she looked at me once or twice? He wondered, too, what had roused her so. Well, he might find out tomorrow. But Hester would never tell him that the spark which had freed her had been ignited by himself.

School Board parties were not, as Hester could have guessed, the most exciting of affairs. But, to her starved senses this, the only one which she was ever to attend, seemed almost more than she could bear. She knew that, in a room full of not very well-dressed men and women, she was the worst dressed of them all. Even Lucy's lace could not save her gown.

On the other hand there was food, lots of it, so that her mouth watered and her empty stomach clenched. She forced herself to be ladylike, to take only a little on her plate when it was handed around, and to eat it as though it were not manna in the desert to the starving Israelites.

Tom was at the top table and he watched with pity her efforts to disguise her hunger. He had dressed magnificently for the occasion, wearing a waistcoat with peacocks embroidered on it, and a black pearl in his cravat. He wondered whom he was trying to impress.

Hester was in a very different mood from the day before. The food pleased her, but the euphoria of her visit to Lucy had worn off, and she was overcome with shame at the memory of her behaviour, not only to Lucy, but also to Tom Dilhorne.

Whatever must he have thought of her? Recalling her last remark to him made her go hot all over. She could not imagine what had provoked it.

If anyone had told her that, deep down, she was becoming sexually attracted to Tom Dilhorne of all people, she would have denied it with her last breath. Even the revelation that Captain Parker's attraction had dimmed had not revealed the truth to her. Nor did her shortened breath and the feeling of excitement which swept over her when he approached her after the meal had ended and the company was relaxing over a little, a very little, strong drink.

Hester immediately became prey to the most unnatural feelings. It was almost as though she were wearing no clothes at all! A strange odd fluttering started in the base of her stomach. Nothing in her short life had prepared her for such sensations, and she feared that she was sickening for a fever, she was so aware of her whole body—and, what was worse, of his.

Everything about him seemed so bright and clear, his sandy-blond hair with its slight wave, his deep blue eyes, the strange twist of his mouth which betrayed the sardonic humour with which he so often spoke to her, the breadth of his shoulders, the depth of his chest, the length of his legs, his height—he had to bend slightly to speak to her.

Oh, she must not be so forward with him, so unladylike, she must not. Finding it difficult to breathe in his presence on top of her shameless feelings about herself and him, made her manner to him as blunt and spiritless as he had ever known it. She was back to the hunted Miss Waring of the interview.

So sour had yesterday's strange joy turned that when he asked her most kindly, 'Are you enjoying yourself, Miss Waring?' she heard herself replying discourteously,

'Very much, but no thanks to you, I fear. Had you had your way, I would not have been appointed in the first place.'

Tom's face tightened. He had been long aware that she thought this, but strangely, for the cold, uncaring man he usually was, it hurt him to hear her say it. He bowed and this time his gravity was real, not mock, as Hester, growing increasingly sensitive to his moods immediately, and contritely, grasped.

'Nevertheless,' he replied, his manner to her as kind as hers to him had been harsh, 'it is Christmas, after all, Miss Waring, and any reservations I may have felt about your appointment have disappeared before your splendid performance.'

Hester turned away from him so that he should not see her eyes filling with tears at his forbearance. She reproached herself inwardly and bitterly for her churlishness. She also saw that Jardine, who had heard the interchange, was looking at them both curiously.

Tom took his peacocks miserably away and sourly regretted putting them on. Jardine leaned forward in his usual deferential manner: he was always courteous to everyone, and Hester's shame grew when he said gravely, 'Miss Waring, a word with you.'

'Indeed, Mr Jardine.' She looked away from him. She had never been more aware of her plain appearance and her dowdy dress.

'Miss Waring, I can understand why you feel as you do about Mr Dilhorne. All Sydney knew of your father's dislike of him. But, I assure you, you misjudge him. Far from attempting to prevent your appointment, the opposite is true. Were it not for his intervention, the Board would never have offered you the post at all. He spoke most feelingly on your behalf.'

Jardine thought that Hester was going to faint on the spot. Her face went an unpleasant yellowish-grey and she swayed on her feet. Tom, who was talking to Godfrey Burrell, but had kept an eye on her, saw what was happening and moved quickly to her side.

'Miss Waring, what is wrong? What has caused this, Jardine?'

Jardine had no intention of telling him the truth. Let him find out from the girl.

'I think that Miss Waring may be feeling the heat.'

'Then we must get her out of here, man.'

He lifted the half-conscious Hester as though she weighed even less than she did, and carried her into an ante-room, away from curious eyes, and set her gently on a chair. 'Water, Jardine. Immediately.'

Jardine, all his suspicions about Tom and his interest in Hester finally confirmed, sped off to find water.

'I am not really fainting, Mr Dilhorne,' Hester faltered in little more than a whisper. 'I am only feeling weak and ashamed.'

'Hush, Miss Waring,' he said, in a voice which Hester had never heard from anyone in all her short life, so full of concern for her that her eyes filled at the sound. 'You may not feel faint, but you look very ill.'

'That is because I have eaten too much, and I have behaved dreadfully.'

'I cannot believe that, Miss Waring.'

'Oh, but you must, Mr Dilhorne. I have behaved very badly to you today and you know it. What I said to you about preventing my appointment was unforgivable. Mr Jardine has told me what you did for me that day. Do not be cross with him for doing so. He was quite right. He could not let me go on insulting you when you had been so kind.'

They looked at one another in silence. Tom, for once, was bereft of words.

'I like your waistcoat,' Hester said unexpectedly.

'Do not reproach yourself,' he told her gently. 'Under all the circumstances, it was natural that you should think what you did.'

'Not at all,' she replied. 'I was quite wrong to leap to such dreadful conclusions. You have always been so kind to me on your visits, bringing me the books, and the sweets for the children, but I didn't like to think so. We had peacocks at home,' she finished inconsequentially.

He saw that she was wretched and tired beyond belief,

lying back in her chair, wearing her ugly dress, her face ashen.

'When Jardine comes back with the water, and you have drunk a little, I shall drive you home,' he said. 'You are exhausted and need to rest.'

Hester's eyes closed. 'How do you know that I am feeling tired? I think that I should like to sleep for ever, only it's an odd time of day to want to.'

Tom could have told her that it was the unaccustomed food and drink which she had taken and the shock of Jardine's news which had reduced her to this state coming as it did at the end of months of suffering. But he said nothing, only helped her to drink the water, for even that seemed to be beyond her.

When she had finished and lay back again, her lips livid, he scooped her out of the chair, carried her to his gig and drove her home before the astonished eyes of School Board and teachers alike.

Another fine piece of gossip about Tom Dilhorne, was the general cry!

Just before the Christmas Party, Hester had visited Jem Larkin and asked him if she could leave her payment beyond the December Quarter Day when it fell due. Larkin had leered at her and told her that it was fair enough so far as he was concerned, if she were prepared to pay the extra interest for going beyond the due date.

Hester had swallowed hard, but had agreed. She needed a little ready money to buy kind Mrs Cooke a Christmas fairing and some comfits and sugar plums for the children at school.

Shortly after that, Tom had arrived at the schoolroom with a bag of sweets and a plum cake for herself and the children. He had insisted that she take some of the plum cake home for herself, and she had found it difficult to refuse.

Lying in bed on the evening of the party, she remembered with some pain all the similar little kindnesses she and the children had received from him in the weeks leading up to her dreadful snub. The day, for example, when she had met him in the street. He had told her that she looked tired and had insisted on driving her home.

It was as though all the poison about him that her father had poured into her for so many years had prevented her from realising how kind he had been to her, and how different he was from the ogre which almost everyone said he was. Well, he might be an ogre in his business dealings, but in his dealings with her, no such thing.

She writhed at the memory of her behaviour to him at the party, but at the same time she could not help remembering the warm feeling which she had experienced when he had carried her up to her room, calling on a surprised Mrs Cooke to come and help her. Cradled in his arms, she had felt not fear and hate but a sense of comfort and security.

Mrs Cooke's face had been one giant question mark, and after Tom had gone and she had helped Hester to undress, she came upstairs with the queerest expression on it. She was carrying a glass of hot toddy in her hand, and some delicious sweet biscuits on a small plate. All of which, she said, had arrived at the hands of Tom Dilhorne's man, with his best compliments, and she and Miss Waring were to share them together.

'He's a card, is Tom,' said Mrs Cooke. 'Mary Mahoney said that you never knew where you were with him. But I don't mind drinking his fine liquor and eating his good food.'

Hester could not but agree, and she and Mrs Cooke,

sitting on her bed, divided the food and drink between them and chatted together. Mrs Cooke was slyly trying to find out why Tom should be driving Hester home and plying her with goodies.

Hester could not have told her. She had slept a little before the toddy arrived, had woken up feeling refreshed and was only too happy to sit with Mrs Cooke, getting slightly drunk—Tom had sent word to Mrs Cooke to give Hester as much drink as she could take, and to deny that it was alcoholic. Mrs Cooke was also given *carte blanche* to drink glass for glass.

Finally the two of them fell asleep together, Mrs Cooke in her shawl on top of the bed and Hester in it, both waiting to greet Christmas morning with slightly thick heads.

Hester gave Mrs Cooke her Christmas present and Mrs Cooke gave Hester her Christmas dinner, thus making two good meals in a row for Hester. They were busy mopping up the gravy when Tom's boy arrived again with a letter for Hester from Tom, a bottle of port and a large plum pudding for them both, as well as Mr Dilhorne's compliments of the season.

Hester opened her letter in front of a Mrs Cooke bursting with curiosity. The superscription on the cover was in an elegant classic script, and Hester wondered for a moment if Tom's clerk had written it, so unlike was it from anything which she had expected. But the letter inside was in the same hand and was undoubtedly from him.

In it he hoped that she was feeling better, begged her to accept the bottle of port and the pudding as a Christmas gift, and hoped to see her well and back in the schoolroom by the New Year.

She puzzled over his beautiful handwriting: it was to be some time before she discovered where and how he had acquired it. She also fended off as best she could Mrs Cooke's questions. She had no more idea than her landlady why Tom should suddenly favour her with his attentions.

A diet of more good food, the plum pudding and the port found her on her highest ropes and telling the gratified Mrs Cooke about Tom's peacock waistcoat, black pearl and elegant fob watch.

'Fancy!' was Mrs Cooke's most frequent exclamation. 'I remember him running around Sydney when he first came here, a cheeky long-legged lad as I recall. Who'd have thought to see him dressed so fine and speak so grand?'

Hester fixed a slightly drunken eye on Mrs Cooke: the port had done its work.

'Fine isn't the word,' she announced, slightly belligerently. 'You'd have thought he'd worn clothes like that all his life.' She smiled at a sudden reminiscence. 'We had peacocks at home when I was a girl. Noisy things. They used to screech. Mama didn't like them. But then there wasn't much Mama liked. Apart from Rowland,' she added.

Mrs Cooke had to stop herself from agreeing heartily with Miss Waring who now sank dreamily back in her chair, waving her glass, and looking around Mrs Cooke's neat parlour while she demanded that they both join in a toast to Mr Dilhorne and his boy for the gift of the port and the plum pudding.

After the meal and the drink both women subsided into a pleasant doze, Hester on Mrs Cooke's hard sofa and Mrs Cooke in her big armchair. Later they soothed their thick heads with some excellent tea—bought from Tom's Emporium—and the rest of the bottle of port which happily rounded off Hester's best Christmas for years.

For some reason just before she staggered up to bed,

Hester found herself buttonholing Mrs Cooke owlishly, and informing her that she thoroughly approved of Mr Dilhorne. 'He looked a very tulip of fashion,' she added, recalling a dim memory of her brother Rowland's slang, long ago.

Mrs Cooke was happy to agree with her. She would have agreed to anything, and watched Hester reel upstairs feeling full of a vague benevolence towards Hester, Tom, his boy, and life in general. Both women enjoyed an excellent night's sleep.

Christmas over, it was back to hard pounding again for Hester. Larkin had given her until the fifth of January to pay the interest still outstanding, and so, after morning school, she gathered it together, put it into her reticule and set off for his little counting-house. She was glumly aware that the money which she was about to hand over would have fed and clothed her adequately for the rest of the quarter. As it was, life would be harder than ever because of the extra interest to be paid for being late.

Larkin's clerk looked rudely at her and pointed mannerlessly with his quill to Larkin's room when she asked to see him. She was used by now to insolence from underlings who found it amusing to taunt a poor, plain girl, and walked in to find Larkin writing in a big ledger.

'Good afternoon, Mr Larkin,' she said, opening her reticule and beginning to count the coins out on his desk, 'I have brought you what I owe you.'

Larkin looked at her strangely, and said, 'No need, no need, Miss Waring.'

He had no idea whether she was aware that her father's debts had been paid by Tom Dilhorne, but he never told anyone anything which might give them an advantage over him.

'No need, Mr Larkin? How can that be?' Hester's face was a picture of bewilderment. He had dunned her father and then herself so mercilessly that she could not believe that he had succumbed to a late access of Christmas spirit.

'I have to inform you, Miss Waring, that your late father's debts have been bought by a business colleague of mine, who then proceeded to burn the papers before me. The debts no longer exist. You may keep your money.'

There was a chair just behind Hester. She slumped down into it rather than lower herself in her usual ladylike manner.

'Bought my father's debts and cancelled them, you say, Mr Larkin?'

'Indeed, Miss Waring, you have it.'

'But who?' she began, until a monstrous supposition overcame her. 'Are you at liberty to inform me precisely which of your fellows paid my father's debts, Mr Larkin?'

'No, Miss Waring. He gave express orders that his name should not be revealed.'

For some reason Hester felt almost indignant about the whole transaction, though God knew how happy she was that this millstone had disappeared from around her neck. She felt light-headed with relief, but angry with the man who had done it.

'It was Mr Dilhorne, was it not, Mr Larkin?'

He bowed politely to her. Given that Tom Dilhorne had made himself her protector, it would be politic to be at evens with her, and not at odds.

'I am not at liberty to say.'

'There is no need for you to say anything, Mr Larkin. I know perfectly well that it was Mr Dilhorne. Who else could it have been? What business did he have buying up my father's debts without speaking to me?'

'I can say no more, Miss Waring. If I may give you a

piece of advice, Miss Waring, it is this: that you should be grateful to the person who paid me and relieved for your good self.'

My good self, she thought indignantly, is about to ask Mr Tom Dilhorne what he thinks he is doing by buying up my father's debts. Bottles of port, biscuits, toddy, plum puddings, best wishes for Christmas! Has the man run mad? she asked herself, echoing Robert Jardine's self-same query made earlier.

She set off for Tom's Counting-House, determined to beard him there. Yes, beard was the only word for such an officious man! But the nearer she got to his office, the greater her understanding of the service he had performed for her grew until, by the time she arrived before his polished cedarwood door in George Street, with its fine brass plate and handles, all the anger had run out of her, and she hardly knew what to say to him. But something must be said.

If Joseph Smith was surprised to see Miss Waring advance towards his cubby-hole, he did not show it.

'Sir,' said Hester awefully, 'I desire to speak to Mr Dilhorne. Pray tell me whether he is in and if he will see me.'

'Certainly,' replied Smith, all courtesy, with a slight inclination of his head. 'Miss Waring, is it not?'

In the face of her determined stare he disappeared into Tom's office. As though he has not known for years who I am, thought Hester rebelliously. She had reverted to the slightly giddy mood in which she had been so impertinent to Lucy, Frank and Stephen. Yes, it must be Tom Dilhorne's proximity which was having such a dreadful effect on her!

Smith returned from Tom's office. 'Mr Dilhorne is in and is at liberty to see you. Please come this way.'

Tom's office was a large room with two high windows

in it. He had installed himself in one of the first buildings which were the result of Governor Macquarie's desire to turn Sydney into a beautiful town in the European mode. His desk was massive, and he came from around it to wave her into an armchair.

He was immaculately dressed, and his effect on her was as strong as it had been at the Christmas party, but in some odd way she was growing used to it and she was filled, not with fear, but with a strange excitement. Instead of ducking her head and appearing shy, she stared at him. Pay her father's debts, indeed! Who had authorised him to do that?

'Good afternoon, Miss Waring. To what do I owe the honour of your visit?'

The honour of my visit, indeed! He was not wearing the peacocks, was dressed very soberly, but was still magnificent. There was a look in his bright blue eyes which she was not sure she cared for.

She said, in the awful voice which she had used to Joseph Smith, 'I have come to speak to you, Mr Dilhorne.'

He gave her his engaging, crooked smile, and in her strange state she registered the way in which his mouth curled at the end and one eyebrow rose, giving him a piratical appearance, which, far from frightening her as it would once have done, almost disarmed her. But she would not let that deter her from pursuing her quarrel with him. No, indeed not!

'Yes,' he said, 'yes, I see that, Miss Waring. What may I do for you?'

'It is not so much what you *may* do for me, Mr Dilhorne, it is what you have *already* done.'

Somehow, everything came out all wrong as it usually did when she confronted him, for he simply smiled again and asked, his head on one side, an expression of intense curiosity on his face, 'Now, what is that, Miss Waring? I do not quite follow you.'

In her excitement she found herself saying, 'As though it is not enough that you plied Mrs Cooke and myself with food, drink and *plum pudding*, you have also bought up and destroyed my father's debts. Pray have the goodness to explain yourself.'

He bowed very low and said most earnestly, 'I thought that you and Mrs Cooke would enjoy the food and drink which I sent you. Was I wrong?'

Hester fixed him with a basilisk eye. 'That is not it at all, Mr Dilhorne. Of course we enjoyed it. We enjoyed it so much that we were overset for two days. That is not the point. The point is that you bought up all my father's remaining debts and destroyed them. By what right did you do that, and for what reason?'

She ran out of breath.

He pulled up a chair opposite to her, sat in it, and leaned forward, his mouth twitching. 'Well, I might have thought that you would like to buy your own port and plum pudding in future.'

He was now so near to her that she could see the tiny laughter lines on his face, the strength of the hands which lay in his lap, and could catch the scent of a clean man, so unlike the sour smell of her late father in his last days. Her indignation began to dissolve, her own mouth began to twitch. Her sense of humour, of the ridiculous, long hidden beneath oppression, drudgery and neglect, began to assert itself as before in their impossible conversations. His impudent refusal to come to the point had its charms for her.

'You know perfectly well what I mean, Mr Dilhorne. How in the world did we come to be talking about plum puddings?'

'I believe that it was you who introduced the topic, Miss Waring.'

'Then it was very wrong of me,' she wailed. 'Oh, why will you not be serious?'

'Because you have been serious long enough. A moment, Miss Waring.'

He rose from his chair, and crossed to a splendid oak sideboard on which stood decanters of rum and brandy and an open bottle of red wine. He poured out two glasses of the wine and returned to his seat. He then handed her one of the glasses. Dazedly, she noticed that it was of the most exquisite quality, like everything else in the room.

'Now you are plying me with wine again, Mr Dilhorne.'

'It is usual, Miss Waring, when businessmen and -women end one deal and start another, that they take wine together.'

Hester was so stunned by this remarkable statement that she drank her wine in one vulgar swallow.

'Another glass, Miss Waring?'

'Certainly not, Mr Dilhorne. Are you trying to make me drunk?'

'Not today, Miss Waring. Another time, perhaps.'

The glance Hester threw him was tragic. She was almost ready to clutch her head in despair. How had her perfectly reasonable request of him led her to this strange pass? End one deal and begin another, indeed! What could the man be talking about?

'You mentioned business deals, Mr Dilhorne. What business deals are these? And how am I involved?'

'Well, the first one is my buying up your father's debts, as you so cleverly surmised, and we are celebrating the fact that I burned them so that you may buy your own port and puddings. The second deal I am prepared to put to you when you are feeling a little more composed.'

'I am perfectly composed, Mr Dilhorne.'

Hester made her voice as cool and firm as she could. To no avail.

'I said *more* composed, Miss Waring. Now I am going to ask my clerk to bring in something to eat. It is my usual habit at this time. I hope that you will see your way to sharing my nuncheon, and when we have finished we may have a little chat together on matters of mutual advantage, which is the sort of nonsense fine gentlemen usually talk when they wish to impress fools. But you are far from being a fool, Miss Waring, and we shall, I hope, meet on terms of equality.'

Hester's first reaction to this speech was, Where on earth has short-spoken Mr Tom Dilhorne gone to? as these Gibbonian periods rolled out. Despite her determination not to become even more indebted to him in the matter of food and drink than she already was, she found herself salivating at the mere idea of partaking of what Mr Tom Dilhorne thought was a good meal. Judging by everything else about him, it would be remarkably fine.

'I cannot imagine what business deal you can be proposing to me, Mr Dilhorne, but yes, I will take luncheon with you.'

He rose, rang a small bell on his desk and Smith came in.

'The usual, no, rather better than the usual, Joseph, and for two today. As soon as possible, please.'

Tom turned to Hester. She now sat almost crouched in her chair, her eyes as wary as a hunting cat's.

'Come, Miss Waring, what shall we discuss? I believe that it is considered the thing for ladies and gentlemen to mouth polite nothings at one another when they are in our situation.'

Nothing for it but to join him in his idiocies.

'We could discuss the news from home, perhaps.'

Tom smiled his crooked smile again, and sat down. 'Seeing that it is nearly a year out of date before it reaches us, I agree with you. It is certainly nothing.'

Hester could not prevent a giggle from escaping. He greeted this with approval. 'Excellent, Miss Waring. I believe we understand each other very well.'

Several moments more of the most impolite banter followed, with each party trying to outdo the other in outrageousness. Hester had never felt so carefree in her life. Fun and banter were new to her and the ease with which she found herself responding to Mr Tom Dilhorne's naughtinesses surprised her. Excitement gripped her to the degree that she thought that her head might fly off, it felt so light.

'You see how easy it is to engage in small talk,' Tom said when Smith returned, carrying a basket of food. Smith then went over to the sideboard and fetched out china plates and silver knives and forks, more glasses, some spoons of varying sizes and fruit knives with delicate ivory handles. Drawing up a small drum table, he arranged these before Tom and Hester, finally handing each of them a damask napkin from a drawer in the sideboard.

That done, he bowed and left, and Tom began lifting bread, butter, cheese, cold sliced meat and fruit out of the basket.

'I can safely say that I am able to recommend everything, Miss Waring, including this bottle.'

He lifted another bottle of wine out of the basket and began to open it.

'You may not believe this, Miss Waring, but I am an abstemious man where drink is concerned. I am, however, prepared to make an exception today in your honour.'

He poured her more wine in yet another elegant glass;

this time she drank it with proper decorum, and began to attack the beautiful food, not trying to conceal her hunger, for she had scarcely eaten since Boxing Day. Tom watched her with approval, occasionally recommending to her the choicest titbits from the basket.

The last thing that he lifted out was a large pineapple, which he divided between them. They ate it with a great deal of amusement, the sticky liquid from it running over their hands. Hester, now well into her third glass of wine, had never eaten pineapple before and she found it delicious.

'But a little messy, Mr Dilhorne, is it not? Pray, is there no polite way to consume such a delicacy?'

She gave him a smile of such sweetness that Tom began to wonder what a properly fed and cared-for Miss Waring might look like.

The pineapple disposed of, its remains neatly wrapped in some of the paper from the basket, he rang for Smith to bring them a bowl of water and a towel so that they might wash and dry their sticky hands. After that, Smith and another man came in and took away everything but the bottle of wine and their glasses.

Alone again, Tom poured Hester more wine. Her third or fourth glass? she queried hazily. He was evidently trying to turn her into a toper as well as a glutton, but oh, what a delicious sense of well-being eating good food brought on! She could forgive him almost anything for that.

He was opposite to her again, his manner now quite serious.

'Miss Waring, I have a proposition to put to you. Pray do not dismiss it out of hand. Think carefully about what I am saying. Your future happiness may rest on it.' He paused.

What could the man be about to say? My future happiness? I must be mishearing. It is all the wine I am drinking, thought Hester, absent-mindedly taking another great swallow in order to clear her fuddled head.

More elegantly arranged sentences followed. 'As you may or may not know, Miss Waring, I am shortly to lose my housekeeper, who is getting married and going to live at Paramatta. I need not say what a blow this is to a man who likes an orderly life. Now, you, Miss Waring, would make an excellent person to run my home. You have a good mind, a bright wit, and would also make me an informed companion with whom I could usefully converse.'

Hester heard all this with her mouth open—not an uncommon occurrence when she was talking to Mr Tom Dilhorne. She tried to imagine herself usefully conversing with him—on what? Whilst thinking this over, she finished her wine and he neatly filled her glass again. She failed to notice that he was not drinking anything.

'But we have a problem, Miss Waring: much though I should like to employ you, and much though you might want to come—' this fascinated her, how could he really think that? '—there is no way in which a charming young lady such as yourself could agree to live in the house of a man like me who has a certain reputation—you take my meaning, I am sure. Think of the gossip which would ensue!

'Now, I also need a wife. A lady who knows what's what about etiquette and the proper thing to do. And you would make an excellent wife, Miss Waring, but I fear that you do not really wish to marry me in the true sense. I am right, am I not?'

Hester found herself nodding her head, quite unable to speak. She was not sure whether it was the wine, or the shock which his words were bringing on which held her paralysed and mute. He took her nodding head for agreement to his last proposition and smoothly continued.

'That being so, and I see that, as usual, we are in complete accord, you will understand why I am making this purely business proposition to you, Miss Waring. What would you say if I asked you to marry me, in name only, so that I would acquire a wife and a hostess, and you would acquire safety, respectability and a good home?'

He had finished, and was sitting back and smiling at her, the blue eyes dancing, his crooked smile more crooked than ever. He repeated his earlier words. 'What would you say, Miss Waring?'

Miss Waring took another swallow, hardly able to credit what she was hearing—for more reasons than one. She wanted to ask him, What on earth has happened to your diction, Mr Dilhorne, to transform you from the poorly spoken brute my father despised? And how in the world did a felon from the gutters of London, transported for theft—or worse—acquire such a superb command of the English language?

She merely said instead, 'That I think that you have run mad, Mr Dilhorne, except that you sound so eminently sane, which I admit confuses me more than a little. Are you really serious?'

'Yes, I am really serious.'

Hester had to admit that he must be. Through the haze which had begun to surround her she could detect that he looked more serious than she had ever seen him before.

'In name only?' she asked him. 'With all that that implies?'

Hester felt that it would be grossly indelicate to put it any more plainly, to say, We are not to go to bed together, Mr Dilhorne? or, You will not demand your marital rights? She dismissed from her mind what her mother and father would have said to…all this. After all, it was not they who were living on a knife edge with the gutter and the brothel staring them in the face.

Was she really having this remarkable conversation with her father's ogre, or was she dreaming it?

'Yes, in name only, Miss Waring. You understand me, I'm sure.'

'How do I know that, once married, you will keep your word?'

'I always keep my word, once given. Without my word, I may do anything…anything at all. And if the other party breaks *their* word, then, again, I am free to act as I please. Perhaps you would like Joseph Smith to draw up a contract for us to sign, Miss Waring? We can get him and one of my clerks to witness it.'

Another dreadful giggle escaped her at the mere idea of such an outlandish notion.

'I think not, Mr Dilhorne, it would not be fitting. Tell me, are there many businessmen like you?'

'Fortunately not, Miss Waring, else I should not be so disgustingly rich.'

Thinking this over, rather hazily, Hester nevertheless thought that she took his meaning. She mumbled, rather than replied as decorously as she would have wished, 'Do you expect an…ansher…answer immediately, Mr Dilhorne?' For some reason it was getting harder and harder to speak. Her tongue was thick and she needed to rest. Oh, how she needed to rest!

'No, Miss Waring. You may give me an answer when you wish. Except that I hope that you may not be too long. We are neither of us getting any younger.'

'Indubitably, Mr Dilhorne.' This proved surprisingly difficult to say. 'Not too long then.'

Why was it that lately, when she met him, she always wanted to sleep? Even the food he had sent her had put her to sleep. Part of her wanted to say Yes, immediately, to his disgraceful proposition. The other part, the part her father and mother had nurtured, told her that she was mad to trust this ruffian, no matter how beautifully he now dressed and spoke.

Her vulgar Mentor suddenly popped up again—having been asleep, no doubt, while Mr Tom Dilhorne was cunningly bending her to his will—and said loudly, But think of the comfort, the good food, the conversation—you like talking to him, you know you do—and you will be safe from the Larkins of this world and their impudent clerks.

She refused to admit to herself that Mr Tom Dilhorne still frightened her a little even though she was beginning to find him disturbingly attractive.

Hester gave a great yawn and surrendered. 'I will give you an answer in a week, Mr Dilhorne.'

Carefully placing her empty glass beside the nearly empty bottle, she settled back in her chair and went to sleep as quietly and properly as a fuddled lady could.

His face a mixture of amusement and tenderness—an expression which would have astounded everyone who knew him—Mr Tom Dilhorne looked down at her and, moved by some impulse he could not define, bent down and kissed the top of her head.

That done, he rose, walked to his desk and resumed his interrupted work, but not before he had looked across at her face, serene in sleep, and murmured to himself, 'And if I don't get you willingly into my bed in a few weeks after marriage, I shall be the most surprised man in Sydney!'

\* \* \*

Hester awoke with a sense of well-being and a strong desire to use the place of easement, as Mrs Cooke genteelly called it.

He seemed to understand that, too. For, on looking up and finding her stirring, he pointed to the door behind him, and said, 'Through there, Miss Waring.'

Hester was out of the door and into the courtyard where the place of easement was before she had time to be flustered or concerned about the delicacies of life. Using the primitive facilities provided, she pondered on the strange nature of her unlikely benefactor and the curious intimacy which they had achieved in which the unspoken needs of men and women could be treated so rationally.

After that, she was taken home again, like a lady, in his gig, with her promise to give him an answer soon. His man delivered her to her doorstep and to Mrs Cooke's resigned ecstasies about her lodger's sudden rise in the world.

# Chapter Five

Hester did not need a week to make up her mind, but she had promised Tom a week and she kept to her word. She was not sure whether at the end of it she was to visit his office in order to give him her decision. In the midst of worrying about this, she sensibly decided that a man of his resourcefulness would create his own opportunity in order to discover it.

She had known from the moment that he had made his offer that she would accept it. Scandalous and shocking as it might be, she was prepared to sell her soul for security. She would not have agreed to a true marriage, but to be his wedded, un-bedded, housekeeper, and hostess, that was different, wasn't it? He had told her that he would keep his word and she had to hope that he would.

She would be settled and life would not be dull if her meetings with him so far were any guide. He had said that he wanted to converse with her. She wondered wherever these discussions would take place. Over tea, perhaps, or during a genteel walk in the garden.

Somehow, such imaginings did not accord with the un-ruly and unstructured nature of the conversations which they had already held. Her dreadful Mentor had constantly provoked her into making the most improper remarks. What would it do when she was alone with him and the doors had been locked for the night?

Hester shrank away from this aspect of his proposal and concentrated firmly on the more impersonal parts of it. There was nothing to fear, she was sure. After Mary Mahoney, her Mentor said unkindly, why should he want to take you to bed?—adding slyly, More's the pity.

She put a hand to her flaming cheeks and willed the horrid voice to stop. It is not that at all. I do not wish to be his true wife, and I am afraid of him.

Not so much as you were—her Mentor's voice was almost agreeable—and when you know him better you'll fear him even less.

In the middle of her deliberations Mr Dilhorne's boy came—again!—with a basket of fruit and some hothouse flowers for Miss Waring and Mrs Cooke. He had more than he needed for himself, said his note, and he hoped that they would do him the honour of eating up his surplus so that it would not go to waste.

'If I did not know you both better, I would say that you had an admirer there, Miss Waring,' was Mrs Cooke's dazzled comment as she ate the fruit.

Meeting Hester in the street the next day, Tom bowed genially to her and wished her a cheerful 'Good morning'. By his manner she knew that he was going to play what her Mentor had christened his cat-and-mouse game with her.

'I have no answer for you today,' said Hester repressively. 'The week is not yet up, and you do not assist matters by bombarding me with fruit.'

'Ah, you and Mrs Cooke do not like fruit? A pity. Shall I send you some more wine, instead? I know that you like that.' His merry eyes were mocking her, even though the rest of his face was grave.

'You must not send me anything until I have made up my mind, Mr Dilhorne. Or I shall think that you are trying to influence my answer in your favour.'

'And you do not think that would be wise of me, Miss Waring? But such conduct is usually considered good business practice.'

'But this is not business, Mr Dilhorne,' said Hester unwisely, immediately realising that her haste had left her exposed to his raillery once again.

'Is it not? I was under the impression that it was. Correct me if I am mistaken. We even, I seem to remember, spoke of a written contract.'

'*You* talked of a written contract, Mr Dilhorne,' replied Hester, wondering why it was so easy for him to wrong-foot her in such a way that she had a wild desire to laugh—if a mouse ever laughed at a cat. 'I believe that I spoke very little.'

'Very wise, most commendable of you, Miss Waring. The less one says, the less one gives away.'

'I apparently need to say nothing for you to shower me with fruit and wine and…' Before her Mentor began to speak aloud for her, as it was threatening to do, and disgrace her entirely, she stopped and almost wailed at him, 'Why do we have such ridiculous conversations, Mr Dilhorne?'

He considered her gravely. 'If you would accept my gifts in the spirit in which they are made, Miss Waring, we could perhaps embark on a discussion of something more substantial and serious. The nature of the Trinity, perhaps?'

A passing matron was treated to the scandalous sight of

Mr Tom Dilhorne assisting Miss Hester Waring who was reeling with uncontrollable laughter.

'Oh, you are impossible!' she finally achieved. 'We must say no more. I will give you my answer on Tuesday and you must promise to be serious—otherwise I cannot answer for my conduct.'

Leaving her school after a busy day's work on the following Tuesday, Hester found Tom waiting for her outside the back door. He was smartly dressed, as usual, and had his hat in his hand. He took from her the bag which she carried, full of her small possessions and walked along beside her. He was obviously determined to be serious on this important occasion and Hester was surprised to find that she regretted this a little.

'Have you had a good day, Miss Waring?' This came out so solemnly and was so unlike his usual mode of speech to her that Hester had to suppress a desire to giggle, similar to those other unsuitable occasions for mirth—such as when she was in church and the Vicar was at his most pompous.

'Yes, indeed, Mr Dilhorne,' she managed to say, 'and you?'

'Tolerable, Miss Waring, tolerable.'

Neither of them said anything further as they walked briskly along towards Mrs Cooke's, drawing a few surprised stares on the way. What could the so-proper Miss Waring be doing in company with an Emancipist rogue such as Dilhorne?

Once they had reached Mrs Cooke's front door and Hester was assailed by the parrot's usual greeting, Tom removed his hat again and asked, 'Have you done me the honour of coming to any decision about my proposition to you, Miss Waring?'

Hester found herself trembling. Now that the moment of truth was on her she was fearful that she would not be able to say what must be said.

She had thought and thought about Tom's offer. In the end she had concluded that the only person she needed to please was herself. He was offering her so much in return for so little, and the only payment required of her was that she was to present herself to the world as Tom Dilhorne's wife. All those who would be prepared to criticise her were so comfortably placed themselves that they could have no idea what the alternative was.

All this flashed through her mind as she looked up at him. He was so tall and she so small that he towered over her. For the first time the power of his presence was almost too much for her. He seemed to sense this—he was as sensitive as a cat—and stepped back a pace. Liberated a little by his action, Hester was able to give him her answer.

'Indeed, Mr Dilhorne, I have. I shall be happy to accept your offer of marriage on the terms stated, and will marry you whenever you think fit.'

He bent from his great height and gravely lifted her hand to his lips, surprising not only Hester, but an old lady who was crossing the road. We are becoming the spectacle of Sydney, thought Hester with the ghost of another giggle.

'Then, Miss Waring, I think it is my duty to tell you that now that you have given me your answer, and I am truly honoured by it, you should visit my home, as soon as possible—for it will be yours, too—so that you may make any changes you see fit.'

'I shall be happy to do so, Mr Dilhorne, and to take tea with you, if I may. But I also think it proper that I should bring along a female companion, seeing that you have no lady in your establishment to entertain me.'

He bowed to her again. 'Ah, Miss Waring, I can already

see how necessary your presence will be in my future life. You will be sure to know the correct thing to do without thinking. Who do you propose shall accompany you?'

'I thought that Mrs Wright might like to be my chaperon.'

'But what would Lieutenant Wright say to that?'

'Well, I'm bound to tell you that somehow Frank always agrees with what Lucy wants, and besides…' she looked shyly up at him to see how far *she* could go in teasing *him* '…I think that Lucy would love to see what all Sydney calls your barbaric home, don't you?'

'You never cease to surprise me, Miss Waring.' And that statement, he thought with amusement, was a true one. 'When shall I expect you to call and at what hour?'

'Next Friday, if it pleases you, and at four of the clock. By then we shall all have dined and a dish of tea would be welcome.'

'I shall be ready for you both at that hour. It shall be my housekeeper's swansong before my wife takes over.'

He bowed to her again and handed her bag back to her. She thought, amused in her turn, that only Mr Tom Dilhorne would have consented to have his proposal accepted in the street, and by doing so had saved her the embarrassment of having to invite him in, thus exposing them to Mrs Cooke's curiosity. She wondered whether anything he did was ever unconsidered.

She took his final words in with her. 'I am sure that you will not regret our bargain, Miss Waring.'

He left her with a spring in his step and with his hat on his head at a jaunty angle. Tom Dilhorne was pleased with life and with himself: Hester Waring was not quite sure how she felt.


Hester put on her best gown, which was not saying much, she thought ruefully, and went to call on Lucy

Wright. Lucy received her warmly and reproached herself
for the long time which had passed since Hester's last disastrous visit.

She had behaved so peculiarly then that when Lucy had
tried to invite her to their Christmas festivities Frank had,
for once, put his foot down, and said that he would not
have her, and Lucy, for once, had given way.

Welcoming Hester reminded Lucy that Sarah Kerr had
recently suggested that Hester did not look as if she had
enough to eat. Her dress was just as shabby as the one
which she had worn before Christmas. Well, there was
nothing Lucy could do about that, but she could arrange
for Hester to enjoy some food.

She rang for tea, ordering bread and butter and some
slices of plum cake.

'What's the Missis want nursery tea for, then?' asked
Lucy's skivvy, only for Cook to sniff, 'Oh, it's for that
poor, plain Miss Waring who doesn't get enough grub
since her pa died.'

Hester's predicament was common gossip among the
servants of Sydney even if their betters weren't aware of
it, and only Tom, for his own ends, had cared to do anything to help.

Hester tried to eat her tea without being overtly greedy.
A difficult task. Her extra money was bringing her a little
more food, but still not enough to satisfy her. She twisted
her hands together: it was going to be harder than she
thought to ask her improbable favour of Lucy. She said
abruptly, 'Lucy, there is something I have to ask you.'

'You know that I'm always ready to do anything for
you.'

Lucy liked to think of herself as generous to a fault, and
always had what Frank called 'her lame ducks'. He

thought that Hester Waring was the lamest duck of all, as
Hester well knew. What she was about to say would surprise Frank as much as anyone.

'Lucy, I am going to be married to Tom Dilhorne, quite
soon.'

Having thrown this grenade on to Lucy's best carpet,
Hester fell silent.

'Married! To Tom Dilhorne? Oh, Hester, is this wise?
Are you sure that you want to? Is there no one else? You
surely know that he's an ex-felon? Came here in chains,
they say! Besides, you are a lady!'

'No, there's no one else,' said Hester painfully. 'Nor
will there be. Ever. I quite liked Captain Parker, but you
know that he'll never offer for me. I've no money and I'm
not even pretty. It's obvious, in fact, that most people think
me plain. I know the other officers think me a bit of a
joke.'

She said this last in a stoic voice, but behind it was the
bitter memory of Captain Jack Cameron and the nickname
he had coined for her, 'Fred Waring's plain piece'.

'Oh, no, Hester,' cried warm-hearted Lucy. 'You can't
believe that.' But one look at Hester's face told her that
she did.

'But…Tom Dilhorne, of all people. Why, I didn't even
know that you were acquainted with him.'

'I met him through the school. He has been very kind
to me. I thought that he didn't want me to be a teacher
because of Father, but it turned out that it was he who
made sure that I was appointed.'

She stopped and decided to tell Lucy a little, a very
little, of the truth.

'Besides, I think that Tom wants a housekeeper as much
as a wife, now that Mrs Jones is leaving.'

If Lucy thought that this was the saddest reason for getting married she had ever heard, she did not say so. She also decided not to deter Hester from marrying Tom, however unsuitable he might once have been as a husband for Miss Waring of Essendene and Lighthorne House. Looking at her, it was plain to Lucy that Hester's future as a single person was little short of hopeless. But Tom Dilhorne! And why on earth did Tom Dilhorne want to marry Hester?

'I really know very little about him,' Lucy said, her voice full of doubt. 'I have never spoken to him, of course, nor he to me.'

She remembered suddenly what Sarah Kerr had said to her once when she had criticised Sarah and Alan's friendship with 'that rogue Dilhorne': that she and Alan would sooner lose all their other friends than break with Tom.

She brightened a little. 'But I do know that Sarah and Alan Kerr think a great deal of him, and that must say *something* good about him.'

'Yes,' said Hester. She had no intention of discussing Tom or her marriage with Lucy. She merely wanted to move on to the favour.

'Would you mind very much, Lucy, if I asked you to come to tea with me at Tom's villa on Friday? He feels that I ought to see it before I marry him, and your presence would make everything proper. Would Frank mind?' she asked, apparently ingenuously.

Goodness, I must be catching Tom Dilhorne's deviousness! She knew perfectly well that such a question would ensure Lucy's participation.

'Mind!' exclaimed Lucy energetically. 'He'd better not mind! I shall only be helping my best friend visit her future husband. What's wrong with that?' She looked suddenly enthusiastic.

'Besides, Hester, I'm dying to see inside his new villa.

Rumour has it that it's splendidly barbaric. I can't wait to see it! By all means, I shall come, and we must go together in my carriage. I can't have you walking all that way. Most improper, if I am to drive there, that you are left on foot.'

Friday duly came and Lucy, resplendent in a new gown of cream muslin made up from the latest pattern book to come from England, arrived at Mrs Cooke's to collect Hester. She instructed her astonished coachman to drive on to Mr Dilhorne's new villa.

'Does the master know?' he enquired impudently.

'My husband's permission is not needed for my actions,' Lucy informed him loftily. 'Drive on.'

Externally, Tom's villa, out on the Point with a superb view of the harbour, was a classical mansion of beautiful proportions. Inside, however, everything was different. The vast entrance hall contained only two blue and white Chinese vases of immense size and a giant bronze urn mounted on a wooden base.

The urn was covered with intricate carving, and around it was twisted a realistic dragon, its tail disappearing into the base and its head raised to roar at visitors. The floor of polished stone had one covering, a large washed Chinese carpet in the most delicate colours.

The disdainful Mrs Jones—so soon to leave—who thought her employer mad to fill his home with treasures from the Far East, led them into a huge room where Tom was waiting for them. To the eyes of most Englishmen and women, accustomed to Georgian elegance, this room was, if anything, even more startling.

There were more Chinese carpets on the stone floor, more porcelain vases in every shade imaginable, more bronzes, as well as lacquer cabinets and a Japanese screen which ran the length of the room. A tiger prowled along it, one sardonic eye cocked at the spectators. It resembled, Hester thought, its owner, who was watching them, an enigmatic smile on his face. Before the screen stood a long table, whose top was made from one block of polished black wood.

Behind Tom was a giant hearth made from uncut stones, over which a Samurai sword hung. Beside the hearth stood a full suit of Japanese armour. Three or four chairs and several lacquered tables, one set with teacups without handles, and several delicate little cakes on even more exquisite porcelain plates, awaited his guests.

Lucy's eyes were like saucers. Hester, who was determined to take everything which came her way without comment, sat down and at Tom's request began to serve the tea and generally play hostess.

'Well, Mrs Wright,' said Tom, after the preliminaries were over, 'would you care to see more of my home when we have taken tea?'

'Oh, yes, please…it's…unbelievable.'

Hester knew Tom well enough by now to know how he was reacting to this, although his face remained impassive. 'So it is,' he said. 'And you, Miss Waring, what do you think?'

'I think that it's beautiful,' she told him truthfully.

He looked at her sharply. 'Yes, I believe you do. But you know that if you don't like anything you have only to say, and I shall change it at once. Mind you remember that.'

Lucy listened to him in some surprise. She had not known what to expect of him, but looking at him as he lounged back in his intricately carved Japanese chair of state, and listening to the kind way in which he spoke to Hester, she thought that perhaps her friend could have made a worse choice.

But this house! Well, one thing you could say about it, it would be easy to clean.

The rest of it, when Tom showed them around, was the same. In the bedrooms there were beautiful silk hangings and great divans with long bolsters and giant cushions covered in wonderful fabrics. No dark fourposters for Tom Dilhorne. Tiny rice paper paintings of exquisite birds and flowers hung on otherwise empty walls. Outside the master bedroom two fat-stomached Chinese idols kept guard on either side of bronze doors. The impression of savage beauty was overwhelming.

After that, to find a modern kitchen and a severe study-cum-library with its shelves filled with books and papers was almost too much. Hester was acquiring a treasure house.

Tom watched the two girls in some amusement. His Hester had been correct in saying that curiosity would bring Lucy Wright here if all else failed, and he could imagine Frank and his fellow-officers being regaled with details of how an Emancipist lived.

He was also wryly aware that Lucy had succumbed to his personal attractions, although he had made no conscious effort to win her over. He would not have been surprised to learn that she had already decided that he was a fascinating man and that Sydney society was wrong to snub him.

What pleased him more than anything, though, was that by her expression and comments Hester was not going to turn his home into an imitation of an English country house. They lived in the Pacific, after all, and his home reflected that. So far as he was concerned he never thought of England as home: it did not exist except as a place to be traded with, and these days his trade was more often with the ports and centres of the Far East. He took the world as his oyster and he had no regrets. New South Wales had rapidly brought him a fortune which he intended to make even greater than it already was.

It was also bringing him a wife who was a lady, one who because of her sad situation was happy to accept him, an ex-felon, a man whom in normal circumstances she would have refused to know. But, having risen above his dreadful start in life, he was now determined that the lady who was his wife would never regret her bargain.

And if love, and the softer emotions, played little part in the considerations which lay behind his choice of Hester, why, that was an advantage, too. For to love anyone was to give a hostage to fortune, and Tom Dilhorne had no intention of putting himself in the way of ever getting hurt again. His marriage was yet another of his business propositions and he had not deceived Hester when he had told her that.

Nor did he deceive himself over the fact that one of the reasons for it was to defy the conventions which governed Emancipist behaviour by demonstrating that, providing he was successful enough, an ex-felon could even marry a lady of such impeccable lineage as Hester Waring was, and to that extent poor, plain Hester was a trophy.

When, finally, he managed to make her his wife in the truest sense, as he fully intended to do, so that he might have a mother for his children, that, too, he told himself firmly, would merely be another business decision.

'No, you must be funning, Lucy. For Tom Dilhorne to marry Hester Waring is of all things the most ridiculous. She brings him neither looks nor money…and for her to marry an Emancipist! Remember what her papa thought of them…and Tom Dilhorne in particular.'

Lucy Wright's mama's reaction was the normal one as

the news ran around Sydney like wildfire, and the gentry who gathered in Hyde Park that week spoke of little else. Gossip was the fuel of Sydney's small social world, and here was a morsel so prime that it eclipsed even the Governor's latest vagary. This also involved Tom Dilhorne, whom Macquarie intended to make a magistrate as well as his crony, Dr Kerr.

'Thought Dilhorne had more sense,' guffawed Jack Cameron to his hangers-on in the Mess, 'than to marry Fred Waring's plain and penniless piece.' He was always nastily eloquent about Hester—for some reason her helplessness offended him.

He thought the joke an exquisite one, the unmentionable marrying the unfortunate. Like many he considered that Dilhorne's usual common sense and his eye for a bargain had deserted him. What kind of a bargain was Hester Waring? Unless of course he was taking her on merely because she was a gentlewoman—which just went to show how desperate an Emancipist rogue could get in his struggle for respectability.

Even the Governor, when his wife told him the surprising news, had raised his eyebrows but made no verbal comment. He thought that whatever Dilhorne did was carefully considered, so this marriage, too, must have its reasons.

Not only the Exclusives were entertained by it. Tom Dilhorne's latest coup was celebrated with derision in Sydney's grog shops, much reduced by Governor Macquarie's latest edict which had closed many of them—another count in the tally against him. Rich Tom, who could have had anyone—well, almost anyone—had chosen the schoolma'm, Fred Waring's dreary dab of a daughter. Past it, or desperate for some reason, was the general verdict.

If Hester knew none of this by direct report, she could

not but be aware of the furore which her proposed marriage to Tom had excited—turning heads, meaningful stares, and almost sneering congratulations from people who had hardly spoken to her for years.

Far from weakening her resolve, this criticism strengthened it, and her Mentor's comments on the response of the respectable was even more unprintably harsh than usual. After all, few of her critics had so much as offered her a crust—only Mrs Cooke had helped her in any way before she had met Tom.

Even Mrs Cooke was as surprised as the rest since Hester was so different from Mary Mahoney, who was intrigued by Tom's choice of a wife. While the rest of Sydney thought that Tom had, for once, shown less than his good sense, Mary, who knew him well, wondered a little. With Tom there was always more than met the eye.

The arrangements for Sydney's oddest wedding went ahead rapidly. Neither Tom nor Hester wanted a great fuss. They were both privately agreed that, providing the banns were called and they both stood before a priest, the presence of others was not needed. Nevertheless, there were some whom both bride and groom agreed must be present.

There were other problems to solve. Hester was worried that her marriage might mean that she would leave her children without a teacher. She confided in Tom and, knowing his resourcefulness, was not surprised when a few days later he told her that he had found a solution.

'Quite by chance I spoke to Captain Ramsey about our wish not to let the children down. He had a word with Sergeant Fenton whose wife has been running a Sunday school for the garrison's children and she would be only too happy to take your place in the little school, provided that you assisted her to begin with—seeing that you have been so successful with them. Will that do?'

'Oh, yes,' said Hester eagerly. 'I would like to continue teaching for a little time, at any rate, but in future my first responsibility must be to you.'

And so it was settled.

One Saturday Hester accompanied him on his visit to the Kerrs. They had particularly asked that she be present. Hester had no real wish to visit them; she was still a little frightened of Tom, however, and dared not tell him that she did not wish to go with him. At the back of her mind, he was still the Tom Dilhorne whom her parents had hated.

Lucy had said, after their little tea party, that Tom would look after her, but Hester was not so sure. Catching sight of him sometimes, when he was frowning, knowing that there were those who cringed away from him when he spoke to them, she wondered what she was marrying.

His great physical strength alternately attracted and frightened her. What, if after the wedding, he insisted on his marital rights? Could she take him at his word? She knew of his reputation for deviousness; after all, had he not practised it on herself? She knew, too, that there were dark stories about how he had acquired his wealth, and he had certainly arrived in the colony in chains. It was rumoured that he had been a successful thief in London's underworld.

She would also have been worried if she had heard Sarah Kerr's reception of the news of Tom's choice. He had wanted to tell Alan and Sarah of his intention to marry Hester before he told anyone else, but a series of circumstances deprived him of the chance.

He was only able to speak to Alan briefly, one morning when he met him on his doctor's rounds, before the news reached them from other tongues.

'Tell Sarah I'm sorry I wasn't able to inform her my-self,' were his last words.

Alan was as disbelieving as the rest of Sydney. Hester Waring! He could think of no one less suited to be Tom's wife and the mistress of his grand home. Much later Sarah was to say of this time that every occasion on which Hester's name was mentioned there was an exclamation mark behind it. Her own reaction was the same.

'Hester Waring! You are funning, Alan!'

'I know how you must feel. I felt the same myself. But no, I am not funning. I had the news from Tom today.'

More exclamation marks followed, with a few question marks thrown in.

'But why Hester Waring of all people? I always imagined that Tom would marry someone grand, handsome and clever who would stand up to him. What can he be thinking of? More to the point, what can *she* be thinking of? He'll eat her.'

'Perhaps she wants to be eaten. Or to eat,' offered Alan helpfully.

Typically Sarah rounded on him and on herself. 'What a cat I am! Poor, half-starved monkey. What on earth will the wedding be like? I know one thing, everyone will want to go, just to make sure that it's really happening.'

'Oh, it's happening,' replied her husband cheerfully. 'Tom gave me the date. He says that the banns are being called straight away. And I invited them both for dinner on Saturday.'

'It explains why Tom hasn't been visiting us lately,' Sarah exclaimed. 'The dog! He's been courting. I'm glad you asked them. Whatever I think of the marriage I mean to do my best for them.'

'What will amuse you,' went on Alan, watching his wife bound about the room, exclaiming further and rearranging

things in order to give vent to her feelings, 'is that she
took Lucy Wright with her to have tea at Tom's new villa,
and that Lucy went without consulting Frank. The first he
knew of it was when Pat Ramsey twitted him about it in
the Mess after he heard the news.'

'Now, how did you find that out?' asked Sarah, fascinated.

'After I met Tom, Pat came over and told me that apparently Frank tried to reprimand Lucy over the visit. Lucy
told him roundly that Hester needed her support, that Tom
Dilhorne was a much misjudged man, and sent Frank back
on duty without any dinner!'

Sarah exploded with laughter. 'How like Lucy. She re-
sembles her mother more every day.'

'Yes, Pat says Lucy's given everyone a guidebook tour
of Tom's mansion which made it sound like a cross between the Imperial Palace in Peking and the British Mu-
seum. All the old cats who have refused to know him will
be queuing up for an invitation to his dinner parties now
that he has a wife. Just to see it for themselves.'

Sarah dried her eyes. 'Well, Villa Dilhorne—' her nickname for Tom's home '—*is* rather splendid. But isn't there
a danger that Hester will want to make it over into something cosy?'

'Not according to Pat. Lucy said that Hester apparently
fell for it hook, line and sinker.'

'What gossips you men are,' said Sarah. 'If I'd come
home and told you all that, you would have said, "Just
like women".'

'Seriously, Sarah,' her husband replied, 'we must support Tom. Hester is his choice of a wife. He's been a good
friend to both of us and we must try to help Hester. She
has hardly a friend in the world.'

'But is catching the richest husband in Sydney. Yes, yes,

I know. I will be a good girl and not say or think naughty things. But she never liked me much.'

'I expected you frightened her,' offered Alan slyly.

'Me? Frighten anyone! What nonsense!'

Sarah welcomed Tom and Hester to dinner with all the warmth of her warm-hearted soul. She took Hester by the hand when she entered the house, kissed her cheek and said, 'Tom's wife is always welcome here.'

Privately she was shocked. She thought that Hester looked ill, and was not sure whether or not she was frightened of Tom. Hester spoke little at dinner, except once when Tom leaned over and asked her opinion of the pudding which, to prevent herself from gobbling, she was eating with elaborate slowness. Her self-control at meals was still frail.

She looked at him and said, 'It is excellent, Mr Dilhorne. The food of the Gods.'

Tom's mouth twitched a little at this.

'And what is that, Miss Waring?'

'Well, sometimes it's plum pudding, and sometimes it's anything I really like when I'm eating it: Ambrosia Mr Dilhorne.'

Sarah's antennae told her that there was more to this exchange than met the eye or ear. Hester's soulful expression and Tom's satiric one were not lost on her.

Later, when Tom was talking of some deals with Sandy Jameson, and how Jameson's clerk had tried to set him down, Hester said slyly, 'Tried to set you down, Mr Dilhorne? It would be a brave man or woman who would try.'

'Come, come, Miss Waring,' he asked, 'am I to consider that a compliment?'

'If you like, Mr Dilhorne, if you like. Now, if you had

been wearing your waistcoat with the peacocks at the time, he wouldn't even have tried.'

'I must remember that the next time I do business with Jameson, but as it was...' he paused, tantalisingly, until Sarah gave way, and said impatiently,

'As it was, Tom?'

'As it was, I took him by the nose, twisted it, told him to mind his manners, knocked him to the floor—quite gently mind, no rough stuff—and then walked over him into Jameson's office.'

'And what did Jameson say? Seeing that Macquarie wants to make you a magistrate, and you had just assaulted his clerk?'

'He didn't say anything. I said it. I told Jameson that my memory of him went back to the time when he had no seat to his breeches, and if he told his clerk to insult me again, it would be *his* nose which got the treatment—and, by the by, I was thinking of calling in the money he owed me over the quarry. That took the roses from his cheeks and made him more than uncommon polite, I can tell you.'

'I'm glad you didn't do business with me like that,' said Hester, her face grave.

'Ah, but you've always been so polite to me, Miss Waring,' said Tom untruthfully. 'Polite people get wine and plum puddings. I should have told Jameson that.'

Alan was laughing. 'You'll make a splendid law-abiding magistrate, Tom. I thought that you'd left rough-housing behind.'

'Well, I have, pretty largely. But it never hurts to let people know that you're still fly. Take that clerk, for instance—he's so polite when I see him now, he could almost give lessons to Miss Waring, except that you don't need lessons in that area, do you, Miss Waring?'

'I fear that I do sometimes, Mr Dilhorne. But if I do need correction I trust that nose-pulling is out!'

'Depend upon it, Miss Waring—' Tom was earnestness itself '—I should find a more appropriate punishment.'

Later they discussed the wedding. Alan was to be best man, and Tom had proposed that, of all people, Robert Jardine be asked to give the bride away.

'For,' said Tom, 'were it not for Jardine, I should not have the pleasure of marrying Miss Waring.'

To Alan and Sarah's surprise, Hester blushed a rosy-red which was not entirely unbecoming. Before she could stop herself, Sarah said, 'How was that, Tom? Jardine, of all people.'

'He kindly gave a character reference for me to Miss Waring who was a little dubious about my credentials as they related to the principles of education and the advice I might give to the Board.'

Alan threw his wife a warning look and said solemnly to his friend, 'Only you, Tom, could come out with something so totally meaningless that sounds so grand. But we take the point; we'll enquire no further.'

'So, if Miss Waring consents, Jardine it will be. I take it that you had no one else in mind,' he asked Hester politely.

Hester replied no, she thought not, with as much sincerity as she could muster, seeing that there was no adult male in the whole of Sydney whom she had any claim on.

'Unless, of course,' Tom murmured wickedly, 'Captain Parker might like to take a hand.'

To Sarah's delight Hester slapped at him gently and said, 'No, thank you, Mr Dilhorne. Mr Jardine will do as well as anyone.'

'And we want a quiet wedding,' continued Tom, 'But I

do have business interests which require to be satisfied, if Miss Waring does not mind too much.'

'Like Jameson's clerk,' muttered Hester *sotto voce*, and tried to look as though she had said nothing. It was not, even now, always possible to silence her Mentor.

'I should like Lucy Wright to come,' she added, 'and that will mean inviting Frank. I don't know how he will feel about attending an Emancipist's wedding.'

'Oh, he'll come,' said Tom with a grin. 'Like the rest of Sydney he'll want to see the fun the day I get married. And Captain Parker, Hester. Surely you'll want Captain Parker?'

'Why should I?' was Hester's response to this sally. She had no idea of how Tom had discovered her early *tendre* for Captain Parker, but he was already the subject of one of their private jokes, like the plum puddings which were puzzling Sarah.

'And, Sarah,' said Tom, 'we shall want your help over a housekeeper for Hester when Mrs Jones goes. Hester will be in charge, but we shall need someone to supervise the kitchen. So far the only one we can find is Mrs Hackett and I can't say I fancy employing her.'

Sarah made a face. 'I'll try my best, but I'm not hopeful. You know what a shortage of women there is in the colony, servants included.'

Sarah and Alan looked at one another after their guests had left.

'I still don't believe it,' Sarah said, 'she's such a half-starved scrap. But I do believe he cares. More, perhaps, than he knows. I never thought to see it. What's more, they understand one another. I would warn anyone who values their safety not to say anything against her, in or out of his presence.'

Alan nodded. 'He's still dangerous. People forget that

he is because he's suddenly acquired perfect manners and perfect clothes. On top of that he's taking a lady for his wife. Very much a lady, too, for all her terrible history. God knows how high he will rise at his present rate. But beneath it he's still the same man he ever was. And you don't twist tigers' tails, even though they might look as though they've turned into tame cats.'

'Does *she* care for him, Alan?'

'I'll use your words—more than she knows,' said her husband. 'And she's got spirit, Sarah. You were wrong about that.'

'So I was,' replied Sarah generously. 'But Tom's doing that, bringing her out. Making her talk. I wonder what all that was about plum puddings. I should dearly like to know.'

'It will do, then?' Alan was serious. He had always been Jonathan to Tom's David ever since they had met on the transport which had brought them to New South Wales and he'd been taken under the fly criminal's protection, for even though Alan had been the older of the two, he had been an innocent in the young Tom Dilhorne's world, and now he wanted David to be happy.

'Oh, yes, it will certainly do, my love.'

To universal surprise Miss Hester Waring, spinster, aged twenty-one, penniless gentlewoman, come down in the world from a family which boasted a lineage back to the Conquest, married Mr Tom Dilhorne, bachelor and ex-felon, transported for God knows what, who did not know exactly how old he was, except that he thought that he might be in his mid-thirties, who was almost certainly illegitimate and who had no idea of who his father might have been, and who by his own efforts had made himself the richest man in New South Wales.

The wedding ceremony in Villa Dilhorne was as small and private as Tom had said it would be, with only Alan and Sarah Kerr, Robert Jardine, Will French, Joseph Smith, the Wrights, Mrs Cooke, Kate and Mr and Mrs Smith, present. The latter because of the chickens, Tom had said gravely—leaving Sarah to wonder exactly what he meant.

Hester, of course, appreciated his innuendo, and was already learning to listen carefully to everything Tom said and detect the hidden meaning which often lay behind his apparently careless utterances.

Tom, being Tom, had taken up Sarah's joke, and had had Villa Dilhorne carved on a great block of stone at the entrance to the long drive so that the guests would not lose their way.

Governor Macquarie sent Hester a beautiful bouquet of flowers from his own gardens and Tom bought her a new gown to wear, over her protests that it was not proper for the groom to do any such thing.

'But I can't have you wearing one of those made-over efforts on your wedding day,' he had replied reasonably. 'It's not fitting.'

Hester thought, looking at herself in the glass at Mrs Cooke's on her wedding morning, that it didn't help much, she was still so thin and plain, even though Tom had artfully managed to feed her once or twice in the few weeks before the wedding.

She told Sarah Kerr, who was her matron of honour, that hers must have been the only wedding where the groom's appearance outshone the bride's. This was so evidently true that even Sarah could not think of anything witty to say which might cheer the bride up. Hester's inward misgivings were so great that she was surprised that they did not cause her to sink through the floor before the eyes of the admittedly limited congregation.

The groom, however, wore an expression which could only be compared to that of an extremely satisfied cat who had just got away with an extremely large quantity of cream. Which, looking at the bride, the congregation found a little strange.

After the ceremony they all enjoyed the wedding breakfast, though why it was called breakfast at such a late hour baffled the bride.

Tom, being Tom again, there was an unparalleled array of food, though God knew where it had come from, Sydney not being quite the thing in the food line, but as more than one guest said, driving home through the moonlight, 'Well, you know Tom.'

All the guests ate and drank mightily, except the bride, who for once felt sick at the sight of food, but found that her husband was as adept after marriage as before it in getting her to drink a rather large quantity of wine.

'Come on, my dear, it will put roses in your cheeks,' he told her, pouring her out yet another glass.

Sarah thought that she had never seen anything quite so forlorn as Hester Dilhorne in her splendid new home on her wedding night. She hoped that Tom would be kind to her.

Surprisingly, after everyone had gone home and husband and wife were left alone in their great barbaric mansion to retire for the night, Hester felt an enormous unreasoning resentment that they were keeping to their bargain when Tom took her up the wide staircase, kissed her hand and said, 'Goodnight, Mrs Dilhorne,' to her outside her room before retiring to his.

Of course, the bride did not really wish him to come in with her. The mere idea that he might made her breath shorten, her heart beat violently, and a dreadful flush mount from her toes to her head and back again. She felt so excited and queer, what with the wedding and the wine, that it needed a long drink of water and a cold flannel on her face to restore her composure.

The groom was well aware of what the bride was thinking, and was certain that good food, affection and comfort would bring them to a true wedding night before long.

# *Chapter Six*

Tom Dilhorne's marriage was more than a nine days' wonder. Even when the initial excitement over it had died down, what passed for society in Sydney had so little to occupy it that, every time gossip flagged, someone was sure to start talking about it and wonder how the newly-weds were faring. After a short time even Sydney could not have foreseen what a remarkable titbit was going to keep their curiosity fed and their tongues wagging.

Often, in those early days, when Tom drove out in his gig, Hester sat beside him, and a mocking world noticed how solicitous he was in his care of her, helping her down, carrying her little reticule, and when it was very hot tenderly holding her parasol over her head for her.

'He's like a man with a new toy,' one wag said. 'Who'd have thought it of old Tom, eh?' as though Tom were sixty and not in his mid-thirties, but he seemed like an institution these days. It was difficult to remember the time when he had not dominated Sydney's economic and commercial life, even if he was not part of the Exclusives' social world—other than being invited to Government House, that was.

Hester had no idea of what marriage to Tom might entail. Any attempt she had made to imagine her future with him had come up against her lack of knowledge of how a man like Tom Dilhorne would live, and what he would expect of her in the odd bargain she had made with him.

In the event her life was strangely easy. Her day began at breakfast, which was a leisurely affair, not a leisurely affair in Fred Waring's manner, but one peculiar to Tom. He took the opportunity each morning to read through his papers and correspondence while eating and drinking at a slow pace, making the odd comment to her. He also made notes on small pieces of paper which he put in his pocket—and forgot.

Occasionally he threw a letter, or a piece of paper, over to Hester and asked her for her opinion of it. At first she was timid and said something noncommittal in the hope that he would not do it again. A useless tactic. Very soon she realised that the only way to satisfy him was to make some substantive comment, however slight.

It was obvious that he saw her dislike at having to commit herself, equally obvious that he was determined to make her do so. One morning he tossed across a letter from a business rival making him an offer, which on the surface was attractive, but which he sensed was dubious after some fashion. There was little in the letter to support this, only his own intuition which had stood him in good stead over the years.

Hester read the letter through carefully and then put it down with a sigh.

'Yes, Mrs Dilhorne?' He always called her Mrs Dilhorne now, whether to impress on her that, despite all, she was his wife or as a means of not using her Christian name—she was not sure which. She looked across at him. He was totally relaxed, like a great cat, she thought. His

face was unreadable, immobile; only his blue eyes, hard
and cold, watched her.

'I don't like it,' she told him, her voice slow and hesi-
tant. 'I don't know why, but there's something wrong with
it.'

'True, Mrs Dilhorne. And I can't tell you why either.'

He reached for the letter. 'We shan't be dealing with
him—at least not on this offer.'

Relief swept over Hester. She had said the right thing.
She was aware that Tom was still watching her while he
swept his papers together and prepared to leave for his
office.

'What if I had approved?' she asked.

He treated her to his grin. The one that said to friends
and enemies alike that Tom Dilhorne knew what was what.

'Oh, I knew that if you gave me an opinion that was
the one you would give me.'

'Just like that.' She was as short as he usually was.

'Just like that, Mrs Dilhorne.' The grin grew. 'You've
a good mind there, be sure you cultivate it.'

She was suddenly Fred Waring's high-bred daughter.
'You patronise me, sir.'

'No, indeed. Merely compliment you. The name is Tom,
or Mr Dilhorne. No sirs from my wife—or anyone else—
in this house.'

Cat and mouse, thought Hester furiously. That's the
game Tom plays with people. He won't eat me, he won't,
he won't. But her smile at him was as friendly as she could
make it, and his response was to kiss her hand as he left:
a response which somehow seemed to excite not just the
hand, but her whole body in the strangest fashion, leaving
it dissatisfied for the rest of the day.

I'm Tom's pet mouse, she raged, when she went through
to the kitchen to supervise the day's work, tingling all

over. He won't even eat me, not he. He'll keep me to prod
with a gentle paw, to let me know who's master.

But you like it, you know you like it, said her horrible
Mentor, and don't you wish that the cat would do more
than play with you harmlessly. How about some more
grown-up fun?

Oh, be quiet, she thought fiercely. Where do such dreadful notions come from?

Then there was the matter of dress. Hester had brought
to her marriage a tiny wardrobe of elderly clothes. Out-
dated threadbare gowns, all of which had seen better days,
and most of which had been made over from her mother's
old dresses. They were dark in colour. Mrs Waring had
been in perpetual mourning for Rowland, and they did
nothing for Hester's complexion and figure.

Sitting at breakfast one morning, and throwing back a
paper on which she had just given an opinion, Hester met
Tom's disapproving stare.

At first Hester thought that the disapproval was for her
opinion, but Tom's next words dispelled that.

'Clothes, Mrs Dilhorne,' he said succinctly.

'Clothes, Mr Dilhorne?' she mocked him gently.

He nodded his head. 'Yours are hardly exciting, Mrs
Dilhorne.'

'My clothes are not meant to be exciting. They are
meant to be ladylike.'

He nodded again. 'Aye, they are that. Go to Mrs Herbert
at the Emporium and order something less ladylike and
more attractive. My wife must not look like a dowd. Her
sempstresses will know what to do.'

To some extent Hester already had Tom's measure. She
knew how far she could go, and that he preferred spirit to
submission.

'Must, Mr Dilhorne? Must?'

'Must, Mrs Dilhorne.' The blue eyes approved her show of spirit. 'We are to dine at Government House on Saturday. I am, among other things, a rich merchant, and my wife must look like a rich merchant's wife.'

'But still ladylike, I hope. What do I use for money, Mr Dilhorne?'

'Why, nothing, Mrs Dilhorne. You use my name. You'll be astonished what it will do for you in Sydney.'

Hester found herself laughing. 'No, I won't. I already know.' And she went and bought herself something less gaudy than she thought he might have chosen—although there she wronged him, as she was later to discover—but sufficiently fashionable to cause Captain Parker to raise his eyebrows when he saw her at Government House on Saturday.

Next it was food. Hester had spent her life since coming to New South Wales feeling hungry. As Tom's wife she was suddenly able to indulge herself. She helped Cook and Mrs Hackett in the kitchen and attacked the results of their work with a kind of frantic delicacy.

One evening when she was eating her dinner with even more appreciation than usual, she looked up to find Tom smiling at her. It was his Cheshire Cat grin which said, I'm amused at something which other people can't see. What in the world could be provoking it? thought Hester irritably. He's seen me eat before.

'Enjoying your dinner, Mrs Dilhorne?'

'Indeed, this mutton is excellent.'

'I think so, too. Compliment Cook for me.'

'You may address your compliments to me, Mr Dilhorne.'

He bowed over his plate. 'I will double them, my dear. Ability as well as beauty becomes my wife.'

'Now you are funning, Mr Dilhorne. Your wife is no beauty.'

Tom looked across at her. Several weeks of good eating and affectionate treatment had made her lank hair glossier, was beginning to give it deep waves, and had improved her complexion, which now wore the look of health. She was beginning to acquire curves where none had existed before. His amusement grew as he watched the well-bred greed with which she disposed of her meal.

'Do you never look in your glass, Mrs Dilhorne?'

'Frequently—how else would I do my hair?'

'How else?'

It was plain that she had no idea of how much she had changed and was still changing.

'I thought that Captain Parker was a deal too attentive to you last Saturday—considering that you are my wife.'

'Nonsense, Mr Dilhorne. Captain Parker has always been kind. Even when I was friendless and poor. He was rather less so than usual last Saturday.'

'Kind, you call it,' murmured Tom, ignoring the truth of the last part of her sentence, and that Hester had not yet changed sufficiently to attract a handsome young man. 'Where I was brought up we had another name for it. I hope that he remembers that you are my wife now.'

Hester knew him well enough to know when he was teasing her. The idle drawl, the slightly hooded eyes, the look to see how the mouse was reacting. And yet, and yet, this time she was not so sure.

Tom Dilhorne's mouse, she thought again. I wonder whether mice are ever allowed to bite back when the cat plays with them.

'I've always thought Captain Parker rather handsome,'

she murmured idly, spooning cream lavishly on to her peaches. 'It is to be hoped that he will find himself a young woman to please him.'

'Careful with the cream, Mrs Dilhorne,' was Tom's answer to this sally. 'We can't have you getting fat. I know for a fact that Captain Parker likes 'em thin.'

It was almost impossible to get a rise out of him, thought Hester crossly, and to punish him spooned out a double dose of cream.

'I like cream,' she said, her manner all defiance, 'eating it is one of the benefits of marriage.'

'Only one, Mrs Dilhorne? What are the others?'

Hester waved her spoon in a totally unladylike manner. Tom had that effect on her. He's corrupting you, her Mentor said. Then I like being corrupted, Hester thought back defiantly, pleased to be naughtier than her Mentor for once.

'Besides eating cream there are comfortable rooms, not worrying whether I can afford a new pair of hose or a new gown—' and before she could stop herself '—and someone to talk to.' Her defiance had, quite without her meaning it, descended into bathos. She wondered what Tom made of this absurd catalogue.

His expression remained impassive. He would not demean her by expressing the pity roused in him by this recital of the ordinary comforts of life as a demonstration of the benefits which she felt marriage had brought her. Not for the first time he cursed Fred Waring's lamentable selfishness which had so deprived his daughter. It would not do to let her know of his pity. Either she would not believe him, or she would resent it furiously.

'And me, Mrs Dilhorne? Am I one of the benefits of marriage?'

The spoon was carefully put down. What was she to say

to that? The truth, of course. The mouse could not escape the cat's paws, but could avoid a mauling.

'Indeed, Mr Dilhorne, as I said. The pleasure of your conversation more than makes up for the disadvantages of the situation in which we find ourselves.'

'We could always remedy that, Mrs Dilhorne.'

Hester's response to this dry suggestion that they dispense with their white marriage was immediate. Her hand flew to her mouth and her eyes were suddenly wide and startled.

Tom watched her ruefully. For all her gallant manner and apparent bravado she was not yet ready to contemplate being Tom Dilhorne's wife in more than name. It was all a game which she could safely play with him, secure in the knowledge that there would be no consequences.

Well, let that pass. He would reassure her now. His time would come. He yawned and made no effort to speak again, to provoke her into saying something which she might later regret. If he made no move now, she would think that she had misunderstood him. Men and women had great powers of self-deception as he well knew to his own frequent profit.

Meantime he must try to make her see that she was slowly turning into an attractive woman, and when she smiled and defied him she was more than that. He had only been half joking when he had twitted her about young Parker. After all, he was near to Hester in age and his fresh, blond, good looks made Tom feel even more battered than he was.

For her part Hester, as Tom had thought, concluded that she had misunderstood him. The cat did not intend to pounce and Mrs Dilhorne might go safe to her lonely bed.

Hiring Mrs Hackett because Sarah could find no one else was an even greater mistake than Tom thought that it might be. To begin with she disliked Hester because she disliked all women younger than herself; besides, Hester was so plain, and drunken old Fred's daughter to boot, who had no business marrying wealth, even Emancipist wealth. Tom she disliked because he had always frightened her from the days when she was Corporal Hackett's wife, and he was a thrusting newcomer.

She was no fool, though, and soon grasped that her employers were man and wife in name only and were sleeping in separate rooms. She spied on them, watched them furtively in order to make sure that her suspicions were correct, and then took this gleeful gossip, too good not to share, and sent it on its way around Sydney.

What next? It beggared belief. Clever Tom Dilhorne had no more sense than to marry a wife who wouldn't let him get into her bed! At last, gossip had something real to get its teeth into. Madame Phoebe's rocked with the news; the garrison crowed with mirth. Jack Cameron started a book, taking bets as to when Tom Dilhorne would get into his wife's bed, how long it would take, and whether it would last. Pat Ramsey told Lucy and Frank the unbelievable news one afternoon, after he had heard it at Phoebe's the night before.

They all looked at one another and laughed immoderately. Even Lucy laughed, and hardly reprimanded Frank when, wiping his eyes, he said, 'I didn't think that plain piece had it in her. The great Tom Dilhorne outwitted by a woman, and too gentlemanly these days to give it to her without permission. Sorry, Luce.'

Other gossip was even more indelicate. Running around Sydney, the unlikely tale even entered Government House and reached Lachlan Macquarie, who pulled his lip and said to his wife, 'What is that devious devil up to now?'

He knew Tom better than most and could not believe him put upon by Hester Waring. Others, though, wanted to believe him bested, and even Mary Wilkinson, late Mahoney, thought it likely that Tom had been cheated, and felt sorry for him.

The last to know were the Kerrs. Most people were too afraid of them to pass on the news, but Sarah, while visiting Lucy Wright one afternoon, overheard some rude laughter about Tom and Hester, and said as fiercely as only she could, 'What is that, Mrs Middleton? You are speaking of my friends. What slander is that?'

Before her mother could answer, Lucy, fearing an explosion if Sarah were publicly informed of the gossip, signalled to her and took her into another room to tell her what all Sydney already knew.

'I don't believe it,' said Sarah sharply, and then fell silent, as everything she had wondered about the marriage, and how the pair had behaved after it, fell into place.

Lucy watched Sarah's face change, and thought, It's true then, the gossip is true, and somehow, Sarah knows. Since, for all her matronly assumptions and her pretty child, she was young and careless, she thought gleefully, What larks!

'Can it be true, Alan?' Sarah asked her husband—he was the last person in Sydney to know. 'Poor Tom. If it is true, what does it mean? Whatever can he be up to now?'

'Yes, I think it's true. I've suspected so for some time. Hester does not look, or act, like a married woman. Her appearance is healthier than it was, but that is the result of having enough to eat and drink at last. But, Sarah, you know Tom nearly as well as I do. Believe as I must that there is more to this than Sydney thinks. Trust him, as I do.'

* * *

Aware or not aware of what was being said about his marriage—and it would have been strange if he did not know, for it was always held that whatever happened in Sydney, Tom Dilhorne somehow knew of it—Tom continued his wife's education in the ways of his world.

First, he insisted that she learn about his business. He had seen too many self-made men's widows cheated of the fortune their husbands had left them. He was determined that Hester should not be left unprotected.

Throwing the letters to her at breakfast was only part of his method of instruction. In the evenings he went further. The week after their marriage he called her into his study after their evening meal.

'This room is yours, as well as mine,' he told her.

Hester looked about her, a little bewildered. He was standing at his desk and patiently he showed her his records, his private ledgers and the order in which his books and papers were arranged on the shelves.

Slowly Hester learned the mysteries of bookkeeping, discounting, money-lending, the running of his Emporium and his warehouses, the building and maintenance of ships, carriage building, the hauling of goods, the upkeep of quarries and the brickfield, and even the arcana of auctioneering—of which Tom was a master.

Some of this she found tedious, some of it interesting, if not exciting. She had a good mind, learned quickly and impressed him with her rapid grasp of affairs, and the matter-of-fact way in which she accepted what must have seemed to her an odd education for a gentlewoman.

Once, puzzling over his explanation of a deal with Sandy Jameson involving the brickfields and which owed more to Tom's intuitive understanding of the world than to his manipulation of figures and contracts, she put one word to him. 'Why, Tom, why?'

Oddly now, whenever they were speaking seriously together, it had become Tom and Hester. Mr and Mrs Dilhorne were reserved for the comic banter with which they had begun their acquaintance and which had continued into their marriage.

He knew exactly what she meant. 'I want you to understand everything I do, Hester. You are the only person in whom I confide and I want no other. You are my wife, even if in name only. You follow most ably all that I explain to you. If I should die suddenly—or be killed, for this is still a dangerous place—I do not want to leave you to be cheated.'

At his mention of dying Hester shuddered, and without thinking, pressed herself against him. Instinctively she wished to be reassured, to feel his strength, to know that he was there, that she could call on him for help. To think of losing him was suddenly an idea so hateful to her that she could not endure it. So far he had kept faithfully to their strange bargain and she had come to trust him absolutely. Living with him, fear had been replaced by liking—and more than liking.

She could hardly wait for him to come home so that she might be with him. When they went out together she watched for him if they were compelled to part, and the strange feelings which the sight of him had provoked before marriage were growing stronger and stronger…

She wanted…oh, what did she want? You know perfectly well what you want, what you wish he would give you, said her naughty Mentor. You are beginning to regret your bargain. Suppose he kissed you now. Passionately. Would you like that? Of course you would. To kiss him back would be of all things the most delightful…and then…

Tom put his hand absently on her head and stroked her

hair to comfort and to reassure her. He felt her quiver beneath him while he did so.

'It seems so strange,' she said at last, 'you are the last person I would have thought of as instructing a woman in business practice.'

'Well, Mrs Dilhorne,' he said playfully, 'you know that a wife's first duty is to please her husband and you please me mightily by doing this.'

'Then I shall try even harder to understand it all, Mr Dilhorne.' She waved her hand at the desk and the walls of books and papers. 'But I trust that you do not expect me to officiate at your next auction!'

Later that week Tom came home early and called to Hester to come into the garden, he had an entertainment for her.

Putting down the fine silk shirt which she was making for him, she slipped on her shawl and went outside. The garden was large with an English-style shrubbery and lawn. At one end was a small Japanese pagoda with a wooden table and chairs, painted white, set out before it, where they often took tea.

Tom had carried out a large mahogany box. He opened it and placed on the table a brace of pistols, a powder horn, balls, and a ramrod to load the pistols. Some distance away from the pagoda he had placed in the soft earth of the border a crudely worked piece of wood in the shape of a man.

'Goodness, Mr Dilhorne, what are you going to do now?'

'Not what am *I* going to do, Mrs Dilhorne, but what *you* are going to do.' He had begun loading the pistols while he was speaking.

'Watch me carefully, Hester,' he said. 'Later on I shall want you to load them.'

'Oh, no, Tom—' Mr Dilhorne was forgotten, for she could see that he was deadly serious, all banter gone '—they're horrid things!'

'Oh, yes, Hester. New South Wales is a dangerous place, and even women should be able to defend themselves. I want you to be able to load and fire a pistol without flinching as though you were really trying to kill a man.'

It was useless to protest. Somehow he always won such battles. It was hard to argue with him. He was so very reasoned and sure.

'You really mean that you want me to fire one of these things?'

'Exactly. Let me show you.' He was being as short with her as though they were engaged in a business deal.

Patiently and carefully he taught her how to shoot. She was not strong enough to hold the pistol in the dueller's traditional stance, left arm behind her back, right arm extended: but neither did he want her to. Instead he taught her to hold it in front of her, in both hands, to keep it steady.

'You aren't going to fight a duel, Hester, so there's no point in learning a lot of nonsense. No one's going to drop a handkerchief and wait for you to fire. First shot, dead shot is my maxim.'

She looked at his hard determined face as he continued. 'Only a fool waits for the other fellow to fire first, and you aren't a fool.'

There was no point in doing anything but obey him. He was quite adamant, so, although to begin with the noise and the recoil of the pistol disturbed her, she gradually became used to them.

'We're not playing at Lords and Gentlemen in Manton's

rooms in London,' he said drily while teaching her to shoot in a crouching stance far removed from the polite forms of the duel.

'No funny little targets here,' he told her, making her fire at the man-shaped board. 'You'd be shooting at a man, Hester, not a little circle. Always aim at his chest and never the head. The chest is a bigger target and you're certain to damage him if you hit him there. No pistol is accurate beyond a shortish range, any road.'

Hester soon understood that, although he made something of a game of it for her and called it an entertainment, this was no game he was playing. She tried to please him by losing her fear and improving her skill. It was one way in which she could thank him for rescuing her from penury, and for his forbearance over the physical side of their marriage.

In the first stages of teaching, however, they inevitably came into close contact when he stood behind her and helped her to steady the pistol. Hester found Tom's nearness exciting. Her heart beat faster, her breathing changed, and she found that not only did she not want him to move away, but that she resented it when he did.

He was scrupulous in gaining no advantage for himself in their nearness, but Hester began to wish that he would show her some sign of affection. She even found that her desire to kiss his warm cheek whenever it was placed next to her own grew stronger every day of their practice.

She was waking up to the world of the senses which had been denied to her all her life by her parents' indifference to her. She hoped that Tom did not observe her strange reactions, but he was well aware of them. He knew what they meant, but also knew that he must be patient, not push or force her, or she might retreat again.

* * *

Once Hester had learned to use the pistols skilfully, he
made her load and practise with them every day. She grew
to be proud of her accomplishment, but the other consequence of their continued intimacy was a disturbing one
for her. On the evenings when they practised together sleep
was long arriving. She lay restless in her bed, wondering
what on earth was coming over her.

Tom could have told Hester what was wrong. He
watched her face flush when he touched her to correct her
aim, or to steady her, and felt her leaning against him
unnecessarily. She would have been surprised to learn how
much he longed to take her in his arms and begin to teach
her the arts of love for which she was almost ready.

He, too, lay restless in bed. The more so since he was
determined not to find solace at Madame Phoebe's. His
patience with her would be rewarded, he knew. With each
change in body and spirit the time was fast approaching
when she would welcome him, not repel him, and he
would become her husband in fact as well as in name.

Husband and wife in separate beds found comfort in
different ways. Tom fixed his mind on his next deal, and
dreamed of the beauties, not of women, but of porcelain
and silk.

And Hester?

Hester did what she had so often done in Sydney. She
imagined herself back in the garden at home in England.
Only, when she drifted into sleep and the door in the wall
opened, it was Tom who walked in to greet her, and not
her dead brother.

Tom was not surprised by Hester's good head for business, or at her growing ability with a pistol. His view of
men and women was essentially a pragmatic one and was
as practical and down-to-earth as his advice to Hester on
shooting.

He had early noted that Madam Phoebe had a better business brain than most men, and that his own mother's bravery, half-remembered from his lost boyhood, had been exemplary. Both before and after her father's death Hester had displayed a stoic courage—indeed, it had been that attribute which had first brought her to his notice.

He didn't think that men and women were equal. In Tom's world there was no such thing as equality, but he thought that most women he knew were silly, trivial and incompetent because their lives and men had made them so. Not that they were more trivial and silly than all the parsons and most of the gentlemen he had met, but that they had had less chance to be otherwise.

His understanding of human motivation and his ability to manipulate his fellows arose from the fact that he had no theory of life, but worked solely on the basis of observation, allied to the intuition which arose from that observation and which allowed him to make startling leaps of understanding. It was one of these which had informed him of the innate possibilities of Hester Waring.

The sight of Hester daily growing in confidence and beginning to enjoy her new-found skills, added to his determination to bring her gradually to be his true wife and the mother of his children.

# Chapter Seven

Hester stood at her bedroom window looking out over the broad sea across which the First Fleet had sailed to reach Botany Bay on January 2, 1788. First Fleet day was usually celebrated by the Governor in fine style. A holiday was proclaimed, even convicts sharing in it; rum was distributed to the garrison, and the Governor gave a great dinner party to every person of consequence in the colony.

This year, although a holiday had been granted on the proper day, the official ceremonies had not been carried out because the Governor had been detained at Paramatta and only now, in late February, was Macquarie's dinner party being held.

The Dilhornes had been invited, although as an Emancipist Tom would be snubbed by everyone else who was present, other than the Governor himself and the Kerrs. Hester was curious to find out how her old friends in the Regiment would treat her—and, more to the point, would they snub Tom?

Her thoughts were interrupted by a knock on the door. It was Tom, she knew. He was always scrupulous about never coming into her room unannounced and, when she called 'Come in', he pushed the door open, hesitantly for

him, and advanced on her, holding the crumpled linen of
his cravat out to her, a rueful smile on his face.

'I can never get the hang of these damned things, begging your pardon, Mrs Dilhorne. Thought you might have
the knack of it.'

Hester looked at him severely. She did not believe a
word of what he was saying. She only knew that lately he
had taken to asking her to help him to finish dressing.

'Need to be just so, Mrs Dilhorne,' was his usual excuse.

Now what would that lead to? she wanted to know.
Something you might like, whispered her naughty Mentor.

'I used to do Papa's,' she said, 'after he could no longer
afford a man.'

She knew that Tom kept no valet and allowed few servants in his home—other than Mrs Hackett who had a
room near the kitchen. The other servants' quarters were
apart from the house, over the mews.

She dragged a stool up to stand on it after he had handed
her the cravat and briskly began to arrange its folds for
him.

'This one is called a waterfall,' she announced. 'Rowland always liked a waterfall. I think that the one Papa
preferred was more suitable for an older man.'

'You don't consider me an older man, then,' murmured
Tom. 'Pity, that. I thought that now I am not only your
husband but one of Sydney's more prominent citizens I
might qualify in your eyes as someone grave and reverend,
to be respected. Why, I even had to be quite elderly with
Macquarie or he would have announced the appointment
of myself and Alan to the magistracy today at dinner—to
spite the Exclusives who try to tell him what to do as much
as to honour Alan and myself, I suspect.'

'If appearing grave and reverend are the qualifications
for being an older man,' said Hester naughtily, smoothing

the final pleat, then stepping down and standing back to admire her handiwork, 'then I doubt whether Mr Tom Dilhorne will ever qualify—even if he should reach ninety!'

'I shall certainly never qualify if I have such a disrespectful wife,' he said, bending his head to kiss her fingers when she leaned forward to give her creation a last approving flick.

'Tell me, Mrs D.—what happened to the meek and mild creature we appointed to be school-ma'm last year? She seems to have disappeared quite. More such advice and you will qualify as a nag.'

His voice was amused, not reproving, and Hester gave him another sly look from under her lashes; she enjoyed teasing him back these days.

'Why, Mr Tom Dilhorne happened to her, sir. Now, your hair, Mr Dilhorne, your hair.'

Tom rose, stared at himself in the mirror. 'My hair? I thought that I had made a good fist for once of rivalling all those lively young officers after whom my wife hankers. You do hanker after lively young officers, Mrs Dilhorne, don't you?'

Hester ignored him. 'You rival the riff-raff in the Rocks as you are,' she informed him with mock severity. 'Pray sit down and allow me to make you over.'

'Nag, nag, nag,' he said. 'I suppose all this is because you have given up the school and no longer have the children to master.'

Nevertheless he sat down again and held his head so that she could brush his unruly sandy crop forward into a windswept coiffure *à la* Brutus, thinking while she did so what a comfortable old married style they shared these days—except, of course, that they were still not truly married.

'Now,' said Hester, admiring the pair of them in the

mirror, 'pray tell me why you do not wish to be a magistrate. I am sure you are aware that every Exclusive in Sydney thinks that you are positively burning for the honour, and cannot wait for the Governor to name the day.'

'Too soon,' said Tom, reverting to his usual short self before growing expansive again—he was always careful to explain his sometimes cryptic utterances to her. 'Macquarie goes too far and too fast. I shall never be accepted in polite society, such as it is in Sydney. Alan might be. He was a gentleman before he was transported, whilst I—' and he shrugged '—was Yorkshire, and then London, scum. I don't even know who my father was. The shadow of my origin and my chains will always hang about me, however rich and powerful I may become.'

His face changed suddenly, all the banter and mockery usually visible on it quite gone as he inspected himself in the mirror.

'Between us, wife, we have created a pretty fraud, have we not? Under your final ministrations and tricked out in these clothes, speaking as I do—and not as I used to do— I look and sound a perfect gentleman.

'No, I have no real wish to be a magistrate, although I may end up as one, if only to be able to prove that Tom Dilhorne, thief, felon and merchant, is Tom Dilhorne still and may laugh in the faces of those who consider themselves his betters.'

'Oh, but you do that without needing to be a magistrate,' said Hester, to have him rise, swing her off her feet into the air, and shake her, oh so gently, and laughing, say,

'Now I know why I married you, Mrs D. I shall think of that when we sit, grave-faced, among the respectable tonight. That I am no longer alone, and that I have someone to share my secret thoughts with—even if you do not grace my bed.'

He put her down again. 'We are ready to face them in every sense, my dear, and Miller shall bring the carriage round so that we shall arrive at Government House in state.'

Of course, Hester had been right in thinking that Tom would be snubbed. He sat opposite to her at dinner, in Government House's beautiful dining room, chandeliers blazing and the Regimental band playing popular airs while they ate. Not a soul, other than the Governor, spoke to him.

At the end of the dinner official toasting began. Until now both ladies and gentlemen had toasted one another privately, leaning over to clink glasses and to offer each other salutes. Pat had toasted Hester, but no one had toasted Tom, and his wine stood untouched in the glass before him.

Hester knew that, although he valued its qualities as a life-giving restorer, he did not like to drink overmuch of it, and here, surrounded by men and women, many of whom were already fuddled, he showed his indifference to their customs by barely drinking at all.

The band began to play, softly this time, and with great feeling, the Regimental march, 'My love is like a red, red rose', to usher in the official toasting. The flunkey who was acting toastmaster began to instruct the guests to raise their glasses. The noise of the company rising was accompanied by the sound of a sudden commotion at the far end of the table, away from the Dilhornes.

A young lieutenant who had drunk more than was good for him had risen before the command was given, and had begun to shout in the direction of the Governor.

'No!' he bellowed. 'Drink the Loyal Toast to His Majesty King George III in the company of felons and scum who should still be working in chains, not I! You may be Governor here, sir, but you strain my loyalty if you require me to share the Loyal Toast with him.'

He waved drunkenly at Tom, and, lifting his glass high began to pour the bright red liquid in it on to the tablecloth in a steady stream.

The uproar grew.

Colonel O'Connell, his face as crimson as the spilt wine, shouted down the table, 'Be quiet, you young fool. Have you lost your wits?'

Other officers, seated near him, embarrassed that the lad in his cups should say publicly what they all privately thought, began to pull him down, but he would not be silenced, shouting again before Major Menzies clamped a hand across his mouth.

'No, it is he who is mad,' he roared, indicating Macquarie who sat, unmoved, with a stone face while the uproar continued. 'To ask officers and gentlemen to sit here and consort with such as Dilhorne, to think of making him a magistrate—and the rest of you are hypocrites...' The remainder of his outburst was lost behind Menzies's large palm.

Heads turned. Men guffawed. Women tittered. The only unmoved person in the room beside Macquarie was Tom himself.

He smiled, picked up his glass, and watched the young man being dragged struggling from the room by his embarrassed fellow officers, his muffled protests continuing until he was finally hauled through the double doors at the far end.

The expression on his face was unreadable. He turned to Mrs Major Middleton sitting on his right, who had shown her displeasure at his presence by not addressing a word to him, saying, 'Come, madam, drink a toast to the only honest man in the room. He, and only he, had the courage to say what you are all thinking. He deserves a bumper for that—you will surely not grudge him one.'

Mrs Middleton looked him straight in the eye and said, her voice ice, 'That being so, Mr Dilhorne, one wonders why you chose to attend.'

Tom continued to hold his glass out but, seeing her lack of response, his mouth curled again.

'No?' he said. 'Why, madam, I am here because the Governor invited me, as he did you. I cannot say fairer than that. You would not have had me insult him by a refusal, surely?'

Hester watched him, fascinated. Oh, she knew that face and that voice. She heard Pat Ramsey suck in his breath, saw Mrs Middleton's face flame as red as a turkey cock's wattles.

'The Governor should have more sense—' she began, then realised what Tom had done. He had compelled her to speak to him, not once, but twice, even though she had inwardly vowed, once she had seen who her companion was, that he would receive no such favours from *her*. Worse, he had made her defend herself when he was the one who should have been doing the defending!

'Some people,' she announced firmly to the table at large, 'know their place in life and keep to it!'

Tom drank his wine, emptying his glass before he replied to her, 'I do so agree with you, madam.' His smile was deadly. 'And my place tonight is here, at this table, beside you.'

He looked at his glass. 'Why, Mrs Major Middleton, is it not? I do believe that I have emptied my glass—and left nothing for the Loyal Toast. You see, you do not have to drink with me, after all.'

Pat Ramsey began to laugh, he could not help himself.

He remembered what he had advised Jack Cameron— never to cross verbal swords with Tom Dilhorne for he would surely lose.

'Your husband compels my admiration,' he said to Hester. 'I only—'

'You need say no more,' said Hester, cutting him short. 'I know exactly what you are thinking, Captain Ramsey, and it is the same as that poor young lieutenant. You know as well as I do that Tom was right. He is the only person at this table telling the truth, and he will be punished for it.'

'He will have a thick head in the morning, and time to think on his folly,' said Pat, unrepentant. 'Now we must drink the Loyal Toast, you and I.' He lifted his glass, Tom held his empty glass before him and bowed low, first to Mrs Middleton, and then to Hester.

Still defiant, she drank up her wine, saying loudly to an amused Pat, 'For both of us, Mr Dilhorne and myself,' to hear Pat reply,

'Bravo, Hester, my dear. One can only hope that your loyalty to him will gain a reward commensurate with your courage.'

Hester thought that he might be taunting her, but perhaps not. She was beginning to discover that Pat Ramsey had hidden depths.

After the toast the company were released to stream into the grounds outside, golden in the late afternoon sun, to discuss with great animation, some amusement and much anger, all that had passed.

The general opinion was that Macquarie had deserved such an outburst for daring to foist the unacceptable on his superiors in Government House where one supposed that such outcasts as Dilhorne would not be received.

Hester, followed by curious and sneering eyes, refused

Pat Ramsey's offer to escort her outside and made straight for Tom. He was as unmoved as ever, talking to the Governor who had made a point of going over to him the moment the dinner ended, taking his arm and walking him outside as a plain indication of his displeasure at the behaviour of the officers of his old Regiment.

Seeing Hester coming towards him, a defiant expression on her face, Tom excused himself, took her arm and walked her away from the disapproving company to a small grove of Norfolk pines through which, far below, the distant sea could be seen rolling.

He felt her arm tremble beneath his hand and said softly to her, 'Come, Mrs Dilhorne. You were a brave girl in there. Give them no satisfaction by showing distress.'

'Distress!' exclaimed Hester, her voice rising. 'It is they who should be showing distress—'

'Hush,' he interrupted her, and his voice was gentle. 'It is no more, and no less, than I expected. Perhaps Macquarie will now see that my advice is sound. I have to confess that his conduct in first inviting us, insisting on our attending, and then making such a point in coming over to honour me afterwards, whilst personally gratifying to us, was neither wise nor sensible. Alan taught me a scrap of Latin once which the Governor would do well to ponder on. *Festina lente*, Make haste slowly.'

He smiled wryly. 'You must understand their resentment, Hester, and learn to live with it. Now, smile with me. We are enjoying the afternoon, are we not? There will be fireworks soon, you will like them, I know, and the band is about to play, which, seeing that they have all been drinking hard while they waited for us to finish, will be an adventure in itself.'

Hester suddenly understood that he was speaking to calm her, that nothing which had been said or done to him had the power to hurt him, and that he was trying to make her respond in the same way.

As though he had read her mind, he said quietly, 'They want to see you distressed. Smile and be happy, and that will annoy them the more. It is like the Japanese, you see, who have this exercise called Judo where you turn your opponent's strength back on them.'

Despite herself, Hester began to smile. It was so like Tom to take an insult and use it to draw some strange moral, some lesson in living, instead of allowing it to distress him. He saw the smile and pressed her hand lovingly.

Will French, one of Tom's business rivals and friends, came up to them—everyone in Sydney was allowed to enter the grounds on these fête days, once the dinner was over. High and low rubbed shoulders together, another source of irritation to the respectable.

'Mrs Dilhorne, Dilhorne,' he said in his bluff way. 'You are looking well, Mrs Dilhorne. Rosy, in fact.'

'Oh, that is merely the effect of temper, Mr French,' returned Hester spiritedly.

'Aye,' said French, 'I heard that one of the young officers disgraced himself.'

Tom laughed. 'Even for Sydney, that gossip travelled rapidly.' The humour in his voice was real, not pretended.

French looked at him sharply; there was no fathoming Dilhorne. 'Yes, well, but that isn't what I came to speak of. Mind if we talk business, Mrs D.?'

Before Hester could reply, Tom said, 'If you have anything to say, French, you may always say it before my wife.'

French did not allow this to surprise him and said, 'Eh, well, you've been a good friend to me and you've dealt fairly with me since. Thought you might like to know that there's an underhand market in Government spirits and stores these days. Thought you had an understanding with O'Connell that what was here, in bond, came out to be distributed through you, kickbacks to you and the military both.'

This was news to Hester, and she thought again how strange it was that the very men and their wives who were making private fortunes for themselves by appropriating Government liquor and by selling it off, through Tom, should follow a social code which allowed them to insult him at will.

Tom knew what she was thinking. 'Time you learned how these things are organised, Hester,' he told her. 'So, French, someone, an officer—or officers, perhaps—is stealing, unofficially, that is, instead of officially, and the stuff is being sold around Sydney?'

French nodded.

'And it's being done without O'Connell's knowledge?'

French nodded again.

'My thanks,' said Tom seriously. 'I'll put out feelers. Can't have someone walking off with the cream of the crop and cheating his fellow officers—to say nothing of Tom Dilhorne.'

Hester could not help herself. She began to giggle. Tom looked at her with mock severity. 'Find it funny, do you, my dear? That someone is doing Dilhorne and partner down.'

'Partner?' interjected French, a little puzzled.

'Partner,' repeated Tom, waving his hand at Hester. It was her reward, she knew, for working hard with him and trying to behave as he would. He was now beginning to tell the world that he and she were more than a simple married couple. She could not thank him now, not in front of Will French and hostile spectators.

Instead, she watched some of the private soldiers of the

73rd walk across the lawn, flaming brands in their hands, to set alight tall branches cut from one of the great pines which stood high above the sea. Others were lighting lanterns among the groves to illuminate the growing dusk, and the first fireworks began to flare and sputter. The band's beery version of Handel's *Fireworks' Music* made a suitable accompaniment to the jollification.

Hester, her face alight, enjoyed the fireworks, insults to Tom and thieves who looted stores alike forgotten. Tom watched her, not the fireworks, such innocent delight wrenching unexpectedly at his hard-bitten soul.

French, staring at him, was suddenly surprised. So Dilhorne did have a soft spot, after all—and it was for his plain wife, of all people. Who would have thought it? A judgement which many others were making with cruel amusement.

Tom might once have agreed with the unpleasant gossip which went on behind his back. His entry into marriage had been cold-blooded enough and Hester being a kind of trophy had been the best part of the game. And if to coax her into bed with him had begun as simply one move in that game, it was rapidly turning into something more than that.

It was not only living in close proximity to her which was making him desire Hester, so that to possess her fully was not simply to satisfy an itch of the flesh, but it was Hester herself who was beginning to compel him. It was an emotion which the hard man had never felt for any woman, however kind he had been to his mistresses, and it was to some extent divorced from sex.

He had experienced such a feeling only once before when he had come upon Alan Kerr, bewildered and lost on the transport, abandoned among human wolves who saw him as sexual prey, all the certainties of his old life destroyed, and with no understanding of the brutal realities of his new one.

The urge to protect someone as helpless as Alan had been in his misery had overcome Tom then. It had made him offer a fierce friendship which had enabled Alan to survive, and the result had been the forging of a lasting relationship.

In Hester he had found someone else who needed him if she were to survive, and the same impulse which had led him to save Alan had moved him from his first real sight of her at the interview to the day on which he had married her—even though, as with Alan, he refused to face the reality of what he was doing, burying it beneath the cynicism which was all the surface man ever showed.

To his everlasting surprise he was beginning to fall in love with her in the truest sense.

The innocent joy with which she embraced her new life, her good mind, her gradually blossoming face and body, and her fierce and unthinking loyalty to him at the banquet, were all beginning to have their effect on him.

He found himself thinking of her all the time. If he did, or saw, something interesting when he was away from her, he reminded himself to tell her of it when he reached home. A new pair of gloves, a pretty fan, seen as they arrived in his Emporium, were picked up as presents for her, sure to make her face glow.

The smallest gift gave Hester, who had seldom been given anything, immense pleasure. Yesterday he had gone into his Emporium to oversee the unpacking of bales of priceless Chinese silks and he had picked up a roll of the purest, palest lemon, held it in his big hands, the nails scrupulously trimmed so as not to snag the delicate stuff, called over Mrs Herbert, who arranged these things, and ordered a dress to be made for Hester.

'A surprise, mind,' he said to her. 'You have her measurements, and I want it quite *à la mode*, you understand, but simple, nothing fancy. Use one of the fashion plates which came in from England—and she's not to know. No meaningful looks and all that.'

Mrs Herbert was always respectful of her employer's taste and feelings for female dress—she had clothed Mary Mahoney for him—a taste she thought incongruous for such a big and physical man.

His employees laughed when he had gone.

'Sweet on her, ain't he? Look at what he's taken home for her already this week. Not his choice he goes to bed alone, I'll be bound. Madam thinks she's too good for him,' was the general agreement.

If Tom knew what was said behind his back, he was quite indifferent to it. The game he played with life dictated that he knew and understood what people thought, said and did—and then he used it against them. Only a fool cared about the opinion of fools and, to Tom Dilhorne's cold eye, most people were fools.

They had been married for nearly two months when Tom came home early one afternoon and told Hester that, when he had been going down King Street earlier in the day, one of the aborigines had stopped him and told him that there was going to be a great storm that night.

Most of the Europeans would have laughed at such a prophecy, but Tom had learned in his hard life that nothing was to be ignored. Aborigines had told him similar things before, and they were usually right. He had tossed the man a coin. He had shown his teeth at Tom, and said something in his own language which Tom hoped was thanks, but thought was more likely to mean 'you poor white fool'.

'In case he's right,' Tom said to Hester, 'we'll drive out with a picnic and have a look at the storm in the open. Have you ever seen one, Hester?'

Hester confessed that she had not.

'Well then,' said Tom, 'there's nothing to lose, and if there's no storm we shall have had a pleasant evening out.'

His man of all work, Miller, harnessed the big carriage, and Tom brought food from Sydney for the picnic. He drove them through the bush to an open space, well beyond the town, which overlooked the sea on one side and the distant mountains on the other.

At first, as Hester said, it was all a hum. There was no storm. But they ate the food and drank the wine which Tom had so thoughtfully packed.

'More wine!' exclaimed Hester. 'You are turning me into a toper, Mr Dilhorne.'

'But you hold it so much better now,' said Tom, who never tired of plying her with food and drink and little attentions these days. He put her shawl on and let his hands linger on her neck. He felt her shiver at his touch and asked her anxiously, 'Do you feel cold, Mrs Dilhorne?'

In reply, Hester flushed slightly and said 'No', but leaned ever so slightly against him while she did so.

If propinquity was affecting Tom, it was affecting Hester even more. Her fear of all men had begun to disappear, and what she was beginning to feel for Tom was far removed from fear.

To enjoy a picnic meal on the edge of the bush which they often did—for Tom liked eating in the open—meant Tom feeding Hester titbits, and Hester managing to lick his fingers when he offered them to her. Just as though I were an intelligent horse, she thought with amusement.

The ogre Dilhorne had long since disappeared from her internal monologue, to be replaced by Tom, who brought her presents and thought of so many amusing and interesting things to do.

He had promised her that they would go swimming one day, and then had said slyly, 'But seeing that we're not really married, Mrs Dilhorne, the question of what to wear becomes difficult.'

Hester had fallen straight into the trap.

'Oh, why is that, Mr Dilhorne?'

'Well, swimming is only worthwhile when one isn't burdened by clothes.'

For the first time he saw that she did not flush when he said something which she might previously have thought over-daring, but appeared to ponder on what he had said.

'Never having had such an experience, Mr Dilhorne, either with, or without, clothing, I cannot say whether you are correct.'

On this evening they made the picnic last and Hester began to offer him the choicest parts of her share, putting orange segments on her palm, and raising them to his lips, saying, 'Your turn to be a horse, Mr Dilhorne.'

Tom in reply licked her hand as though he were an overeager pony who somehow managed to eat halfway up to her elbow before stopping.

After they had drunk their wine and were lying on the grass there was some interesting, if rather mild, horseplay involving Hester's wide-brimmed straw hat which Tom demanded as forfeit if Hester were unable to inform him what the current rate for Treasury Bills was in Sydney.

'What use would my hat be to you if you won?' asked Hester, who had just discovered that her wineglass was unfortunately empty.

Tom looked at her as she reclined beside him. She was

wearing a dotted Swiss muslin dress, a cobweb of a shawl, and a straw hat with a blue ribbon twined around it in such a fashion that it tied under the chin. Her looks had improved beyond belief; her complexion was clearing, was turning into a delicate pink and white, her hair had regained its lost lustre, and her expression these days was one of innocent mischief.

'Your hat looks so fetching, my dear, that wearing it could only improve my looks, too.'

This rather feeble sally by Tom's standards struck Hester as most uncommonly witty. Admiring him in his black silk trousers and shirt, a scarlet sash about his waist, she told him that she had really no answer to such an ill-judged statement.

Where it would all have ended Tom did not know. Hester's mood was so relaxed that anything seemed possible, even out here in the open. The storm, however, now took a hand in the game, and events followed a slightly different turn.

Just at the moment when Tom said that Hester's collar needed a little rearranging, a clap of thunder announced that the promised storm was arriving.

Hester agreed to let him straighten it.

'My fingers are all thumbs tonight, Mr Dilhorne.'

Surprisingly Tom managed, with remarkable lack of skill, to start to undo the collar rather than to fasten it up, stroking Hester's neck absent-mindedly while he did so, causing little shivers of delight to run up and down her body: a truly delightful sensation which she had never experienced before.

Hester jumped at the next violent crack of thunder, and Tom resigned himself to the fact that the first assault had not been so much repelled as not registered at all!

Hester's mood, however, was such that he had a small

private bet with himself that Mrs Dilhorne might find herself a truly married lady by morning.

They watched the distant storm for a long time engaging in much imaginative byplay until Hester gave a series of little screams when the thunder rolled and the lightning cracked. This enabled Tom to offer her a great deal of manly protection which involved him in putting his arms around her and encouraging her to hide her face in his chest when the thunder grew really loud.

This was yet another experience for her which proved strangely satisfactory to them both so that they quite forgot to notice that great curtains of rain were coming nearer and nearer.

By the time that they did so, it was too late. Their enjoyment had led them to end up some way from the carriage, the better to see the spectacle. In a moment they were drenched, which, for some reason neither of them understood, they found the biggest joke of the night.

An even bigger joke was to rescue their rug, the picnic things, Hester's parasol and Tom's light silk coat, all of which had been rapidly drenched in the torrential downpour. Far from quenching their excitement, for both of them had been on the verge of breaking their bargain, it added to it, and if Hester did not fully understand where matters were rapidly leading, Tom had no doubts at all.

Still laughing, they ran to the carriage. Tom almost threw Hester into it, and, whipping up the horses, he drove them home as rapidly as he could. Hester, who had always been afraid of storms, found herself strangely exhilarated by this one.

She clung to Tom while the carriage careered through the evening, thunder and lightning rioting overhead.

'Hang on, Mrs Dilhorne, we'll soon get you safely home.'

Improbably her response was to laugh. The downpour was relentless. Water streamed from Hester's hair and her clothing was sodden. Their evening trip had been transformed into something almost resembling a swim. Tom turned his head towards her and his eyes shone as the lightning flashed across the sky.

'Not frightened, Mrs Dilhorne?' he shouted above the thunder.

'No!'

And that was the truth. So long as she was with him she was not frightened. There were only the two of them in the whole wild world. Hester almost wished that this mad ride might never end. She clutched at Tom's arm and he turned again to reassure her. Her face told him that no reassurance was needed. The exhilaration which gripped him was affecting Hester, too.

They were at one in their joy of themselves and of the wild night. The few months which they had lived together had brought them to this moment of shared pleasure. All deceit, all trickery had leached out of Tom. If he had married Hester partly to scream defiance at the world from which she came, he would make her his true wife this night because she was Hester and he was Tom, and Exclusives and Emancipists, his past and hers, were alike irrelevant.

For Hester what was happening was almost like some powerful dream. The happiness which the past weeks had brought her, the gradual loss of her fear of her strange husband and its replacement by affection, which was rapidly turning into a passionate love which she did not yet know how to express, was something which she had never thought to experience.

She had told him that she was not afraid and that was the truth. Once she would have been, but that was before she had known him. Common sense might say that she ought to fear him, but whatever he was to others, to her he was the man who had delivered her from the prison in which she had lived for over twenty years. Unconsidered, passed over, slighted, left to starve or be condemned to become a prostitute, like Tom the external factors of their world meant nothing to her in the face of what she was coming to feel for him.

Their journey was nearly over. The villa loomed before them, white in the darkness.

# Chapter Eight

One last giant crack of thunder heralded their arrival. Tom helped Hester down, and then swung her off her feet, calling for his stable hand to take the horses and the carriage round to the mews.

The lad ran out, mouth open and, staring at Tom, watched him stride into the house cradling Hester in his arms.

Tom took the stairs at a run, water streaming from him. Mrs Hackett, unseen by them, opened her door and watched him carry Hester upstairs into her room, kissing her at every step he took. Her face was rigid with disapproval of their laughter. Then Tom emerged to run into his own room—to reappear almost immediately on the landing, a brandy bottle in his hand and towels over his shoulder.

He knocked on Hester's door and entered to find her trying to dry her streaming curls. She stared at him: the water was running down his face from his sodden hair, and—like hers—his face was alight with mischief. He strode to her dressing-table and poured a large tot of brandy into her water glass and thrust it towards her.

'Drink this, Mrs Dilhorne. Make you feel better.'

Hester felt as though some restraining hand which had held her back all her life had been removed. She took the glass from him, and remembering her father, tossed the drink back in one swallow—then choked and spluttered, the alcohol burning her throat and sending a warm river down to her stomach. Eyes as well as hair streaming, she turned to Tom who was laughing at the expression on her face.

'Bravely done, Mrs Dilhorne!'

He advanced on her, brandishing one of the towels, 'Here, let me dry you, Mrs Dilhorne.'

She should be refusing him, retreating from him, reminding him of their bargain, but Hester found that the strangest excitement was gripping her. Far from coming out with a maidenly 'Oh, no, Mr Dilhorne, I am quite capable of drying myself', she was welcoming his intrusive hands and the feel of them on her body.

Worse—or was it better?—the closeness of his body to hers which should have had her recoiling in disgust from him, was bringing on a fit of the giggles instead. Somehow Tom drying Hester involved him not only in towelling her hair, but in loosening and removing her clothes, and oddly enough in removing his as well!

'They are so very wet, Mrs Dilhorne, mustn't risk a fever.'

A statement which, far from frightening Hester as it would once have done, provoked her to an unreasoning amusement so that presently he had succeeded in wrapping them both, now quite naked, in one of the giant towels which he had brought with him.

That was not all, however. In the middle of doing these immodest things to her he also announced briskly, 'You will take an ague, Mrs Dilhorne, if you continue to shiver so. Allow me to assist you to re-cover yourself.'

Tom's re-covering Hester meant that he stroked her all over. True, he was doing it very gently, but now the shivering was not being caused by her being chilled, but by the effect his hands were having on her.

At first his stroking was quite innocent, but slowly he moved from a chaste massage of her back and shoulders, to one which encompassed her flanks and then her breasts. His thumbs on her nipples raised and quickened them in the oddest fashion. The pleasure that this induced had Hester not only crying out, but also leaning on him for support—which merely served to afford him even more opportunities to pet and caress her, all with muttered assurances that she would soon be warm again, he could guarantee that!

The melting sensation inside Hester grew stronger and stronger. She welcomed his impudent hands, and when they deserted her breasts she felt annoyed, only to discover that he had transferred them to the inner side of her thighs, and then to her most secret parts of all, still stroking and caressing.

He had also become silent, and instead of caressing her with his voice, he was kissing her face and shoulders and finally her deserted breasts, which found that his artful mouth on them was even more satisfactory than his hands had been in giving her pleasure.

All of these attentions produced a sensation inside Hester which was so powerful that she thought that she was literally about to burst. All sense of shame, of modesty, had deserted her.

She found that she was pressing herself against him and all that she could think to say was, 'Oh, please, Tom, please.'

What further she wanted him to do to her she could not think, except that somehow, she knew that there was more to come and that she wanted it. To compound her immodesty, she seemed to have lost control of herself to the degree that when she was not asking him to do something to her, she was stroking and caressing him!

Hester was not entirely sure what to do to please him as he was pleasing her. She only knew that his breathing, too, was becoming quite ragged, so she must be doing something right, which was a relief to the passionate maenad Mrs Tom Dilhorne, late Miss Hester Waring, had turned into.

His hands were suddenly in her drying hair and he had taken her right breast into his mouth and was teasing it with his tongue so that she was writhing against him. She was lost to everything, propriety, maidenly modesty, bargains arranged before marriage, and codes of conduct involving young gentlewomen, Exclusives and Emancipists.

She only knew that her whole body was craving for fulfilment, and that the man whose hard erect sex she could feel against her naked stomach was the one person in the world from whom she wanted it.

His mouth had deserted her breast and he was kissing her, first down her willing and yielding body to where the ache for fulfilment was at its strongest, so that she cried out, and then up, up, to her ear.

He was whispering into it, his voice hoarse with desire, 'Warmer, now, Mrs Dilhorne? Still want to keep to our bargain?'

She should be thrusting him away, shocked, but instead her hands clutched at him with such ferocity that her nails scored his back.

'Gently, Mrs Dilhorne, gently,' he murmured, and lowered her on to her bed, the two of them still half-smothered in the towel.

Fright flared briefly in Hester's eyes when she felt the

bed and took a little of his weight. Instantly aware of her reaction, he rolled away from her, and gave her a look so purely wicked that she giggled involuntarily when she felt his lips travelling down from her ear to her throat, down to her stomach leaving a trail of fire.

'Has anyone ever told you how sweetly you smell, Mrs Dilhorne? Captain Parker, for instance?'

Hester could not prevent herself from laughing. Her passionate response of a moment ago returned and she responded to each caress with caresses of her own, so that when his tongue entered her mouth to tease hers, she not only wantonly welcomed him, but used her own tongue to tease him back.

She felt that she was about to dissolve. The brandy, the excitement of the storm, mirroring their own, the enclosing towel, and now the unmistakable attentions which Tom was paying her, began to have their effect.

Her last thought as he threw off the restraining towel and began to make love to her in earnest was, Can this really be prim Hester Waring drowning in a sea of passion?

'Don't be frightened,' he whispered when he prepared to enter her, her body open and willing before him, 'I may hurt you a little to begin with, but afterwards, why afterwards, I promise you, you will enjoy yourself and we shall die the little death together.'

He was right again, Hester found, for by the time that the pain of first entry was on her, she was almost past normal sensation. She only knew while they mounted towards fulfilment, her hands on his back, his on her flanks, that if between them they had broken their contract of non-involved marriage, she did not care, no, not at all.

Thought departed: she was lost in a sensation so exquisite that she was crying out her joy, and afterwards she melted into the sleep of fulfilled exhaustion in her lover's arms, the lover who was her husband, who had married her as a jest, and had now found that the joke was on him.

Hester awoke the next morning to remember that some time during the night, they had made love yet again, but this time slowly, oh, so tantalisingly slowly, the pleasure being long drawn out, so that her cries and Tom's mingled at the point of release. After that they had achieved a half-reclining position in which Tom held her cradled in his right arm, with her head on his chest.

She looked up to find that he was already awake; seeing that she was also stirring, he gave her a quick kiss on the top of her head. After what had passed during the night, and her own passionate response to it, she felt a little shy, but the comfort of his warm body, the reassurance of his hard arm and his matter-of-fact acceptance of their situation made any reservations she might have had seem absurd.

She fell into a contented half doze. A little while later Tom slipped out of bed and left her and she began to wonder if she had dreamed it all. Her body told her, No! An emphatic no! She further wondered if he would return. Her bed felt strangely empty without him. She slept again, only to wake when the door opened and he came in.

He was wearing a military-style dressing-gown, ornamented with gilt frogs, much braid and epaulettes. Above it his knowing face was oddly incongruous. She began to smile.

He came over and sat by her on the bed. 'Why are you smiling, Mrs Dilhorne?'

'You look just like a member of the dandy set.'

'When I wear this, woman, I'll have you know I *am* a member of the dandy set!'

Quite without her willing it, as though they had a life of their own, she lifted her arms and pulled his head down to hers.

There was some brief scuffling and a touch of intricate manoeuvring on his part, at the end of which it seemed right and proper that his left hand was in her hair, cradling her head, his right hand was under her body, and his mouth was on her breast. He paid it some urgent attention.

Hester's breathing, which had become shallow, turned into a series of rising gasps as other parts of her body were explored and then into a repetition of his name on a rising crescendo.

Some further deeply interesting action, initiated by Tom, which resulted in yet another explosion of pleasure, highly satisfactory to them both, took a little time before he collapsed across her, his face in the pillow, and it was her turn to stroke his head until she fell asleep in mid-stroke.

Waking, she found him fully in bed with her again. 'What happened to your dressing-gown, Mr Dilhorne?'

'Lost it, Mrs D., but I shall find it again.'

'Not too soon, Mr D., I trust.'

His answer was to take her into his arms, not to make love to her, but to hold her while he whispered into her ear, 'You make an adept mistress, Mrs Dilhorne. You learn quickly.'

'Taught by a master, Mr Dilhorne.'

'That's good. You show me a proper respect.'

His muffled laughter joined hers until she fell into a doze again, wondering as she did so how easy it had become, easier than staying awake.

Consciousness returned again. He was still with her, stroking her hair, and gently kissing her cheek. 'Happy, Mrs Dilhorne? Enjoying yourself?'

She looked at him gravely and examined her condition. It surprised her.

'I'm hungry,' she announced. 'Very hungry.'

'Hard work, loving. Well, we'll remedy that for you.'

He was out of the bed in one smooth movement, and was slipping on his dressing-gown. 'Wait here. Don't go away, mind.'

Now where should I be going? thought Hester drowsily. With nothing on and loved into immobility, for she had no doubt that it was love and it was far nicer than anyone had ever led her to believe, and funny, too. The joy of it all touched her face with a soft hand, the corners of her mouth curled up, and it was thus Tom found her when he returned, a tray in his hand with a great Chinese bowl on it, a spoon and a capacious napkin.

'Sit up, Mrs Dilhorne.'

Hester yawned, sat up and let him drape the napkin around her neck. The bowl contained hot bread and milk, and something else, something rather pleasant which she could not identify. Tom sat on the bed, by her side, and, holding her in one arm, began to spoon the liquid into her mouth as though she were a child again. She had never felt so loved and spoiled in all her life.

'Nice, Mr Dilhorne. What's in it?'

'Bread and milk, my love.'

She slapped gently at his hand. 'I know that. What else?'

'Well, I wouldn't be saying there's not some rum in it. Got to keep your strength up.'

Hester licked the spoon greedily, and swallowed before teasing him gently. 'Well, what would you be saying, Mr Dilhorne, if you weren't saying that?'

'That if you look at me like that once more, I shan't be answerable for the consequences. By the by, I've told Mrs

Hackett that you are not very well, and that you are spending the day in bed.'

'And you, Mr Dilhorne? What will you be doing?'

'Spending it with you, Mrs Dilhorne. Unless you want me to send for Captain Parker. In which case it will be my duty to shoot him dead before giving you what you deserve.'

She had finished her milk broth. He lifted the bowl to the bedside table, and she murmured softly, 'What do I deserve, Mr Dilhorne?'

'This.'

This took some little time, and involved a great deal of kissing, stroking and thrusting on Tom's part, and not a little sighing and groaning on Hester's, to say nothing of exchanged endearments. Afterwards he lay propped on one arm, watching her, rosy and fulfilled, looking less like poor half-starved Hester Waring, and more like some flushed nymph from a Boucher painting.

'How do you like being Mrs Dilhorne, Mrs Dilhorne?'

She considered. 'Pleasant, if a trifle exhausting at times. I'm relieved I shan't be expected to get up today. And you,' she queried him, eyes alight, 'when do you go to your work, Mr Dilhorne?'

'Tomorrow, Mrs Dilhorne, tomorrow. The day after if you're lucky.'

'Tom,' said Hester seriously, letting Tom know by her form of address that she was not bantering him, but needed an honest and straightforward response. They were lying quietly and comfortably in bed the next morning, watching the dawn break, for Tom disliked drawing curtains, although the room possessed a magnificent pair, made of Chinese brocade.

'Yes, Hester.'

'There's something which worries me a little.'

'What is that?'

'Well, from what Mama said—and it wasn't very much—I gathered that going to bed with a man was a cross women had to bear. It wasn't very pleasant, she said, but it had to be done if you wanted to marry and have a family. I know that she frightened me so much that, before I met you, I couldn't look a man in the eye. Not even Captain Parker, whom I used to find attractive, which you know, since you tease me so about him.

'Yet…' Her voice trailed off. 'Now,' she began again, 'but now…'

'Now…Hester?'

'Well, is there something wrong with me that I enjoy what we do so much?'

His shout of laughter covered his hidden anger at what the late Mrs Waring had done to her daughter.

'Of course it's not. It's the most natural thing in the world. There'd be no babies, Hester, if we didn't enjoy ourselves, and you wouldn't like that.'

'Are you sure?' she asked him dubiously, hiding her face against his broad chest.

He took her by the chin and tipped her face towards him.

'Look at me, Hester. You were made to enjoy yourself and so was I. Only foolish parsons and, forgive me, silly women, think otherwise. Why should we torment ourselves over what comes so naturally? It's only when we misuse ourselves and one another that it's wrong.'

'Oh, Tom,' said Hester, 'you comfort me so. I was beginning to think myself quite vicious like the women at Madame Phoebe's.'

'The women at Madame Phoebe's don't enjoy themselves, my love,' he told her softly. 'Which is why I never slept with them. You run out of honest joy if you pay for it, or do it for pay. And that includes husbands and wives if they misuse one another. They're not vicious, Hester, they're earning a living, poor creatures, in the only way they can.'

Hester stirred in his arms. She thought that if he had not rescued her she might have been one of Madame Phoebe's girls if all else had failed her. He had saved her from that… She shivered and turned to him for reassurance. 'You know so much, Tom, and I so little. Tell me, are all men like you?'

'God forbid, no!' he said suddenly, with great violence and deadly serious. 'The only good thing you can say about me, Hester, is that I don't like to see women suffer.'

'Only,' she said softly to the grey light when he finally slept beside her. 'But that's a big only, Tom.'

Crouching at their bedroom door, listening—her face avid and cruel—there was one who did not enjoy their passion, or their new-found happiness. She was only too willing to make a mock of it about Sydney.

'Well, he finally gave it to that haughty madam the night of the storm,' cackled Mrs Hackett to her friends and anyone who would listen. 'Carried her up to bed and stayed there with her for two whole days! Only got up, he did, to come to my kitchen as bold as brass, wearing his bedgown. "My wife is ill," he says, cool as cool, "and won't be up today. I'll take her meals up to her."'

She fell into paroxysms of ugly mirth. 'Ill! Looking after her! Two whole days of it! I wonder you couldn't hear them in Sydney!'

Jack Cameron's book threatened to lose him even more when the news entertained the town and the garrison. He disliked Tom enough to let his emotions control the odds he had offered. When the gossip reached Lachlan Macquarie he grinned at it, and thought, The cunning fox. I wonder what his game is this time?

Alan Kerr heard Pat Ramsey and young Ensign Osborne laughing over Tom Dilhorne's latest exploit, and took the good news home to Sarah. When he had finished telling her, she kissed him.

'I told you to trust Tom,' he said.

# Chapter Nine

Tom and Hester had been truly man and wife for about a fortnight and were still in the first throes of delight when they received their invitation to attend Lachlan Macquarie's ball.

A ball! Hester had never been to one. She had read about them, but had never hoped that she might be a part of the grand company at Government House enjoying themselves in state. On the other hand, neither could she have visualised what had happened to her since she had married Tom.

Each day brought her new experiences—or was it more true to say that it was the nights which pleased her the most? She must be pleasing Tom, too, for on the night he told her of the invitation, he also said to her, 'For being such a good wife in bed, Mrs Dilhorne, you shall have a new gown for the ball, and be the finest lady there.'

Tom, as usual, was as good as his word and came home with a splendidly simple robe of the finest amethyst silk. He also gave her—she never knew where his treasures came from—a collar of amethysts and a ring to wear with it.

That night he made her dress herself as for the ball in

all her new finery, her hair coiled high on her head and delicate kid slippers on her tiny feet. Then, very slowly, he removed everything with a loving and elaborate care which had her whimpering in frustration. Everything, that was, but the amethyst necklace which remained around her neck during the long night of loving which followed.

Hester had still not yet achieved the looks which Tom was sure she would possess when her flowering was complete, even though she was much improved from the girl he had married.

He was proud to take her on his arm, truly Mr and Mrs Dilhorne at last, to taunt Sydney with his success and her emerging beauty as well as to defy the gossips who had been devouring his marriage like vultures.

Before they left, Hester asked him shyly, 'Do I look well, Tom?'

He looked at her, ran his hand delicately around the column of her neck, and whispered in her ear, 'Very well, Hester, although I prefer you with only the amethysts on—but that would never do for the ball—later, perhaps.'

Flushed and smiling, for Tom had spent the journey in the carriage wickedly teasing her about the delights to come when they finally reached home again, Hester arrived at Government House more sure of herself, she considered, than she had ever been. Which only went to show, she thought wryly afterwards, how poor a prophet she was and that pride was sure to go before a fall.

To begin with she was too happy to do more than enjoy being present. Lachlan Macquarie was kind to her when he arrived. He and his wife had recently been guests at one of her first dinner parties—but after a time she could not fail to notice that she and Tom were the subject of more than common interest, and that, by the way it was expressed, some of it was unpleasant.

Tom noticed, too, and his face hardened, but he said nothing to Hester. He shrugged off his uneasiness and concentrated on trying to secure her pleasure. Hester tried to put the nods, winks and leers out of her mind. Living with Tom was giving her armour.

After a light collation had been set out on tables at one end of the vast ballroom she expressed a desire to sit away from the heat. Tom immediately took her to a corner of the room by the newly built glasshouse where it was pleasantly chill and there were no other guests.

They sat together for a little while, watching the passing show, until Tom suggested to Hester that she might like a cooling drink and, on her agreeing, strode off to collect it, leaving her alone to listen to the band and admire the dancers. Tom rarely danced.

'Not part of my education,' he explained. Hester often wondered exactly what his education had consisted of and how he had obtained it, but he never spoke to her—or anyone—of his past life.

A pair of officers, one of them Jack Cameron by his voice, and another whom she did not know, walked into the glasshouse, to smoke a cigar, away from the ballroom where smoking was frowned upon. They stood near the open door and appeared unaware of Hester's presence nearby. She could hear them laughing and talking.

The talk and the drifting smoke disturbed her. She was about to move away to try to find Tom when she heard her name, and his, repeated.

'So he got his plain piece into bed, after all,' the unknown officer said coarsely. 'A fortnight ago, I hear, and a high old time they seem to be having: in bed for two days, they say. All bets due should be paid off, Jack. When do I get my money?'

'Don't know, old fellow. He's got her there, true, but

will he keep her there? Tom Dilhorne knows how to rig the odds, you may be sure, but can you be certain that she'll want to go on having her jollies with a brute like him? No, we'll wait to see what happens before I pay him—or anyone else.'

'You're nearly as devious a devil as he is, Cameron,' complained the other officer. 'I'd like to see the colour of my money.'

'Well, it took him over two months to get her there, it might not take so long for it to be off again. Even Dilhorne can't win all the time.'

The other man said nothing to this, then asked, 'Have you seen her tonight, Cameron?'

'Can't say I've had the pleasure,' guffawed Jack. 'If you can call it a pleasure!'

'Well, I own she's not quite as plain as she was. But that bastard Dilhorne's put his brand on her. She's wearing a fortune in amethysts around her scrawny neck.'

Cameron guffawed again. 'I thought that it was Sarah Kerr Dilhorne was sweet on. This one's a bit of a come down, I must say. But if he wants to drape her in amethysts, that's his bad taste. I suppose he spent his winnings on them.'

They moved off and Hester heard no more. She had sat as though paralysed, unable to move as the dreadful truth unfolded itself. Tom had broken their bargain, not because he loved her, but to win a bet. Had their whole marriage merely been a callous joke played by a man who loved another woman, and that woman, Sarah Kerr?

Jack Cameron carelessly stubbed out his cigar in one of Elizabeth Macquarie's pot plants before he left the conservatory. Arriving late in the ballroom, he had seen Tom leave Hester alone and had manoeuvred Menzies into a position where he was sure Hester could hear every cruel and deceiving word.

If she didn't think that her husband had made her the subject of vulgar bets and even more vulgar jokes, it wasn't Jack Cameron's fault. If that didn't take the shine off Master Tom's marriage, then nothing would.

Better still, if he had made sure that the marriage was off again, he might save himself from the financial ruin which was staring him in the face. That would teach Dilhorne not to humiliate an officer and a gentleman in Madame Phoebe's.

Hester sat rigid. The amethyst collar seemed to burn her neck. So the bargain with Tom was not a secret after all. Tom had told. Worse, he had bet on getting her into bed. Everyone knew everything, hence the looks and guffaws in the ballroom. How else would Jack Cameron know what she and Tom were doing if Tom had not told? His words could have no other meaning. Alternate hot and cold chills racked her. The glow on her face had disappeared.

How much had he told? Why had she ever trusted him? Her father and mother had been right about him. He had gained his revenge on her father by making her his wife and then publicly humiliating her. She thought of their lovemaking and the joy it had brought her, and she was near to fainting where she sat. The brute, the odious lying brute. He had treated her like a whore and she had thought him so kind, so considerate. The room reeled about her.

Tom returned with their drinks. He knew at once that something had happened. Hester's face had changed and shrivelled. She was once more hunted-looking Hester Waring; even her eyes seemed to have sunk back into her head and her pallor was ghastly.

'Hester! What's wrong?' he exclaimed, putting the

glasses on a table by her chair. He made to take her hand in his, but a look of horror passed over her face.

'Don't touch me, you are not to touch me. Take me home.' She made as if to push him away, her voice faltering on the word home. She had no home…

Tom straightened up, his face stern. 'Why, Hester, why?'

'I heard,' she whispered. 'I heard them. They were laughing about Tom Dilhorne's plain piece whom he got into bed with him to win a bet.'

He stood quite still, face impassive. 'Hester, you cannot believe that.'

'Oh, but I do, I do. They knew everything. Exactly when it happened. That we had two days in bed together. How we enjoyed ourselves…' Her voice broke. 'I thought it a secret between us, and it is the joke of Sydney.'

She stood up and put her trembling hands to her neck, unclasped the amethyst collar and handed it to him.

'I'll not wear your brand, Tom Dilhorne. That's what they said it was. Your brand. Now take me…home…'

She had begun to shake. Tom put out a hand to take her arm, but she flung it off. 'You are not to touch me.'

He held the collar in his hand, his face grey.

'Hester, please.' It was the first time he had ever pleaded with her—or with any man or woman for that matter. 'Please put the necklace back. If they don't know now that you are throwing me off, they will when they see that you are not wearing it. And believe me, Hester, I love you. For my sake, put it back on. For Tom, Hester, for Tom.'

There, he had said it at last, what he had never said directly to her during all their lovemaking. What he had thought that he would never say to anyone, ever: I love you.

'For your sake! Why should I? They seem to know everything else about us so I *want* them to know that I've thrown you off, and then you'll lose your damnable bet and Jack Cameron can collect his winnings.'

He was putting the collar carefully into his pocket until he heard Cameron's name.

'Jack Cameron? Was it Jack Cameron you overheard? How can you believe a scoundrel like that when you don't believe me?'

'Because you're a bigger scoundrel than he is, and all Sydney knows it. Yes, he knew. They both knew. I think by the way that people have been looking at me that they all know.'

Her voice trembled on a sob.

'They knew what we were doing, and that you betted on me. Did you tell them the next day? Oh, please take me home. I cannot bear to be looked at any more.'

Tom, for once, was defeated. Hester began to walk away, head high, and he walked beside her, not touching her. They crossed the ballroom not touching, looking at nothing and nobody, her face as impassive as his: Mrs Dilhorne well taught by Mr Dilhorne.

More than one person noticed that Mrs Dilhorne was not now wearing her amethyst collar, among them a grinning Jack Cameron.

But it was Tom's face which held most people's eyes. It was as set and grim as though he were going to his execution.

All the way home Hester huddled herself away from Tom. He drove with uncommon care, and when they reached the villa and were at last inside she left him without a word, mounting the stairs to their room—which not long ago had been her room only.

At the door she turned, mouth trembling. 'You can col-

lect your possessions and go to your old room, Tom Dilhorne! The original bargain between us still stands, that's
all.'

He ignored what she said and walked in after her. 'Hester, you must listen to me.'

'Why should I? You cheated me from the beginning. I
can see that now. It was all a huge joke to you, to marry
a lady, and you got a good housekeeper into the bargain.'

'I could have found a housekeeper,' he said, 'without
needing to marry her. Mrs Hackett on her own would have
done—I can't see myself marrying *her.*'

'Why did you marry me? Because you wanted a lady
for a wife? They said that you loved Sarah Kerr, and what
a come down I was.'

He closed his eyes. The careless banter he had used to
her since the day of her appointment could no longer serve
here, and yes, to some extent, she was right. He had begun
his pursuit of her quite cynically and cold-bloodedly. He
had manipulated her into marrying him, and then he had
manipulated her into bed with him. Even though she had
wanted it as much as he did at the end, it remained manipulation.

His marriage had originally begun as one of the games
he played with life, one of his sardonic jokes. If he were
honest, it had even been a backhanded way of getting his
revenge on that unpleasant swine, her father, to bed his
daughter and have that daughter his willing partner.

Only, at some point, the game had changed, and everything with it, for as he grew to know her, he had come to
care for her. The change had been slow, and it was hard
for him to know when his careless amusement had
changed into love, when his cold heart had been melted.
It was for her sake now, as much as his, although his own
pleasure was great, that they made love. If he had changed

her, transforming her from frigidity into a creature of passion and fire, he had changed himself, irrevocably, and he could even remember when that understanding had come to him…

Early one morning, against their usual custom of him rising before her, she had slipped out of bed quite naked, for she had no false shame before him, however modest and shy she was in public, and had begun to pin up her hair before the mirror.

Lying there, propped up on one arm, watching her, he saw, not for the first time, that although tiny, her body was beautiful, perfectly proportioned and shapely now that good food and happiness were bringing it to full perfection. When she raised her arms and turned her head, the lovely lines of it were fully revealed.

All those months ago he had been right. The promise he had seen in her, when he had caught her unawares in the schoolroom, had flowered into the graceful woman before him—and she was not, he was sure, all that she would yet be. The two Hesters, the one in the glass and the one outside it, moved before him, and the one in the glass saw his eyes on her. She smiled at him, her mouth lifting at the corner.

A wave of something which Tom Dilhorne had never before experienced broke over him. He knew, for the first time, that what he felt for Hester was not simply pride of ownership, or lust for the delights of the body, but was love for her, for something outside of himself, love for the essential Hester. She was not simply to be cherished because she was his, an extension of himself, but because she was herself, was Hester…

Jack Cameron had smashed the love and trust which was beginning to grow between them with a few wicked words. He was sure that it had been done deliberately, and Cameron, he swore grimly to himself, would pay for the doing. Dearly.

He also thought that he knew who it was who had spread the gossip about Sydney which had enabled Cameron to spit his poison. Something would have to be done about that, too. He blamed himself for having ignored it, for thinking that no one would dare bait Tom Dilhorne or his wife with their knowledge for fear of what he might do. He had not thought that vicious gossip would destroy what Hester and he were building between them—a marriage based on trust and joy.

He must, at all costs, try to get Hester back. He could not lose her now that he had found her—and had found himself through her. The last few months had shown him what true love was, and his suffering was all the greater because of it. The Tom Dilhorne whom Mary Mahoney had known would have ridden through this without a thought, a smile on his face. That Tom Dilhorne had gone for good. Improbably, Hester Waring, drunken old Fred's plain daughter, had destroyed him.

He recognised that Hester was still insecure, still emotionally vulnerable because of her years of suffering and neglect, otherwise she would not so easily have fallen victim to Jack Cameron's lies. She was standing with her back to him, her face averted. He made one last appeal to her.

'Hester, please try to believe that Jack Cameron was lying by inference to hurt you, and to get back at me. I have never told anyone of what we have shared. Nor have I made any disgraceful bets involving us. I have never betted over a woman in such a fashion in my life. It's a gentleman's failing. I have no doubt from what I have overheard myself that somehow our life together has become common knowledge, and that Cameron has made a bet out of it—but not through me.'

Hester still refused to look at him. He could see her whole body trembling and shaking, but her voice when she spoke was steady and scornful. Oh, he had changed her, no doubt of it, and now she was strong enough to withstand him, who would once have been broken by him, would have given way.

'Oh, *you* must be honest with *me*, Tom Dilhorne.'

She spat his name out as though it were nauseous medicine. 'I know what I heard, and how else could they have heard it, except through you?'

She was impervious to reason. Worse, it might take time to show her who was behind the gossip. At this point pleading would not work. She was strong—how strong? Ironically *he* had made her strong, and for the first time she was using that strength—and against him!

Tom had always relished life's ironies—even when directed against himself. But he could not relish this. For the first time he would use the whole of his moral and intellectual strength against her. Nothing less would serve, for was she not truly Mrs Dilhorne now, his fit partner?

His face grey, he counter-attacked. He had nothing to lose.

His usual laconic drawl was gone. The elegant, detached classicism which he had used in his office to win her to his bargain was gone. For once unconsidered words poured from him in a stream. Devious Tom Dilhorne was speaking from his breaking heart. The heart which no one, including himself, believed that he possessed.

'Honest! Oh, let us be honest, by all means. It was true that I always meant to get you into my bed once we married. Oh, I'd no intention of keeping to our bargain. I've always wanted to bed you ever since I saw you in the schoolroom, on the day you sat among the chickens with Kate Smith, and the day when I met you carrying that abominable dress. You looked at me as though you could eat me—and you didn't even know you were doing it!

'You be honest, too, Hester. From the beginning, yes, the beginning, you wanted me as much as I wanted you. I could see the red-hot passion roiling round in you, beneath the starch and the ice, if only I could release it, smash the ice.

'Oh, don't deny it, Mrs Dilhorne,' he went on as, shaking her head, she threw up both hands to her betraying scarlet face which she had finally turned fully to him.

'It's the truth and you know it. In the end you lusted after me as much as I lusted after you, only you wouldn't acknowledge it. The worst thing Fred Waring and his high-and-mighty missis did was not to starve you, neglect you and beat you, bad though that was, but to turn you into a frightened prude, ready to hide every time you saw a man looking at you.

'You've enjoyed yourself mightily with me these last few weeks and showed a rare talent for loving, too. I knew that if I'd proposed a real marriage to you in the beginning you would have shied away from me like a frightened mare I was trying to put a saddle on.'

He didn't pause for breath, but continued headlong, throwing out a strong hand to grasp hers, to hold her, even though she tried to writhe away from him.

'Yes, it's true that I once thought that I loved Sarah Kerr, and would have married her, if she would have had me. But that's long gone. It's you I love now, God help me, and you're a fool if you let this come between us. No, I didn't tell the secrets of our marriage bed around Sydney, although I can guess who did. Nor did I bet on bedding you, although there are some who think I did. There are no secrets in this town; you misheard.'

Still she was turned away from him, aloof. Was she

shutting her ears, refusing to listen? No matter. The man who had never before cared to justify himself could not stop doing so.

'Yes, Hester, you misheard. Whatever there was of deceit in our marriage has long gone. Above all else I now love you truly, as I have never loved anyone before, nor ever thought that I should be able to love anyone. I don't love you as a trophy, nor as merely someone to be the mother of my children, but I love you, *only you*, because you are Hester. I have never felt like this for anyone before—not even Sarah Kerr. Don't let them destroy what we have, Hester, don't.'

This uncharacteristic rush of words from the heart, not carefully considered in the manner of Tom's usual speech, which should have told her how deeply he was hurt, how deeply he felt for her, had stopped. It had no effect on Hester. She had been unconsidered Hester Waring for too long, and their love had been too short for her to believe in herself, or in him, when the world had put its dirty fingers into their affairs.

'I don't believe you. My father was right. You are odious. I should never have married you. Do not speak of our time together. I shudder when I think of how I have been behaving—no better than a whore at Madame Phoebe's—'

'But not so inventive,' he put in brutally, since it was apparent that she did not wish to heed him. His strength was rearing up to meet hers, for now they were equal in that, and yes, in misery, too, who had never been equal before.

'Do not flatter yourself, Mrs Dilhorne, you have a deal to learn yet, before you can set yourself up in The Rocks.'

'Oh, you are unspeakable,' she cried passionately, 'Every word you say confirms my father's opinion of you.'

She began to wring her hands; an age-old gesture which

touched him, even through his anger and pain at her rejection of him, and yes, anger at himself for indirectly bringing them to this pass through his own infernal cleverness.

He cursed himself for leaving her alone. Finally he cursed the men she had overheard. He had gone to the ball in such pride, his own true wife on his arm at last, armoured as he thought, in mutual happiness, and it had come to this…

'You must hear me,' he cried hoarsely, finding himself in a situation which he had never before envisaged. Tom Dilhorne had sworn a great oath long ago that he was his own man, and that none should enter the citadel of his heart. He had denied that he had a heart and the world believed him.

In bed with Hester he had, as it were, given her his heart to hold in her hand, something which he had never done before, and her rejection of him was thus the more bitter.

Hester refused to cry—she would not give him that pleasure—but the shock and shame which still gripped her had her sinking into her bedside chair, the chair where he had held her and made love to her. At the memory of it she began to wail tearlessly, to keen almost, like the Irish women at their wakes. Tom dropped on to his knees beside her.

'Come, my love, come to Tom. Let's forget this. We must trust one another. I'd not harm you by word nor deed. You should know that by now.'

Hester flung off the arm he had tried to place around her. The lost expression on her face, which he thought that he had banished forever, had returned again.

'I don't trust you, and I don't want you. I should have known better. Who would want plain Hester Waring except as a trophy? Someone to boast about in your cups at the grog shop. That you had married an Exclusive's daughter, a lady, never mind that she was plain and poor and that she was all that you could hope to win.'

Had the occasion not been so serious he could have laughed at this picture of himself, the most secretive of men, boasting about his life, either in or out of his cups, even if there was some truth in her belief that he had married her because she was a gentlewoman.

Tom stood up. It was useless to persist. To do so would merely antagonise her further, and he was sufficiently wise in the ways of men and women to know that only patience could mend matters here. He must try to show her that Jack Cameron had lied, and that Mrs Hackett, as he suspected, had spread the gossip about them around Sydney, and then perhaps matters could be mended, *would* be mended.

After all, he thought glumly, I am not truly innocent—she was right there. I did deceive her, but only for the best, mind. He thought of her laughing face when she had teased him the night before, until she had almost driven him out of his mind. Afterwards she had surrendered to him with such airy grace that he had sworn to himself that he would always cherish her. Alas, always had turned into a mere twenty-four hours.

'I'll go to my old room, then,' he said slowly, and with perhaps a little hope that she might relent and allow him to stay.

Only to hear her return, 'You may go to the devil for all I care, Tom Dilhorne.'

Well, he thought wryly, at least I've given her some spirit. She was such a mouse before I turned her into a tigress. All your own work, Tom Dilhorne, and look where it's gotten you!

He turned at the door to say goodnight to her, only to

have her swing her face away from him, to hide it in the chair back so that she might not see him.

But, as he crossed the landing to his lonely bed, he said with all the cold ferocity which had turned him from a penniless convict into the richest magnate in the colony, 'By damn, Mrs Dilhorne, I'll have you in my bed again, and liking it, choose how!'

# *Chapter Ten*

Once the tempest of anger and despair which had raged through Hester had blown itself out, she was left becalmed on the high seas of misery.

Sitting opposite to Tom at breakfast the next day, she was afflicted by two contradictory desires. The first was never to see or speak again to the man who could so betray her. The second was related to the fact that both her mind and her body ached for him to take her to bed and make love to her with all the passion of which she knew he was capable. Or, on the other hand, for him to hold her, quiet, almost unmoving, cradled in his arms, as he so often did for long periods of time after their lovemaking was over. She could not imagine a world in which this would never happen again.

And Tom? Seated opposite to her, seeing her unhappy face, the face of the Hester Waring whom she had once been, that complex man was overwhelmed by one simple desire. To take her to bed and to make love to her, so that she would respond to him with all the passion of which he knew that she was capable, or, on the other hand, to hold her cradled in his arms, warm against him, sleeping or awake, as they so often lay after their lovemaking was over. He could not imagine a world in which this would never happen again.

Tom was sure that it was Mrs Hackett who had betrayed them, but he needed hard evidence that she had done so. Simply to confront her without it would be useless. She was perfectly capable of brazen denial. He gave a little thought to the matter before arriving at a possible solution—and one which amused him.

She had watched and spied on them from the day they had been married. On the evening when they came home from the ball she had seen Tom return to his old room with his possessions and had no doubt of what had happened. She was bursting to pass on this latest piece of scandal, and could hardly wait for noon to arrive when she was due to visit an old friend who would be sure to enjoy what she had to say.

While Hester sat alone, repairing a torn frill on one of Tom's dress shirts, Mrs Hackett, in the intervals of drinking tea, was announcing gleefully to her cronies that 'Madam don't want him any more, and fine Master Tom's been turned out of her bed again', thus sending even more lurid news about the Dilhornes around Sydney.

What was even better, on the way home she was stopped by Jack Cameron, who asked her cheerfully whether she could help him again—she had previously supplied him with news of the state of the Dilhornes' marriage. If so, he might be able to advantage her again.

Oh, yes, of course she could. She told him her latest piece of gossip, and arrived home, enriched, in a very satisfied state of mind indeed.

Tom's opportunity to snare Mrs Hackett soon came. Walking down Bridge Street in the early evening, he saw young Ensign Osborne about to turn into one of the grog shops frequented by the younger officers and lesser gentry of Sydney.

Instinct had him following the lad, who owed him a favour. Deep play in which he had unwisely indulged in with his seniors, and in which he had lost heavily, had deprived the boy of the ready. Even more unwisely Osborne had paid his debts of honour at the expense of those he owed to tradesmen, and his IOUs to them had ended up in Tom's hands.

Tom rarely showed sympathy to fools, but Osborne's exploited greenness, combined with information from Hester—gained at the breakfast table—that young Osborne was from a poor family and most of his pay was sent home to his mother, had earned his pity for the young ass.

He had cancelled the debts for less than their value and told Osborne to keep his mouth shut: he couldn't afford to finance the whole garrison. He had also advised him not to play cards with sharpers like Jack Cameron again.

Osborne's gratitude had been pathetic, and he had heeded Tom's advice; that gratitude might do Tom a good turn now.

He gave a start of surprise when he saw the boy, and walked over to where he sat alone, making his one drink last, saying, 'Mind if I sit with you, lad? I'm alone, too.'

Osborne, not unnaturally, liked Tom, and frequently defended him to the other officers. He eagerly agreed to this suggestion.

'Landlord, bring brandy for me and my friend here,' called Tom.

It was a pleasant afternoon for young Osborne. He and Tom drank merrily together, the drinks on Dilhorne, of course.

He found himself muttering blearily to his Emancipist friend, 'Say what they like about you, Dilhorne, you're a good fellow, even if you were a felon. Never mind what Jack and the rest think.'

'You've not been betting with Jack again, I hope,' said Tom, filling Osborne's glass again. His own drinking had not kept pace with Osborne's, but the boy was too far gone to notice such a detail.

'By no meansh. Not even on the book he'sh started over you and Hester.' Drink had made Osborne unwary enough to come out with this, but not so unwary that he did not belatedly realise what he had said. He flushed red, and added, 'Shouldn't have told you that, Dilhorne, not the thing.'

'Never mind that, lad,' returned Tom cheerfully, 'we're all men of the world. Doing it a bit brown, don't you think, to bet on a man's marriage?'

'Sho I told him,' returned Osborne dolefully. 'He laughed at me. Shaid I was green, and felons didn't deserve good marriages. Shorry again, Dilhorne. I think he'sh upset because he shtands to lose a lot if you and Hester make a go of it. Ain't quite the thing, either, what he says about her round Sydney and bribing your housekeeper to tattle about you, and laughing at Hester for being plain. I told him it wasn't her fault she was plain.'

By now Osborne was lost to everything, even the change on Tom's face when he spoke of Jack's comments about Hester.

He looked up at Tom, his face working a little. '*He* ain't quite the thing. Should tell him sho, but I ain't man enough. Even Pat Ramsey don't want to tangle with Jack, best man in the regiment with sword and pistols, boxes like Gentleman Jackson, too. I ain't up to him. More's the pity. Needsh a lesson, take a good man to give him one.'

He yawned, downed one last drink and saying, 'Odd

thing, I'm damned tired thish afternoon, Dilhorne', he put his head on the table and began to snore.

'Sorry about that, lad,' said Tom, fetching a towel from the landlord and putting it under the boy's head. 'But I had to find out—and so I have.'

He called the landlord over, and told him to send for one of his own men to drive Osborne back to quarters when he had recovered.

After that he drove home, feeling rather better about life than he had done that morning, although his thoughts about Cameron were shot with blood. The knowledge that Hester's name was often on his lips, that he was bad-mouthing her about Sydney was the last, worst, insult. The betting and the bribery were bad enough, but the abuse of Hester was intolerable.

'By damn,' he said to himself, 'give me half a chance to have a go at you, Jack, my boyo, and you'll wish you'd never been born.'

Now to deal with Mrs Hackett and after that with Hester. He had no doubt that she was as miserable as he was. Question was, how could he persuade her to come about, and also persuade her not to retreat back into being miserable Hester Waring, and not triumphant Mrs Dilhorne? Well, let him settle with Hackett and Cameron and that might not be too difficult.

Once home, he found the woman in the kitchen. Her look for him was sullen. She had originally feared him, but familiarity over the weeks had dulled that, replacing it with contempt for not being a proper man who would insist on his rights with Hester.

He was peremptory. 'Give me five minutes, and then present yourself in my study.'

With never a please or a thank you, she thought resentfully, but she duly knocked on his door five minutes later.

Tom had his back to her. He ignored her for several minutes during which time he could almost feel her agitation growing behind him.

He turned suddenly, leaned against his old-fashioned tall desk at which he stood, not sat, and surveyed her, his eyes as hard as stones.

'Enjoying yourself, are you?' he asked sardonically.

'I'm sure I don't know what you mean, Master Dilhorne.'

'Sir to you, Mrs Hackett, sir.' That he should insist on the demeaning sir was a sign of his acute displeasure. He wanted to humiliate her as she had humiliated Hester.

'Can you think of a single reason why I should not turn you away, without pay, and without a character, and make damned sure that no one in Sydney would ever employ you again?'

Her face turned an ugly purple. 'You wouldn't do that...sir.'

His face changed and she began to tremble. His expression was purely murderous. The fear of him which she had once felt came back with a rush. As Alan had prophesied to Sarah, for all his changed manner and appearance he was wild Tom Dilhorne still: a man whom it was dangerous to cross.

'Would I not?'

His expression might be hard but his voice was soft. 'I've a mind to do it now, straight away. This minute, and if I did who would employ *you* to spread their affairs abroad? If you tell me what you've said and done about me and mine, why, I might just keep you on. But stand there and pretend that you don't know whereof I speak and I'll throw you out of doors myself this very minute, and joy in the doing of it. Now, think on.'

He had not raised his voice above a whisper, and it was worse and more deadly than if he had shouted at her.

'I may have said something to a few friends, sir…' she began. Her fear of him was suddenly so strong that she could not lie to him.

'And money?' he said, watching her expression change as he spoke. 'Did someone pay you money to tattle?'

She wondered how he knew. She had thought that the matter had been secret betwixt her and Cameron. She wanted to deny it, but in the face of his white-hot anger she dared not.

Tom laughed. 'So…someone paid you?'

'That officer,' she told him despairingly. 'Cameron. He stopped me not long after you were wed. Said he'd pay me for anything about you and Mrs Dilhorne. I never took money before…that was the first, as God's my witness.'

She suddenly dropped to her knees before him. 'Oh, God, Mr Dilhorne, sir, please don't turn me away. I'll have nowhere to go if you turn against me. No one will want me, they'll be too afeared of you to employ me. I'll starve.' She gave a great sobbing cry and clutched at his knees.

Tom looked down at her, the anger running out of him. It was only a poor old woman, after all, who hadn't the sense to see what a cushy berth she had, and that Hester was a kind mistress. Above all, he could not condemn her to what he had rescued Hester from.

'Get up, get up,' he said brusquely. 'What did he pay you?'

'He gave me another guinea today when I told him about last night. God's truth, sir, that's all.'

Tom closed his eyes. So last night, too, would be running around Sydney. Godsend Hester did not hear of it before he could deal with the old hag and settle with Cameron.

'Give me his guinea, and we're quits on that. First there's a spare room over the mews where the other servants live. It's neither so large nor so fine as the one you have, but Miller shall do it up, and when he has, you may move your traps there. I'll have no more servants spying on me in my home.'

He pushed her away. She began to sob her thanks, fumbling in her pocket for the guinea which she placed in his outstretched hand.

'Be quiet, woman, you sicken me. Now for the second condition. If I find you telling tales again, other than ones I might ask you to tell, that is, I'll have you on the street before you can turn round. Mind what I say, and be grateful that worse hasn't befallen you. Now go.'

What to do now? Tell Hester? About Mrs Hackett's tattling, yes. About Cameron, no. He would settle with Cameron before he told her the truth about the bet.

He picked up the papers on his desk. Madame Phoebe wished to speak to him urgently on a business matter. He grinned to himself wolfishly. He would see her this very night, without fail, at her house. The 73rd's officers might be there, Cameron among them, and who knew what Tom Dilhorne would choose to do then?

He took the guinea from his pocket, tossed it spinning into the air, caught it, made it disappear, before plucking it from the heart of a flower in one of the vases Hester had placed in his study. Then, having apparently placed it in the right-hand pocket of his breeches, he spread his hands to demonstrate that he no longer held it—and took it triumphantly from his left-hand pocket.

Tom Dilhorne had not lost his skills, not he. Which of them he would use to teach Jack Cameron a necessary lesson, he did not know.

* * *

Driving to Madame Phoebe's he felt elated. He had told Hester over dinner that Mrs Hackett had been the informant and had so confessed. He also told her of the guinea given to her by an officer. He had not named Cameron.

Hester, sitting opposite to him, face cold and withdrawn, heard him out without interrupting him. But there was a spark in her eye which told him, to his affectionate amusement, that she wanted to believe that he had not been the one who had spread the details of their marriage around Sydney—even if she said nothing. She was disliking their rift as much as he was.

She then said, irresolutely, 'But the bet, Mr Dilhorne. You haven't explained the bet.'

Good! He was Mr Dilhorne again. Before she could stop him, he leaned forward and kissed her on the cheek.

'That shall be explained, too,' he promised. 'Now I have business to transact, and must leave you. Do not expect me home early tonight.'

His last memory was of her face, which betrayed her disappointment at his going.

He entered Madame Phoebe's with savagery added to his joy that Hester was softening towards him, even before he had needed to explain how the bet had come about and why Cameron had lied to deceive her.

Madame Phoebe greeted him affectionately.

'Thought you wouldn't come here again, Tom, after you'd married gentry.'

He grinned at her, 'You know better than that, Phoebe. Besides, Mrs D. won't mind me coming here, so long as we confine affairs to business. She's hot on business, Mrs D.'

Madame Phoebe nodded. Long ago Tom had lent her the money to start her house in Sydney, but once she had paid him off, he had never had any stake in it, although she always sent for him when she needed money or advice.

Mrs Hackett's latest piece of gossip about Tom and Hester had already reached her via Jack Cameron, so she knew that Tom had been banished from his wife's bed again. Now, smiling, she offered him not only the customary bottle of wine to share while they talked, but discreetly hinted to him of her own availability.

As usual, he refused both offers, but was willing to lend her money to extend her flourishing business. She needed to redecorate and refurnish. She even offered him a share of her profits—to see his shaking head.

'It's not that I disapprove, mind, but I have a wife, now, and a future to think on. Yours isn't the kind of business I need any more, Phoebe. But I'll always bail you out,' he added as he rejected her, but his rejection was a gentle one. He admired and respected her—one more woman making her way successfully in the world—and his rejection was not based on any self-serving morality, or on contempt for what she offered.

She was a sensible woman and accepted what he said without offence. 'I offer a necessary service,' she said simply, and wondered how long Tom would go without needing it if his wife proved obstinate, and now that Mary Mahoney was respectably married.

The house was already roaring. Tom made his way to the gaming room which was crammed with the officers of the 73rd intent on making another night of it.

He looked around and found the man he wanted seated at the big main table in the middle of his cronies, and walked the length of it towards Jack, every jeering eye upon him.

Above the noise he heard his own name, and then that of Hester's repeated, followed by loud laughter and Captain Parker's voice saying, 'Steady on, Jack, the lady's a good friend of mine.'

Tom stopped and pushed his way through the group of officers who fell silent at the sight of him. Quite deliberately he had not shaved himself and was still wearing his working clothes: he had visited the brickfields that afternoon.

At last he found himself facing the author of the jests and the man he most wanted to see.

Jack was not a whit abashed by Tom's arrival. He raised his glass, and sneered, 'The man himself', before offering Tom a mocking toast. Parker, standing by him, put a restraining hand on his arm. Jack shook it off.

Tom ignored the mockery and the toast. 'Captain Jack Cameron, I believe.'

'As you well know, dammit, Dilhorne. Now what may I do for you?'

'You can tell me what you have been saying about my wife, Jack.'

'*Captain* Cameron, sir, to felons, Dilhorne, and what I say about your wife is my affair, not yours.'

He drank from the glass, emptied it, and poured himself another. Parker again laid his hand on his arm. Again Jack shook it off.

Tom spoke into the silence which had followed Cameron's last words. 'Oh, but it is my business, Jack. I ask you again: what were you saying about my wife?'

'Leave it, Dilhorne, he's drunk,' said Parker, his pleasant face worried.

Tom ignored him. The attention of the whole room was now centred on Jack and himself as though they were a pair of gladiators homing in for the kill.

No sense of propriety, of what was the done thing, governed matters in a brothel. Many thought that since Dilhorne was an ex-felon and not a gentleman Jack might say anything he pleased to Tom about himself and his wife— who had put herself beyond the pale by marrying him.

Knowing this, Tom put his hand in his pocket, pulled out Mrs Hackett's guinea and flung it on the table in front of Jack.

'If I give you your money back, will you tell me then, or shall I have to beat it out of you, Jack?'

Jack's response to this was a reddened face and a bellow of laughter. He ignored the coin lying before him.

'By God then, Dilhorne, you shall have it. I was saying what a fine fellow you were. Such a fine fellow that even that plain piece your wife, and damme, they come no plainer, ain't so desperate for it that she'll let an ex-felon like you into her bed again. What do you say to that, Dilhorne, hey, hey?'

His drunken laughter pealed into an appalled silence.

Tom had gained what he wanted. Jack had been provoked into saying something which even the class-hardened officers of the 73rd might find difficult to stomach. But in the doing he had destroyed his own iron control. It broke.

He had hardly raised his voice when he had spoken to Cameron. He was indifferent to abuse of himself. He was amused by it, even. He knew that he had been a thief and a rogue: that was a statement of fact, not an insult. What he had not grasped was that he would be so enraged at Hester being bad-mouthed.

To hear her jeered at by a drunken roué in a vile dive before half the officers of the Sydney garrison was almost too much.

'This!' he riposted, and lunged across the table at Jack.

Glasses, bottles, wine, gaming counters, IOUs, and cards sailed in all directions. Before anyone could stop him he had seized Jack by the ears and smashed his face down into the hard mahogany of the table.

He was lifting Jack's now lolling head to repeat the action, but the men around him, initially stunned by the speed and ferocity of his attack, pulled him away, leaving his victim head down, semi-conscious, with the blood from his ruined face mingling with the spilt wine.

Deathly silence was followed by uproar. One group clustered around the fallen Jack and another pinned Tom hard against the wall. He made no effort to resist. His face was suddenly as calm as though he were taking tea with the Governor wearing his beautiful clothes and speaking in the cultured accents of a scholar and gentleman.

'By God,' shouted the officer whose arm was across Tom's chest to prevent him from attacking Jack again, 'it's easy to see that you're no gentleman, Dilhorne.'

'And you call *that* a gentleman.' Tom's quiet drawl was deadly. 'Just let me loose and he'll never insult a lady again. My work's only half-done.'

His voice was all the more disturbing for being so indifferent.

'I've no doubt that he'll call you out when he's recovered,' said the young officer who held Tom by the right shoulder.

Tom turned his head to stare coldly at him. 'So's he can poke his little sword into me, I suppose. I know a trick worth two of that. He'll not insult or tell lies about my wife again if I have to cut his tongue out to stop him.'

This last threat was uttered so pleasantly that the young officer recoiled.

The officers around Jack moved away, suddenly sobered. Parker, his face grave, came up to Tom and said, 'He shouldn't have said what he did about Hester, Dilhorne, I grant you that, but you've marked him for life. His nose is broken and his teeth are loose.'

'Are they now?' Tom's drawl was at its most provoking. 'Do you think that will teach him to be careful of what he says about my wife in future?'

'Well, he was in drink,' said Parker dubiously. 'You should have waited to get satisfaction from him in the usual way, not gone for him like that, without warning. As it is, he's bound to call you out when he's recovered.'

'Is he now? He wants satisfaction from me? I should say he's got it already. I'm not playing your daft games, Parker.'

'If he won't give Jack satisfaction,' said the young officer still grasping Tom's shoulder, 'I vote that we hand him over to the law to be tried for assault.'

Before Parker could answer Pat Ramsey took a hand. He had been leaning against the wall watching the fracas with the sardonic amusement of a man who favoured neither party in it.

He rounded on the officer. 'You damned young fool, what good would that do? Do you want this affair aired more publicly than it will be? A squabble in a brothel? The whole room heard Jack insult Dilhorne, and what's worse, Dilhorne's wife. Hester Dilhorne is a lady. For defending his wife from an insult such as Jack offered her, Dilhorne would be chaired from the court. Do you want to disgrace the Regiment? Isn't what has been said and done enough?'

These evident truths silenced the uproar for Tom's blood. A stalemate seemed to have been reached. In the silence that followed Ramsey dropped the authoritative tone he had been using and, picking up the guinea from the table where it still lay, somehow having avoided the chaos which Tom had created, said, in his usual airy manner, 'Now, what was all that about a guinea?'

He looked at Jack who was being carried from the room, drink and his injuries combined having rendered him senseless. 'D'you think Jack might tell us? If he's able to speak, that is?' His lack of sympathy for the fallen Cameron was obvious.

Young Osborne, sitting in the corner, nursing his thick head, and watching the fun, suddenly spluttered and said, 'Time Guinea Jack got his, you know, and Dilhorne was the man to do it. Shun't have talked like that 'bout poor Hester.'

Tom's revenge was complete. Guinea Jack was Cameron's derisive nickname from then on.

The men around Tom were still reluctant to let him go. Who knew but that he might follow Jack and end what he had begun, as he had promised?

He, and they, were saved by the arrival of Madame Phoebe whom the uproar had brought downstairs, and who had watched it, silent, from the beginning.

She had waited for a suitable moment to intervene, and seeing instantly that the worst was over, imposed her authority. 'What the hell do you think you're doing? Let go of Tom immediately. What's the matter with you all? Has it got so that officers and gentlemen can't behave themselves when they've a bottle of wine in them?

'Tell Captain Cameron he's not welcome here until I give him leave to come again, and he can refrain from mentioning a decent woman's name in a whore-house. Go home, Tom Dilhorne, letting you loose among gentlemen is like setting a tiger at kittens.'

Tom laughed at the offended expressions of the military as she walked to the damaged gaming table.

'God love you, Tom Dilhorne, can't you settle your affairs without ruining a poor woman's business? I shall want recompense for this, mind.'

Tom suddenly felt wonderfully happy. The thought of Jack Cameron's mutilated face filled him with savage pleasure. Madame Phoebe's knowing manipulation of the assembled gentlemen added to it.

'Recompense you shall have, my darling.' He retrieved Jack's discarded shako from the floor and tossed it to Parker. 'Pass the hat around like a good fellow, Captain Parker—and pay for your fun at Madame Phoebe's.'

All Sydney was agog. Typically, in what was a frontier society, everybody knew everybody else's business. The story was too good not to be told. How cool, collected Tom Dilhorne had reverted to his wild origins and wrecked, not only Jack Cameron's face, but Madam Phoebe's gaming hell—for the story grew with the telling.

The cream of the joke was that, at the end, he had somehow made the officers of the 73rd pay for the damage, and when the hat had reached him he had put his hands in his pockets, and said that since he had been considerate enough to provide the entertainment he didn't see why he should have to pay for it as well!

The only person in Sydney who wasn't enjoying the joke was Hester. No one spoke to her of it. She had heard Tom arrive home in the small hours of the morning. He had taken the stairs two at a time, and later she had heard him whistling while he prepared for bed. Despite herself she longed to know what had made him so happy, and the next morning at breakfast he had sat smiling at her with an expression on his face which, had it been on any other man, she would have called daft.

He had decided to tease her a little, to have a grand reconciliation that night, because by her manner she ap-

peared to be ready for one without explanation. He had
laughed to himself at her bursting curiosity and her determination not to give in to it. Oh, we'll celebrate tonight,
Mrs Dilhorne, see if we don't!

When he left her to go into Sydney he had kissed the
top of her head murmuring, 'Tell you all this evening, Mrs
Dilhorne', which provoked her mightily. Nevertheless, as
she watched him drive off, her face had already softened,
and downtrodden Hester Waring had disappeared into a
limbo from which she was never to return.

She decided to go into Sydney to do some shopping.
She was perhaps the only person in the town not to be
aware of what had occurred at Madame Phoebe's the night
before, but she immediately knew that something odd had
happened involving Tom and herself when she saw people's reaction to her, the stares, and the smiles.

She walked into Tom's Emporium. Every head turned
as she entered. Conversation stopped, to start again. She
could hear her name and his being whispered, which was
nothing new, except that this time her presence was creating even more excitement than usual.

When she reached home again the stable-hand who had
driven her into Sydney, greatly daring, thought that she
ought to know how the master had defended her good
name, but after a stammering beginning he fell silent. This
left her to understand that somehow, Tom, the military and
herself were involved in some incident of which everyone
knew but herself. Well, if the military were concerned,
then Lucy Wright would be sure to know of it.

She put on a new gown, something which Tom had
picked out for her before their quarrel, and with it she wore
the new bonnet, parasol and the parure of garnets he had
given her. Thus attired for war, she ordered the carriage

again and visited Lucy, who was delighted to see her after a longish absence.

'Oh, Hester, you do look splendid! Did Tom choose that for you? I will say that for such a masculine man he has the most remarkable taste when it comes to women's clothes. More's the pity he no longer serves in the shop.'

'Yes,' said Hester briefly. She did not want to talk about Tom, but she did want to find out what the gossip was all about. She had learned patience in a hard school, though, and it was only after she had admired the baby, drunk some tea and Lucy was fetching out her needlework that she raised the topic which lay behind her visit.

She looked shyly at Lucy and asked, 'Has Frank said anything to you about some trouble involving Tom and the military?'

Lucy put down her sewing with a gasp. 'Oh, Hester, don't you know? Hasn't Tom said anything?'

Hester's reply was a model of the deviousness which she was learning from her husband. 'You know Tom.'

'Of course, well, perhaps it would be best for you to know. I can't tell you all the details because Frank thought that they weren't fit for my ears, me being a virtuous female and all that. He didn't want to tell me that it happened at Madame Phoebe's—I'm not supposed to know that such a place exists. I ask you! How could I not know?

'But he told me enough to make out that Tom went to Madame Phoebe's last night when all the garrison's officers were there, and had some sort of argument with Jack Cameron and Jack got the worst of it, Frank was there, you see, and saw it all. Apparently Tom half-wrecked the place, too, and the joke of it is, Frank says, is that somehow Tom made the officers pay for the damage while he got away scot-free! Typical Tom, if I may say so.'

She laughed, and was plainly not going to enlarge on what had caused the argument.

Hester was not having this. 'What were they quarrelling about, Lucy?'

Lucy hesitated, and then decided to tell Hester as much as she knew, which was very little. Frank had decided not to tell her exactly what Jack had said, or Tom had done—Lucy's supposed virtue again.

'It was something to do with you and Tom. Captain Cameron was drunk and insulting. Frank thinks he had been telling lies about you and Tom.'

Hester closed her eyes. Then opened them again. 'You mean Tom attacked him because of me?'

'Yes. Frank says he made an awful mess of Jack's face. He wouldn't tell me how. I must say, Hester, I should be happy to think that Frank would be as fierce as Tom if I were insulted in a gaming hell or anywhere else, for that matter.'

'Why did Tom wreck the place?'

'Well, he didn't exactly wreck all of it. Just the gaming table and what was on it when he went for Jack.'

Both girls contemplated the scene Lucy's words conjured up. They knew so little of the places where men and 'those women' went that it was hard for them to work out exactly what might have happened.

So many vital facts were missing, and only Hester knew that Tom had undoubtedly been punishing Jack for what he had said at the ball, for bribing Mrs Hackett, and for any further insults offered at Madame Phoebe's.

'Frank says Jack wants to call Tom out—fight a duel—but there's even an argument about that. Frank says that no one can decide who is the challenging party, Tom or Jack, since Tom broke all the normal rules governing disputes between gentlemen.'

'But why does it matter who challenges whom?' asked Hester, baffled by the silly intricacies, or so they seemed to her, of the gentlemen's code of honour. 'In any case, I don't think that Tom sees himself as a gentleman.'

'Oh, it does matter.' Lucy was earnest. 'You see, the challenged man gets the right to decide which weapons to use—and no one knew who challenged whom. Was it Tom when he hit Jack? Or was it Jack challenging Tom because Tom hit him?'

She suddenly laughed. 'Yes, it is silly, isn't it?'

'Tom would say it was silly,' agreed Hester.

She suddenly felt flattered that Tom had attacked Jack on her behalf. He deserved it for the dreadful things he had made her think of Tom, and the awful way he had mocked her for her lack of looks. She suddenly knew who had been telling Jack Cameron tales, and that the bet Tom was supposed to have made about getting her into bed had never existed.

With the thought came the memory of Tom's face when he had pleaded with her on the night of the ball. She turned slowly away from Lucy and began to collect her belongings. He didn't deserve her stupid anger, he didn't. Not a man who had wrecked Madame Phoebe's for her.

'Must you go so soon?' asked Lucy. 'I haven't told you about the guinea.'

Hester looked at Lucy. Mrs Hackett's guinea. 'It started the fight,' she said slowly.

'Yes. How did you know that, Hester?'

'I didn't. I guessed.'

She must go home immediately and get to the bottom of this.

'I'm sorry, I have to leave you now, Lucy.' She smiled a dazzling smile, and looked better than she had done since the ball.

Lucy watched her walk determinedly to her carriage. Now, what on earth did I say to her to make her leave in such a hurry? Frank said that Jack claimed that she and Tom were at outs. But I don't believe it. Not the way she looked at me every time I said his name.

That afternoon Jack Cameron took his two black eyes, his broken nose, his swollen mouth and loosened teeth into Colonel O'Connell's room at the Barracks. Previously, he had not left his quarters, except to consult Dr Kerr, who had told him that apart from his broken nose, for which he could do nothing, everything else, including his teeth, would mend, given time.

His opening words were peremptory. 'I want that bastard Dilhorne arrested, put in chains, and charged with aggravated assault.'

O'Connell looked at him with weary distaste, but spoke to him as a man, not as a superior officer to an inferior.

'You know I can't do that, Jack. Much as I would like to see Dilhorne in gaol, I can't do anything to him over this.'

Jack pointed to his damaged face. 'The brute nearly killed me last night. Isn't that sufficient?'

'You know it isn't. You provoked him. If you'd merely insulted *him*, well and good. I'd have had him in irons by now. But you insulted his wife, and whatever he is, she's a lady, and what's more, there's never been a breath of scandal attached to her. Other, of course, than that she married Dilhorne. But that ass Fred Waring left her so dirt poor that marriage to him was a better alternative than starvation or Madame Phoebe's.'

Jack began to bluster. 'Well, all I can say is that you've been misinformed. Who told you that?'

'Parker gave me a full account last night.'

'Parker!' Jack's sneer was as vicious as he could make it. 'That green boy. It's what I might have expected of him.'

'Even you, Jack, can't call Pat Ramsey green,' said O'Connell wearily, 'and his account matches Parker's.'

'So Dilhorne gets off scot-free, and he won't even give me satisfaction.'

'Oh, do shut up, Jack. You should learn to hold your liquor.'

Jack's expression was murderous. 'It's the thought of that swine walking around Sydney as though he owns it that I can't bear.'

'Oh, come on, Jack. He does own Sydney, or very near,' growled O'Connell. 'No, Jack, cut your losses, and make sure that you pick an easier target next time. If you don't know by now that Dilhorne's dangerous, you never will.'

Jack turned away in disgust, but was brought back by O'Connell's next comment. 'Plain, I hear you called her. You haven't been looking at her lately, Jack. Loath though I am to say it, since she married Dilhorne that girl has been transformed. She's turning into a regular little beauty.'

O'Connell's last words rankled. A regular little beauty, is she? thought Jack furiously. I can't say I've noticed it, but if O'Connell says so, there must be something there. He's a ladies' man, is O'Connell. I wonder how the devil I can pay that vile brute back—through his wife or his business might be the easiest, but best of all would be to destroy him, see him dead!

Tom sat down to dinner that evening still bathed in the remnants of the exhilaration which he had felt ever since he had assaulted Jack Cameron. He had seen Alan Kerr that morning, and Alan had twitted him on what he had done to Cameron. 'I'd forgotten what a bruiser you are, Tom. You've come such a long way since we first landed in New South Wales.'

Tom looked at his old friend. 'He insulted Hester,' he said simply.

'I know. I don't need to tell you that the story's all round Sydney today. Did you really have to wreck Madame Phoebe's as well, though?'

Tom burst out laughing. 'Is that what they're saying? No such thing. I merely rearranged the table when I improved Cameron's looks. I owe his fellow officers a debt of gratitude. They stopped me from killing him—which would have been the end of me.'

He paused. 'You know, I thought that it was all gone. That I was a civilised man. When he said that about Hester, added to his other misdeeds, I was eighteen again, ready to kill if I were crossed. Not that I ever did, mind. But the thought was always there.'

He shrugged. 'There's a lesson for me to control my temper. Funny, though, if he'd stuck to insulting me, I'd have laughed in his face. It was Hester I could have killed him for.'

Now, sitting opposite to her, Tom wondered what had caused Hester's slightly flushed face, and why she had chosen to wear the garnets he had given her, and the matching gown whose deep crimson matched her cheeks. She seldom wore so elaborate a toilette when they were alone together.

The forlorn look which had returned on the night of the ball was gone, and she ate her soup avidly. He was about to ask her why she was thus honouring their table when she looked up, and said to him in the bantering tone of their conversations before the quarrel, 'What were you doing in Madame Phoebe's last night, Mr Dilhorne?'

'What do men usually do in Madame Phoebe's, Mrs Dilhorne?' he countered.

She primmed her mouth comically. 'I don't like to say, Mr Dilhorne.'

'Well…I wasn't doing that.'

'Then what were you doing?'

'I thought I was paying a business call, Mrs Dilhorne, but then I found out that I was in a mill with one of O'Connell's officers. I think I may have improved Jack Cameron's manners, but I can't say the same for his face.'

'Oh, Mr Dilhorne, it's the talk of Sydney! Tell me, I long to know, why did you wreck Madame Phoebe's?'

His face was as comical as hers had been a few minutes earlier. 'How many times do I have to say that I didn't wreck Madame Phoebe's? Shall I get old Smithson to print me a bill saying so?'

'Well, if you didn't, Mr Dilhorne, and of course, I accept your word, what were the officers paying for?'

'A damaged table, Mrs Dilhorne, and some spilled wine—all done in a good cause.'

'For me, Tom?' Her voice was soft. 'Because of what Jack said at the ball—and at Madame Phoebe's?'

He nodded. 'For you, Hester. Always and only for you.'

They stared at one another across the table.

Hester put her spoon down as he rose from his chair and walked towards her. He knelt down by her side, took her hand and kissed it. 'I am forgiven, then?'

'There was never anything to forgive. It is you who should forgive me. You were right. Mrs Hackett told tales, and Jack Cameron was lying. I don't know why I didn't believe you.'

'Because you were hurt by what you overheard.'

'I was as unkind as I was at the Christmas Party. It was very wrong of me.'

'It doesn't matter now,' he said gently, kissing her hand again.

'Oh, but it does. I was cruel.' She paused. 'I think that it was partly because I couldn't believe that I was intended to be happy, and partly because of all that my mother and father said about you. When Lucy told me this afternoon what you did for me, I felt guilty all over again.'

'Lucy told you.' He was amused.

'Well, not everything. Only the gossip and a little of what Frank said. I'm wearing the garnets, Mr Dilhorne.'

'So I see. I think you'd better take them off. I want to do dreadful things to you, Mrs Dilhorne... On second thoughts, keep them on.'

She leaned against him and put her lips to his cheek. 'Anything you like, anything you like.'

'This is what I like.' He picked her up, and threw her over his shoulder as though she were a sack of coal. She hung there, laughing. 'Oh, Mr Dilhorne, whatever will you do next?'

'This,' he repeated, and strode through the door. At the bottom of the stairs he met Mrs Hackett carrying the roast, the little maidservant behind her.

'Ah, Mrs Hackett,' he said, swinging around so that Hester's face, scarlet with amusement was hidden from her. 'We shall not be wanting dinner tonight. You and the maid may eat it yourselves.'

He laughed into her dumbfounded face. 'And you have my full permission, nay, it is an order, to tell the whole of Sydney that Tom Dilhorne is taking his wife to bed tonight!'

Leaving Mrs Hackett gasping behind him, he took the stairs at a run, and passing through the bronze doors, he deposited his burden on his bed, there to make love to her in a passionate frenzy which did not even wait for such niceties as the removal of clothes, until at last they lay, laughing, fulfilled and exhausted, together again, and this time for good.

## Chapter Eleven

Those first months after they had re-consummated their marriage were for Hester a time when everything was new and exciting, when she and Tom were as wild and irresponsible in their loving as the tigers she sometimes imagined they were.

The morning after their reunion, she was lying in bed, dozing, when her Mentor, who had been quiet since Tom first made love to her, suddenly spoke again.

'Goodbye, Hester,' it said. Always before the voice had been low, but now it was so loud that she could almost imagine that Tom, who was shaving before her long mirror, could hear it.

Why was it saying goodbye? Even as she thought this, the voice said, sadly, 'You don't need me any more, Hester. You're no longer a defeated mouse. You're Tom's mate, his tigress. You'll go hunting together, see if you don't.'

'I shall miss you.'

'No, I'm not wanted now. But if ever you do need me, I'll be back. Goodbye, Hester.'

Silence. It had gone.

For a moment she was desolate before she thought, I'm

no longer frightened Hester Waring. I can say aloud what I think.

To add to her confidence Tom continued her education in life, and now it involved many a seminar in the arts of love. His inventiveness in terms of enjoyment stretched far beyond the physical act itself. He seemed capable of finding something new for them to do on every possible occasion—either at work or at play.

He showered her with presents: fans, clothes, exotic food and wine. He bought her a horse so that they could ride together, had breeches made for her so that she could ride astride. He taught her to swim and made love to her in the water. He made love to her everywhere as the fancy took him.

Happiness enveloped her and the change in her looks became so marked that Tom was astonished to discover that she was unaware of it.

'My Venus,' he said to her once when they were making love in the bush, surrounded by flowers and scents. 'My exquisite miniature love.' She had become what he had always believed she might be, when everyone else in Sydney had merely seen poor, plain Hester Waring.

It was obvious, however, that she thought that it was his love speaking and not the truth. She could never forget that Tom's intervention had saved her from falling into the pit which awaited those who had been swept from life's table.

Tom often took her with him when he was engaged on business, and the way in which he deferred to her and frequently asked her opinion was often noted with sneering amusement. This amusement would have faded if they had known how often she actually advised him and how sure her judgement was.

Sometimes his associates spoke carelessly in front of

her—and she was able to pass useful information to him.
They complemented one another: if Tom was sometimes
too hard, Hester was there to soften him. If she were sometimes too tender, he was there to stiffen her. Even so, she
still remained unaware of what Hester Dilhorne had become: a beautiful woman secure in her husband's love.

It took a ball at Government House to reveal to her that
she had changed indeed.

That evening Jack Cameron entered the ballroom at
Government House determined to have a good look at
Hester Dilhorne. In the weeks which had passed since his
downfall at that bastard Dilhorne's hands he had looked
for her in Sydney, and somehow had never seemed to find
her.

'She's turned into a regular little beauty,' Ramsey told
him one day, echoing O'Connell.

'Pigs might fly,' he had guffawed.

Hester Waring a beauty! If ever he had looked at her,
which wasn't often, thank God, he had seen a plain gauche
child who had blushed an ugly red every time he did. That
ass, Frank Wright, had also said that she was much improved—but what the devil did he ever know about anything!

O'Connell had advised him to cut down on the drink,
so he was sober when he looked around the room for entertainment. His face still bore the mark of that felon's
handiwork. His nose would never be the same.

Where, then, was Hester Dilhorne? He wanted to have
a good look at her, but she was nowhere to be seen. No
matter, as much as a good laugh at her he needed a little
light relief with a pretty woman, before going on duty. A
fellow as ill-done to as he had been deserved no less.

He soon found his light relief.

Across the room, sitting quite alone, was a delectable creature whom he could not remember having seen before. She wore an elegant gown of the palest lemon silk, a rope of pearls of the finest quality was twisted through her lustrous black hair. Around her creamy shoulders was an exquisite Chinese scarf embroidered with mauve irises. On her lap was a half-opened fan, also from China, remarkable for the pure beauty of its porcelain decorations. On her tiny feet she wore cream-coloured kid slippers such as Chinese ladies wore, sewn with pearls.

Dazzled, Jack wondered how in the world such a delicate beauty could have escaped his notice—she must have arrived on the ship which had docked the previous week. He decided to take advantage of the freedom of the ballroom and introduce himself to her. He strode purposefully across the room, all else forgotten.

He was quite unaware that when his destination became obvious a hundred pairs of eyes followed him in hopeful anticipation of yet another delicious piece of scandal. Near to her he saw her beautiful dark eyes widen and a flush colour her ivory cheeks.

Unwisely Jack took this as a tribute to his own advance and his bow was a deep one.

'I never like to see beauty neglected, madam. May I introduce myself to you? Captain Jack Cameron at your service.'

His beauty gave a little gasp. Her flush deepened and she opened her fan to blot out the face which he was gallantly bending towards her.

Enlightenment suddenly dawned.

'Why, I do believe...' Jack stammered. 'It cannot be! Can I possibly be addressing Miss Hester Waring?'

Hester shook her head proudly, half-amused by his evident confusion. 'My name is Hester Dilhorne, sir, as you

well know. I do not think that you should be speaking to
me. It is scarcely wise.'

She had lowered her fan to regard him steadily. Her
coolness, her poise, were doubly surprising to Jack when
he remembered her former manner. O'Connell and the rest
had been right. She was transformed. She had changed into
an elegant and confident beauty.

Rage filled him. What had that brute Dilhorne done to
deserve a pearl of such price? Reason should have told
him to ask what that brute Dilhorne had done to turn her
into this exquisite and composed lady of fashion!

'Mrs Dilhorne, then.' He bowed again. 'I am delighted
to have found you. I wish to apologise for any hurt which
I may have caused you in the past, and to inform you of
my admiration for you tonight. You are beauty's self, madam.'

He was not lying. Before him was the woman whom he
had always felt was his due, but had never managed to
find—but Hester let him go no further.

'No need, sir. I have no wish to converse with you, nor
receive apologies. Pray retire, sir. You must be aware that
you address me at your own risk.'

Useless to speak to him so. Jack was fascinated. Reckless of danger he persisted. His eyes could not leave her
glorious face. There was no one else in the room to com-
pare with her. Beauty and pride of manner alike singled
her out from all others.

Hester looked around for Tom, who stood a little way
away talking to Will French. She could not answer for the
consequences if Tom saw him pestering her—she could
not believe that Jack's admiring stare was genuine.

Too late! Jack made no effort to move and Tom, bored
by Will's long-windedness, looked back at Hester—to dis-

cover that she was being badgered by that swine Cameron. It was plain from her manner that she wished him gone.

'My wife needs me,' he told Will abruptly, and strode across the ballroom floor, every fascinated eye now on him, to where Jack was still pressing his unwanted attentions on Hester.

Tom seized him by the shoulder and swung him round, grimly pleased to see that Jack's face paled at his presence.

'I'll thank you not to trouble my wife, Cameron.'

'I was only trying to apologise, Dilhorne.'

'Insult by apology is not wanted from a swine like you.'

'I was only trying to do the decent thing, Dilhorne.'

'You wouldn't begin to know how, Cameron.'

Jack decided that to back down before the whole room which was avidly watching this exchange would be the last disgrace. He began to bluster.

'Now, see here, Dilhorne…'

The killing rage that had swept over Tom when he had seen Jack talking to Hester deepened. He had difficulty in controlling it. His hand tightened cruelly on Jack's shoulder.

He said, in a voice of ice, 'Do I have to teach you manners all over again? I warn you of the consequences, Cameron, if you try my patience. Stay away from my wife.'

The whole room was staring at them. Hester looked at Tom and saw that his expression was murderous. He was scarcely recognisable as the man she knew. Something had to be done to prevent him from leaving Jack Cameron dead on the ballroom floor.

She rose gracefully, put her left hand on Tom's free arm and at the same time, closed her fan with the defiant swoosh which Tom had told her was the Japanese ladies' way.

'Mr Dilhorne, my love, I feel a little faint. I wish that we might take a turn outside. I am sure that Captain Cameron would not seek to detain us.'

Tom looked down at her. There was not the slightest sign that she was faint or in any way discomposed. She had spoken to him in the voice which she used in their teasing exchanges. Her nod to Jack was dismissive. His rage at the man was swept away, and was replaced by admiration for her cool head. Not for the first time in their dealings with the outside world she was using her supposedly weak femininity to defuse a difficult situation.

Reluctantly he released Jack's arm. He took his wife's instead and, without a backward glance, his head bent solicitously towards hers, he walked her to the open glass doors. The room behind them stopped holding its collective breath. Jack Cameron was left alone and foolish on the edge of the ballroom floor.

Half of the watchers were disappointed that the famous scene in Madame Phoebe's was not to be repeated, this time with more serious consequences. The other half, who liked Tom and were coming to admire Hester, were relieved.

Lucy Wright, who had been sitting next to her, said to Frank, 'You were right when you said that Tom would have killed Jack that night at Madame Phoebe's if you had let him. For a moment I thought that he was going to murder him here, publicly, before us all.'

'Jack's a fool,' Frank proclaimed, 'and someone should tell him so. Did he really not recognise her?'

Lucy nodded. 'I'm sure he didn't.'

Pat Ramsey, who had enjoyed watching Guinea Jack's discomfiture at the hands of both Dilhornes, turned to his fellow officers of the 73rd and drawled, 'Now what I should dearly like to find out is how that devious devil knew that if you fed and thoroughly bedded that plain piece, Hester Waring, she would turn into a raving beauty and fit to help him run his empire into the bargain! That sort of know-how ain't for sale, my boys, else we should all be so lucky!'

Outside Tom led Hester to a white-painted rustic bench standing among some acacia bushes in the Governer's garden.

Neither spoke for some moments until Hester said quite deliberately, 'My dear, you shouldn't be so troubled by Captain Cameron speaking to me. I know that you don't like it, but it does seem a little excessive for you to want to kill him for doing so.'

Tom's grim expression lightened at this, and still more so when she continued, 'It was really the oddest thing. Are you sure that you didn't addle his brains at Madame Phoebe's? He came prancing over to me as though I were the Queen of Sheba, paid me a series of extravagant compliments with the most absurd expression on his face and then tried to pretend that he didn't know me!'

Tom said carefully, 'I think that perhaps he didn't recognise you, Mrs Dilhorne.'

Hester was brisk with him. 'Fiddlesticks! I expect it's these clothes I'm wearing. But that's you, Tom, not me.'

It was useless for him to try to tell her how much she had changed. Tom smiled and said simply, 'Nevertheless…' before slipping an arm around her shoulders. 'You're not really feeling faint, are you, Mrs Dilhorne?'

'Not really, no. But I had to get you away from Jack Cameron somehow. I wasn't wrong, was I?'

'Not at all. You were right. It would be a pity to swing for such an ass. He's his own punishment. But I would have liked to see his face when he did recognise you, though.'

Hester stood up. 'I think that we ought to go back now. We have given them enough time to talk about us, and they should have started on another topic by now.'

He grinned back at her. 'Oh, I doubt that, I really do, but yes, we'll return. I need to placate Will French—I left him rather abruptly, to say the least. Wouldn't do to lose business over Jack Cameron.'

Their return to the ballroom was eagerly watched. Tom led her over to rejoin Lucy Wright and her friends.

He bowed to them. 'Your servant, ladies and gentlemen. I wonder, Mrs Wright, if you would look after Mrs Dilhorne for me while I apologise to Mr French for my late ill manners. She is not feeling quite the thing.'

Every regimental head turned to look at Hester. If she were not feeling quite the thing, then that was the condition to which all women ought to aspire. She had never looked more charming and composed.

The officers who had passed her by when she had been poor Hester Waring were almost officious in their gallantry to her to the degree that she became a little embarrassed.

She said shyly to Lucy, 'I think everyone has run mad tonight. First Jack Cameron and his nonsense, and then Captain Parker has been favouring me with some extravagant rubbish about beauteous nymphs, and even Frank has joined in the game.'

Lucy looked sharply at her. Did Hester really not know how much she had changed. Had Tom not told her?

'Do you never look in your glass, Hester?' she said, unconsciously echoing Tom. 'Is it possible that you are not aware of the great improvement in your appearance? It is so great that you have become the talk of the ballroom.'

She would have said more had not Governor Macquarie and his wife come up to them, only for the Governor to add to Hester's confusion by praising her lavishly—he had always had an eye for a beautiful woman.

'I wish that your husband were with you, Mrs Dilhorne, so that I might compliment him on his wife. If we had the old-style Queen of Beauty at our balls these days there is no doubt who would win the crown tonight. Trust Tom Dilhorne to acquire the prettiest woman in Sydney for his wife.'

The ground opened up before Hester. Jack Cameron had not overset her, but the Governor had. Coming on top of Lucy's remarks, he had finally convinced her that Tom was not paying her loving, but meaningless, compliments. She must examine herself in the glass when she reached home.

The Governor kissed her hand before moving on. The whole room watched him give the accolade to Mrs Dilhorne. Tom, approaching the little group after leaving Will French, was a delighted spectator.

Driving home through a night lit by an enormous moon, Hester spoke to Tom.

'You were right, Mr Dilhorne.'

'I am always right, Mrs Dilhorne. Which particular thing was I right about this time?'

'My looks. I have to accept that I am greatly changed and that it is not solely due to the splendid clothes and presents which you have chosen for me.'

'Oh, yes, Mrs Dilhorne, I was certainly right about that.'

'But why?' she cried. 'And how? What has happened to change me so?'

He grinned at her, his face triumphant. His day was finally made as Hester at last entered her kingdom.

'Good food, Hester, my love, and food and wine, and

fun in bed. Especially fun in bed. Let's get home quickly—
and make you even lovelier!'

Happy Tom might be, but Jack had to be dealt with—
he was a loose cannon. Tom moved swiftly. He heard on
the secret grapevine which existed in Sydney that Jack was
determined to get his revenge for the insults which Tom
had offered him, never mind his broken nose and damaged
looks.

'He's a mad dog, Tom,' his informant, Natty Jemson,
told him. 'I'd be careful if I were you, mate. He'd do you
any damage. Best watch your back.'

Yes, mad dog was a good description of a man who was
wandering around The Rocks, half cut, letting his hatred
of Tom and his desire for Hester become public knowledge.

While there were those in The Rocks who might like to
do Tom Dilhorne a bad turn, there were others who either
feared him too much, or who owed him, either for his
forbearance, or for what he had done in the distant past
when he was still the young London thief let loose in a
frontier town, ready to make it his own territory.

Tom walked to his office, dodging the growing traffic,
thinking over what Jemson had told him, and pondering
on how to cut Cameron's claws. Dealing with a mad dog
was difficult: they were the most dangerous dogs of all
because they were irrational.

Above all, Hester must not know of this. He wanted
nothing to mar their happiness, so Jack must be dealt with
quickly. Chance was kind. He entered his office, saying
abruptly to Joseph Smith, 'I want you to scour Sydney and
buy up as many of Captain Cameron's debts as you can.'

Smith grinned at him. 'No need. Larkin came in not an
hour ago and offered me the lot—and glad to get rid of

them. I havered a bit—though I knew you'd most likely want 'em. Was I right?'

'Very right. Pay him as little as you can—they're worthless, except to me.'

Buy up a man's debts and you could control him. Tom sat down at his desk, laughing and saying to himself, Here's to cutting Master Jack's claws, and wrote him a letter instructing him to visit Dilhorne and Co.'s office in a week's time to discuss matters of business relating to his debts. That should fetch him at the double, reflected Tom, as he handed it to his boy to deliver.

He was particularly merry at dinner that night. Hester said, smiling, 'If I did not know you better, Mr Dilhorne, I would think that you had been drinking.'

Tom began to laugh. 'A good idea that, my dear. We've been neglecting the bottle lately.'

He went over to the great lacquer sideboard and came back with a bottle of red wine which he opened and poured her a glass. Instead of handing it to her, he held it to her lips, saying, 'Drink up for Tom, my love. I did a good piece of business today. No, I shan't tell you what it is this time. Let it mature.'

He laughed at his own cleverness as she obediently drank the wine down while he cradled her head tenderly with his left hand.

Later he was to look back wryly and conclude that happiness had made him careless and over-proud, something which misery had never done. But at the time he celebrated.

The wine was finished off in bed, and it was good.

In the night they awoke to make love again, and it was particularly satisfactory so that at the end they were laughing together with the joy of it.

Tom had raised himself on his elbows above her, and Hester, putting up her hands to stroke his face said, between her gasps of laughter, the most incongruous thing which she could think of, given his size and his strong, quirkily handsome face.

'Oh, you are my pretty boy, Tom! You're my pretty boy!'

He stared down at her, his face working. His own laughter stopped completely. His face then became quite still and, without a word, he collapsed by her on the bed, one arm flung across her body, shaking violently.

At first Hester thought that he was still laughing, but when he raised himself into a crouch, his hands over and protecting his head, she suddenly realised that he was crying. Great racking sobs were tearing apart a man who had not cried since he was a small boy: a man who had little pity for others and none for himself.

Hester was terrified. Tom had become her rock, her foundation stone. He had rescued her from penury and ruin. To see him so broken and distressed shook the underpinnings of her world.

What had she said or done to cause this?

Nothing mattered to her but that she should comfort him as he had so often comforted her.

She sat up and uncoiled him enough to clutch him to her breast as though he were her child. She rocked and stroked him, using only his name, avoiding all endearments since the last one which she had uttered had proved so disastrous.

Gradually he lay quiet against her. Her shoulders and breasts were wet with his tears.

After a little his hand crept out to clutch her own.

'Hester. I frightened you. I'm sorry.'

She stroked the hand. 'I was frightened—a little. But

that does not matter. You have made me much braver than I was.'

He gave a cracked half-laugh. 'Well, that's something good I've done, perhaps.'

He fell silent.

'If it would help you,' she told him gently, 'you could tell me what I did or said that troubled you so. But not if it would pain you too much.'

For a little time Tom did not answer her and, except that his breathing had not changed, she might have thought him asleep.

'Oh, Hester,' he said, at last, 'you broke a childhood memory. Something I had pushed away and forgotten. For years I have acted as though my life began when I reached London. I destroyed my earliest memories quite deliberately because I could not bear to remember them. It was as though they had never been. It might even be true to say that I was only born as the Tom Dilhorne I am when I met Alan Kerr on the transport which brought us to Botany Bay. Between us we changed my life completely.'

Tom fell silent again, and when at last he spoke it was in a flat uninflected voice, quite unlike the many voices which she had heard from him before.

'My pretty boy, you said. My mother used to call me that when I was a little lad. I had forgotten that, too, until you said in love, what she had said to me—also in love. When I heard you I was suddenly a child again, and all I had deliberately forgotten came back to me in a rush—and then all the things which I have done since. God forgive me for what I am and for what I have done.'

He fell silent again.

To say anything would be wrong. To hurry or to question him would be wrong. He only needed to know that she was with him—and that she loved him.

He spoke again. 'You have spoken freely to me of your past life, and I have told you nothing of mine. I have been wrong—there should be no secrets between us. I will tell you what I have told no other. Not even Alan knows what I was and where I came from, although he may suspect from words I have let drop what my life has been.

'My mother was a farmer's daughter, decently brought up in the Yorkshire Dales. She said that her family was comfortable and it was customary for the daughters to be sent to the big house for instruction and experience.'

He laughed shortly.

'Experience! Well, she got that, poor girl, if nothing else. Right enough the son of the house made her his mistress. She said that it was true love. She told me some nonsense about a marriage; said that she would never have lain with him else. The big house was near the moors, but some uncle of his married them, secretly in a little church far away from his home.

'Any road, whatever the truth of it, she found herself expecting. One of the other servants informed on them, and told her lover's father that she was carrying his son's by-blow. The father was a tyrant who frightened them all, her lover included, and the consequence was that my fine young gentleman deserted my mother. She never saw him again after his father discovered her condition.

'Hart, she called him, my dearest Hart. She never really believed that he had abandoned her. It must have been his father, she said, who prevented him from seeing her—he would never have betrayed her else. Whatever the truth of it, she was put out to be a skivvy on a farm far away from both the big house and her own home and family. She never saw any of them again. Her family disowned her— she had brought disgrace on them. She was to exist as a banished whore, to have her bastard—me.'

Tom's laugh was sad, more of a gasp than a laugh.

'I was brought up on the farm. I remember that we didn't have a bad life at first. But the farmer's wife grew old and sick and my mother was a pretty girl. The farmer took her to his bed against her will. I mind the night that he did. I saw her struggle and fight with him... His wife told her brothers what he had done. They came to the farm, thrashed the farmer and turned my mother and me away.

'You can see why I wanted to forget my past, Hester. It's an ugly story. My mother had been raped, but we were punished as severely as though she had been willing. I don't know how old I was then. I still don't know how old I really am. Another farmer took us in. He was a brute who couldn't keep servants. He abused my mother and beat me. She soon lost her pretty looks.

'He began to beat my mother, too. It gave him pleasure—and it's why I can't bear to see a woman hurt. I remember so clearly now what I willed myself to forget—and how it all ended. I suppose that I was about twelve or thirteen, and was big for my age. My mother said that I was growing to look like my father. She taught me my letters and made me keep up my reading and writing. There was a Bible and a Bunyan and Foxe's *Book of Martyrs* in the house and some chap-books.

'One day he came in and found us reading together. For some reason it angered him. He began to beat her cruelly. Always before I had been afraid of him, although I'd promised myself that I would kill him one day when I grew big enough. I was fearful that he was killing her. There was a carving knife on the table. I can see it now. I remember picking it up and plunging it into his side. I never knew whether I'd killed him or not...

'He fell, bleeding, across my mother. She was crying and wailing, "They'll hang you for this, Tom."

'"Never," I said. I was young and stupid and giddy with pride at what I'd done. We left him lying in his blood and ran away to London. It would be hard for them to find us there, she said.

'London! She'd no more idea than I had how far away it was. It was just a name to us. We walked there and it was her death. She'd begun to cough blood at the farm. We slept in barns and under haystacks. I wasn't too young to know that she sold herself for food to keep us alive.

'Somehow we reached London. I remember thinking that we'd arrived in Hell. I knew about Hell from the *Book of Martyrs*. My mother was dying when we got there and it didn't take long for her to go. With her last breath she was babbling about herself and Hart on the moors before I was born. I was left alone. I had no one and nothing— no family, no means to survive, no decent clothing to give me respectability, no trade and not even a home. I slept in the street, under bridges, in inn yards, begging for scraps.

'I soon learned that thirteen-year-old boys can be cheated but I rapidly found ways of avoiding that. I worked for a magician for a time and learned a lot of useful tricks, but he wanted me for his bed, so I ran away from him. In the end I became a thief because there was nothing else for me to be. I was big and strong and clever, and I soon became an organiser of thieves, boys like myself. I was a fence before I was out of my teens. Oh, I was a likely lad, I can tell you.

'By the time that I was eighteen I was fly and rich with it. I'd a pad of my own and a pretty mistress. I often wondered what happened to her after the Runners arrested me when I over-reached myself. I thought that I could take on the masters of my world.'

His laugh this time was a bitter one.

'It taught me to mind my back, Hester, but too late to

benefit me then. My elders saw me beginning to threaten their profits and they shopped me, betrayed me to the Runners. Oh, yes, I was a real threat—I've always known how to manage people and I looked after the boys I ran, my pickpockets. I didn't simply exploit them like they did. They were the ones with the power, though. They set me up for the Runners and I was taken red-handed, with all my gains about me.

'What I'd committed were capital crimes—and to cap it all, I'd even bought the law. An old man in a nightgown with a black cap on his head sentenced me to death. I suppose that it's the criminal bastard's usual end. I couldn't believe it. Clever Tom Dilhorne was to swing. My lack of years didn't save me. The old man said when he sentenced me that I was a dreadful example of youthful vice and he'd do the world a favour by sending me out of it. I can't help wondering how he would have fared if he'd been turned out, quite alone, on the London streets at thirteen.

'I remember now that I lay in Newgate in a stupor. I couldn't believe that I was going to escape this time. I remember vowing that if by some chance I didn't hang, I would be more wary. I'd never trust anyone again—my best friend had informed on me—and I'd never put myself in a position where I could be betrayed by anyone.

'The day before I was due to swing the turnkey came to my cell. I was lying in the straw in a daze.

'"Get up, boy,'' he shouted.

'I thought that he'd come for me a day early, or that I'd miscounted the days. I'd lost all track of time. He let me think that it was Tyburn Tree I was bound for. They took me outside and chained me to another three poor devils and drove us in a cart to the hulks. The talk was that our sentences had been commuted to transportation—and so it proved.'

He gave a great sigh before he started to speak again. Hester realised that in some way he was purging himself—that he must tell her the whole sad story.

'I met Alan on the transport. He was just coming out of his stupor. His case was worse than mine for he was a gentleman and was as green as grass among the hardened felons who surrounded him—myself included.

'He had been a surgeon on a naval ship of the line, sentenced for treason, for unwisely expressing sympathy for the ideals of the French Revolution, something which his captain chose to regard as mutiny. He had been lucky not to be hanged on the spot but to be transported instead.

'I felt sorry for someone who was as green as he was. I don't know why. No one had ever felt sorry for me. I think now that I needed someone to care for, perhaps to make up for what I couldn't do for my poor mother. I befriended him, protected him, saved him from assault—and worse. It was the best thing I ever did.

'He was educated, clever and a natural teacher. And I wanted to learn. How I wanted to learn! I thought that if I had known more I might not have been caught so easily, might not have descended to be a thief. I wanted to dig myself out of the pit I was in. So when he said that he wanted to repay me for saving him I asked him to teach me all that he knew. In the long days and nights on the transport and then on Norfolk Island when we reached New South Wales he educated me.

'I could read a little and I could scrawl something which passed for writing and I was naturally clever with figures, but I spoke like the scum I was. He taught me to read properly and to write an elegant hand, the hand which surprises so many when they see it. I imagine that it surprised you...'

Hester nodded and he laughed drily.

'He taught me to speak like a gentleman. I'd always been a good mimic and I learned quickly. I mastered Latin, too, it helped us to pass the long time on the voyage and to keep us sane. That was why I knew perfectly well what I was doing when I teased you about teaching the little ones Latin. I knew perfectly well what *amo* meant, but I wanted to see your face when you answered me.

'We were off the Cape of Good Hope when he began teaching me a little Greek—which was all that he knew. Alan said that I had the best memory of anyone he had ever met. I never forget anything which I have read, written, heard of, or experienced—which is why it puzzles me that I forgot my early life so completely.

'Why should I remember so much but forget that? Unless, of course, I had willed myself to forget it. I remembered dimly that my mother had been brave and loving, but that was all. And then for it all to come back so suddenly when you spoke just now. That is a mystery, too.

'Alan also taught me medicine and made me his assistant on the transport. He said that I would have made a good doctor or an even better dominie. There's a thought for you! Wild Tom Dilhorne a scholar! So when I interviewed you for that post I probably knew more than the rest of the Board put together, because I've read widely since. An old clerk, transported for theft, taught me bookkeeping and other business skills in return for me helping him as I helped Alan. Between the two of them they educated me so that I was saved from being another ex-thief who didn't know how to earn an honest living.

'I never revealed what I had learned when we reached Sydney and Alan and I parted to go our own ways. Let them think Tom Dilhorne a wild man and an ignoramus. That helped me to grow rich, I can tell you. Many is the time when my rivals or the Exclusives talked in front of me in their superior way, never knowing that I knew exactly what they were saying. Quoting their bits of dog Latin and speaking French—Alan taught me that, too—in front of the stupid felon.

'I've not told you all, my love, not all I've done. It's not fit for you to hear. Even Alan doesn't know the whole truth, but the poor lost bastard survived—if at a price.'

He had finished.

Hester sat up and pulled his head against her breast as though he were her child and rocked him.

'My poor love, oh, my poor love.'

The story of the lonely boy and his betrayed mother had moved her beyond words. And I thought that I had suffered, she said to herself. I hardly know what suffering is.

Tom's lack of self-pity, the matter-of-fact way in which he had spoken, shocked her the most. He had told her his story in a level voice, almost as though he had been speaking of someone else. Whatever she had thought his past might have been, she could never have imagined what he had told her.

For his part Tom lay quiescent against her as she kissed and stroked him gently, bringing him to climax by her own actions. For once he was passive, the loved one, the acceptor of delight, and not the fierce and tender lover who initiated their pleasure.

He had put his past behind him. He had become Tom Dilhorne, rich and powerful, who ruled and controlled his world absolutely. To remember was to become the helpless boy again, to be controlled, not to control. He had conquered his world, but at a dreadful price.

Telling Hester was, they both knew, in some odd way

the greatest gift he could make her. He had surrendered his deepest self to another, although after Newgate he had vowed never to do so again.

Chastened, purged, he slept at last. Hester, holding him against her heart, lay awake until the new day arrived to bring them back to the demanding present. She was no longer Tom's toy, she was truly his partner, as her Mentor had promised. In the future his associates would discover that if they accepted him, they had to accept her.

What he had told her explained what drove him so frantically towards success in everything that he touched and, above all, the energy which had allowed him to find her, to understand her, to change her whole existence, while at the same time not diminishing any part of his busy life. No one, watching him, could have guessed from the man that he showed the world what he had been and how much he had suffered—nor would she ever tell anyone his secrets.

## Chapter Twelve

Tom was sitting at his desk in his counting-house on the morning of the day on which he had asked Jack Cameron to visit him. His concentration was broken by the sound of a struggle outside his room.

He had barely had time to rise to his feet when the door flew open. Jack Cameron stood outside, Tom's letter in one hand, a scarlet-faced Joseph Smith's ear in the other.

'I mean to teach your insolent lackey a lesson, Dilhorne.'

'I merely asked him to wait until I found out whether you were free to see him, Master Dilhorne.'

'Ex-felons are always free to see me when I need to see them,' sneered Jack.

'You mistake,' Tom returned mildly. 'It is I who need to see you.'

He was perfectly cool with Cameron now that Hester was not involved. 'If you don't release Mr Smith at once, I fear that it is I who will teach you manners, since you seem to have forgotten the last lesson I gave you.'

Jack pitched Smith from him. 'Oh, very well, Dilhorne. I'll let your miserable serf start pushing his quill again.'

'I think,' remarked Tom, as smooth as silk, 'that you

have just added two per cent to the interest I shall require
from you in payment of your debts. It shall go to Mr Smith
to compensate him for being manhandled by a poor apology for a gentleman.'

'Two per cent, is it?' sneered Jack, watching Smith
leave. 'What the devil does that mean? And what's this
ordure you've written to me? I must say that I'm astounded
that you can write at all.'

He tossed Tom's letter on to his desk.

'We have some business dealings to conclude,' said
Tom, ignoring Jack's insolence, but having taken sardonic
note that Jack was carefully avoiding coming to physical
terms with him.

'I wasn't aware that I had any business dealings with
you, Dilhorne. I'm always careful to avoid contact with
felons whenever possible.'

'Ex-felon is the correct term,' was Tom's only answer,
'and if you imagine that you have no business dealings
with me, you are as mistaken as when you chose to mis-
name my wife.'

Jack's anger at this was tempered by his wariness in
dealing with the vulgar ruffian before him.

'Captain Cameron to scum like you, Dilhorne.'

'Certainly, Captain Cameron,' agreed Tom in his most
exasperating drawl. 'Captain Cameron. Well, Captain
Cameron, I take leave to tell Captain Cameron that I have
bought up all his debts. They lie on the desk before you,
Captain Cameron. And I shall require Captain Cameron to
agree to three conditions if Captain Cameron will be good
enough to listen to them.'

'Damn you, stop repeating my name, you filth!' roared
Jack.

'I was under the impression that you ordered me to use
your name, Captain Cameron, but as you have asked me

so politely not to, then I shall be only too happy to oblige you and cease.'

'What conditions, Dilhorne? How dare you talk to me of conditions, you damned convict?'

'I shall add another one per cent for vulgar abuse,' said Tom equably, 'and you will talk to me of conditions because, if you don't, I shall set the bailiffs on to you for debt and inform Colonel O'Connell into the bargain.'

Jack was on the verge of gibbering. 'Come to the point,' he finally achieved in a hoarse whisper.

'I fear you mistake again. There are *three* points for you to consider. Firstly, I have purchased all your debts and now hold all those which you have run up in Sydney. Secondly, I shall charge you a percentage on them to be paid each quarter day at an interest which I shall determine, and of which Smith will inform you in advance—and you will not assault him again, or I shall send all your papers straight to O'Connell. Thirdly, any form of default on your part, or interference with me and mine, and again, I shall send in the bailiffs.

'Is that all perfectly clear to you, *Captain Cameron… sir.*'

The 'sir' came out with such studied insolence that it was an insult, not a respectful salutation.

Jack sank into an armchair opposite Tom's desk and stared mutely into the bland, smiling face of the man opposite to him. Then, his voice thick with rage, he snarled, 'By God, you damned felon, I'll call you out, see if I don't.'

'Do so, by all means. Here and now, if you like. Shall I choose fisticuffs, on the spot or later? For be sure I shall never call you out, however tempted I might be to kill you, and thus, by your own ridiculous rules, the choice is mine, always mine.'

'By God, Dilhorne,' cried Jack despairingly, 'I never thought that I'd find myself ruined in a hell-hole like Sydney by a ruffian such as you!'

'Did you not? Then you should have ordered your affairs better. But you have not answered me.'

'What answer can I give you other than yes? You have me by the throat. But I'll do for you yet, Dilhorne, see if I don't.'

Tom leaned back. The smile on his face was deadly. Hester would scarcely have known him.

'I find you a dead bore, Cameron,' he said at last. 'Your vocabulary is limited. You have all the charm of a fifty-year-old whore and your reserves of courage disgrace the army which you profess to serve. You haven't the stomach to call me out, however much I insult you. If it weren't that I can make a useful profit from your inability to manage your affairs, I wouldn't care to know you.'

'By God, Dilhorne, I'll make you pay for this.'

'You mistake. It is you who will pay me. Now take yourself away, I have work to do.'

He sat down, picked up his quill and began to write in the ledger before him.

Jack stared at him, his face alternately white and red, his mouth working. He started to his feet and stamped out, closing the door behind him with a shattering bang.

'Now I wonder if I overdid that,' mused Tom. 'But the fool is such an easy mark.' He shrugged and rang for Smith.


Several nights later Tom and Hester engaged in what they did not know at the time was their last night of unalloyed bliss.

As usual it centred around a picnic. It had lately become unsafe to go far afield. A group of banditti—as Sydney had recently dubbed escaped convicts—had been preying on anyone who strayed near the bush at night.

Tom naturally thought of a variation of their usual excursions. He decided that the shrubbery in his own grounds was safe enough and he and Hester went down there with food and drink, rugs and pillows—and pistols.

Hester was wearing the boy's clothing in which she went riding: a white silk open-necked shirt, black trousers and a black jockey cap. Tom was similarly dressed without the jockey cap. After they had eaten enough food to satisfy them they blazed away at targets in a competition which Tom had invented. The winner had to take two drinks and the loser one at the end of each round.

Tom had suggested that this might be a better way to indulge themselves rather than by simply drinking the wine with their food. He did not have to relax much in order to allow Hester to win a few rounds. Her marksmanship was now almost as good as his.

Their laughter rang out in the moonlit night and their aim became more and more erratic as the game went on, until Tom pointed out that to continue it might become more actively dangerous to them than to the target.

'Besides, I doubt whether I want to make love to a boy,' announced Tom, staring at Hester's breeches when he pulled her on to the rug beneath the trees.

'No, Mr Dilhorne, I can see that that might trouble you. Suppose I removed them, would that help?'

'Do not strain yourself, Mrs Dilhorne, allow me.'

'In that case I insist that I remove yours.'

They fell asleep in one another's arms surrounded by the remains of the picnic whilst, unknown to Hester, Tom's employees patrolled the far perimeter of the Villa Dilhorne to allow its master and mistress to take their pleasure in safety.

A wiser precaution perhaps than either of them knew, for Tom had acquired an enemy whose hatred was implacable. Jack Cameron's detestation of Hester Dilhorne's husband had become so bitter that it seemed like bile in the mouth.

He had been both publicly and privately humiliated by him, and had been brutally assaulted after a fashion which had caused laughter all over Sydney. The last humiliation of all was that he had been nicknamed Guinea Jack because of the coin which Tom had flung at him in Madame Phoebe's—and the name had stuck.

Complaining to Pat Ramsey about this, that cool customer, who disliked Jack intensely because he thought that he demeaned the honour of the regiment, had stared at him, saying briefly, 'You should be pleased that you're not called worse.'

Jack began to splutter and to threaten so that Pat, before walking away from him, said coldly, 'I'll neither fight you, nor gamble with you, Jack, and that's my last word.'

It was all that swine Dilhorne's fault and the interview with him over his debts had been almost the last straw. Almost, because the real last straw had been Hester Dilhorne, and the effect which she had had on him at the ball.

Tom had been right to think that he had overdone it a little in his interview with Jack, for the manner in which he had treated him, coupled with his obsession for Hester, had tipped him over into something resembling insanity. It was fortunate for him that Tom remained unaware of the passion for his wife which had suddenly afflicted a man already made unsteady by his other passions.

Before he had seen her at the Governor's ball he had always boasted that all skirts were the same to Jack Cameron. 'Nothing between them', he had said confidentially to his fellow-officers who thought themselves in love, either with their wives or other women. 'They're all the same in the dark—as well one as another!'

He had mocked Frank Wright for doting on Lucy and here he was pining like a great mooncalf for a woman he couldn't have, and to make matters worse that woman was Dilhorne's wife.

Jack could not drive from his mind, try he ever so hard, the memory of her face as she had looked at him over her fan, the grace with which she had turned away from him and put her tiny hand on that hulking felon's arm.

He tracked Tom around Sydney, burning for revenge, but he also tracked Hester, burning for he knew not what, she seemed so out of his reach. The idea of taking her to bed seemed like sacrilege, and the thought of her in the arms of that brute Dilhorne made him feel faint.

These emotions were so new to him that he scarcely knew how to act. Jealousy had always been a joke. Now he felt jealous of anyone who as much as spoke to her because they were doing what he could not. By chance, though, he had cornered her one day as she walked alone to her carriage after visiting friends in Sydney.

Jack had caught his breath at the sight of her. He moved into her path. No gentlemanly compunction could prevent him from accosting her. It might assuage the strange ache which he felt whenever he thought of her—which, to his offended surprise, he so often did.

He bowed low. 'Mrs Dilhorne, I am at your service— ever and always.'

Hester stared at him. He had no business to speak to her, none at all.

'Please, Captain Cameron, allow me to pass,' was all that she could manage.

'Not until I have offered you my most humble apologies.'

'I believe that I told you once before that you address me at your peril.'

'But I do so wish to take back all that I have ever said of you in the past. You are a nonpareil, Hester—if I may so call you—there are none like you.'

Was the man mad that he persisted so?

'I do not ask you for your compliments, sir, and I do not thank you for them.'

Jack was desperate to touch her. He put out a hand. She drew back.

'You shame yourself, sir, by trying to detain me. Again, pray allow me to pass.'

He would not desist. 'I wish that I had looked closer at you before you married that felon.'

'You did, Captain Cameron, but you did not like what you saw. If you do not allow me to pass, I must inform my husband of your ungentlemanly behaviour. You would not care for the consequences if I did.'

Jack's face contorted. 'Is there no way in which I can convince you of my regrets for my behaviour, and persuade you to speak kindly to me—if only for a moment?'

Hester regarded him steadily. 'If you will allow me to continue on my way, then I will think more kindly of you than if you pester me with your unwanted attentions. You must be aware that even if I wished to speak to you—which I do not—my husband would not allow it, but would hunt you down to punish you.'

Nothing would do. Jack stood back. 'I shall not detain you further, but believe me, my admiration for your looks and spirit knows no bounds.'

Hester closed her eyes, preferring not to see him. She could not imagine what Tom would say or do if he learned of this encounter. Jack watched her until she disappeared around the corner. When he had disposed of Dilhorne she *would* listen to him—he was sure of it.

One morning Hester, instead of rising to greet the new day with joy, awoke to find herself feeling ill, and when she finally rose from her bed she was overcome with nausea. At first she thought that this was a passing ailment, occasionally common to Sydney, but the condition persisted, affecting her only in the early morning, until at the end of the first week she found herself vomiting helplessly.

She said nothing to Tom who invariably rose before her, but on the day when she had been violently sick, he looked at her keenly, watched her eat very little, but said nothing. On the following morning, having risen and left her, he returned rapidly upstairs after a few minutes to discover her lying on the bed, her face damp, having suffered the worst bout of sickness yet.

He wetted a cloth, sat beside her and began to wipe her face gently.

'How long has this been going on?'

'Every morning for over a week now. It seems to pass off during the day,' said Hester faintly. 'I kept hoping that it would go away and that you need not know.'

'Have you any notion of what is wrong with you, Hester?'

'A sickness of the stomach, I suppose.'

'You might call it that.'

Unaccountably Tom was smiling. 'But I suspect that you are increasing. Do you have any reason to suppose that it might be so?'

She sat up suddenly. 'Oh, yes. My courses are late, but they have been late many times before, as you must know, and it wasn't because of a baby then.'

'Then you were recovering from near starvation, which

always affects a woman's courses, and you have never had morning sickness before. If this continues and you continue to miss your courses, we must take you to Alan to be examined. But I am bound to tell you that I have no doubt that you are expecting a baby.'

Hester looked at him anxiously. 'Do you mind, Tom?'

He pulled her to him. 'Oh, Hester, I have never told you, but it has been my dearest wish that we should make a baby. I hope that you feel the same, but remembering how you behaved with John Kerr and your schoolchildren, I need hardly ask.'

She smiled at him. 'It is my dearest wish, too, and I do hope that you are right. How odd that you should know and that I should not.'

'Well, in some respects your life has been very sheltered—although not in others. Whereas I...' and he grimaced '...there is little that I do not know about men and women. Alan certainly added to my knowledge of them when I helped him on the transport.'

'Is there anything I can take to cure my sickness?'

'I remember that Alan used to prescribe gruel and a plain diet in the early morning before the patient rose, and from now on that is what we shall do. It seems to help.'

Alan Kerr duly confirmed that Hester was pregnant and Tom's attitude to it was all that might have been expected. He was both protective and brisk. He bluntly told Hester that once her sickness had abated she must live a reasonably active life: she was not an invalid.

He was encouraged in this by Alan, who was as unorthodox in his treatment of pregnancy and childbirth as he was in his insistence on a healthy diet to avoid sickness and in his rational care of the health of the convicts who surrounded them.

Hester had only one demand to make of them both, and that was that when the baby was being born she wanted to know that Tom was somewhere near. 'You will promise me that, won't you, Mr Dilhorne? It's your child as well as mine.'

'I promise, Mrs Dilhorne, that I shall agree to whatever makes you happy—will that do?'

To his great relief, as her sickness diminished her energy returned and, far from causing her to lose her looks, pregnancy enhanced them, conferring on her a new radiance which more than one who met her privately remarked on.

Lying awake one night, for her pregnancy made sleep difficult, Hester could only marvel at Tom's kindness and consideration for her. Oh, he was still the hard, devious man whom all Sydney knew, and she had no illusions about that. What mattered to her was the private Tom whom only she knew: a complex, many-sided man who had manipulated her into marriage—for which she daily thanked him.

She was also coming to understand him more and more. Recently she was sure that something was troubling him and that—contrary to his usual practice—he was not telling her what it was. Now it was beginning to worry *her*.

At this point Tom stirred and rolled towards her, opening one eye. He pulled her down beside him. 'Still awake, woman? You need your sleep. Is owt wrong?'

'No,' Hester said, not yet ready to question him about possible trouble. 'It's odd, when I first knew you, and then after I married you, I seemed to need to sleep so much—and now I don't.'

'Not odd at all,' he mumbled, but he refused to amplify his answer further, simply putting a friendly arm around her so that she, too, drifted into sleep, since now, when it did come, it always came easily.

\* \* \*

Jack Cameron moped around Sydney. He had done little to advance his revenge on that swine Dilhorne. Anger seethed in him, growing stronger by the day, fuelled by the knowledge that he was finding it increasingly difficult to pay him the interest on his debts.

After his abortive meeting with Hester, to watch Tom walk and drive around Sydney with her by his side, to hear of his business successes, to learn that one of his horses was winning races regularly and that he had made a killing in his deal with the Yankee whalers, all served to inflame him the further. The news that the Governor was about to make him a magistrate was enough to start him gibbering.

To cap everything, he had gone to Lucy Wright's one afternoon and had heard something which finally destroyed his last hold on sanity. To go there at all showed how far he had fallen since young Wright, taking pity on the yellow-faced hangdog he had become, took him home for tea—an entertainment which the old Jack would have heartily despised. The new one accepted the offer lethargically.

A great deal of idle small talk went on about low persons whom Jack normally avoided. He was about to leave when Lucy, feeling sorry for him left stranded and alone, handed him a china cup full of boiling hot tea. He had scarcely taken it from her when a woman nearby said loudly to the company at large, 'Have you heard the latest, my dears? Hester Dilhorne is increasing.'

Before Lucy could reply, Yes, she already knew, Jack gave a strangled cry and created a sensation by crushing his cup in his hand, scalding himself in the process, and cascading boiling liquid and pieces of Lucy's precious china on her carpet.

Such a to-do followed with Jack's cut and burned hand being dressed, a servant being sent for, pieces of china being retrieved, and the carpet mopped, that the reason for Jack's strange behaviour was overlooked. Only that sardonic onlooker, Pat Ramsey, a late arrival come to view the spectacle of Guinea Jack at an afternoon tea party, raised his eyebrows, said 'Well! Well!', to nobody at all—and came to the correct conclusion.

Jack sat in a daze with all the females exclaiming over him. He was the object of more sympathy than he had received for years. Everyone assumed that Lucy had overdone the hot tea and that Jack had had some sort of accident with it. No one—other than Pat Ramsey—could conceivably have guessed that when Jack had learned of Hester's pregnancy he had received an almost mortal blow which was to drive him on to his final acts of madness.

Pregnant! By that appalling swine! Jack rode back to the Barracks, nursing his bandaged hand and his hate, recalling something which he felt made the mere idea of a pregnant Hester Dilhorne even more obscene.

It had happened some weeks earlier when his private hell had become unendurable.

That day he did not know what was wrong with him. The previous evening when he had been in bed with one of Madame Phoebe's girls, trying to forget that he was an unhappy Jack Cameron, Hester Dilhorne's face had risen before him and effectively ruined his pleasure. Even Ramsey, that turncoat whom he had seen in cheerful conversation with Dilhorne more than once, had tried to be kind to him, but damn him, too, a gentleman should know better than to consort with a felon.

Desolation saw him saddling his horse and riding off, alone, towards the bush. He tried not to think, looked about him instead, but sun and scenery had no attraction for him and his mind turned round and round in the ruins of his life.

He came to a great stand of gum trees and shading greenery and rode into it to escape the sun which mocked his dreadful mood. He sat there for some time, hidden from view—until he suddenly had company.

Some distance away, beyond a large level opening in the bush, two riders emerged from another clump of boskage. One of them was that unspeakable cad, Dilhorne, dressed in an odd costume—white silk shirt, loose black silk trousers tucked into beautiful cavalry boots and a grey slouch hat on his head.

The other rider—and Jack's heart leapt with savage glee—was a boy! A boy wearing black and white jockey's silks and a black and white jockey cap whose broad peak obscured his face.

What a tale to tell Sydney! Tom Dilhorne, alone in the bush—with a boy!

Fascinated, Jack watched them dismount. Dilhorne first, and then, steadying the boy, he helped him from his horse. They stood for a moment close together, talking, but he could not hear what was said, they were too far away.

Dilhorne put his hand into his saddle-bag, took something out, and then he and the boy walked towards an open expanse of green, and he saw that it was a ball which they were throwing the short distance between them as they walked.

Tom had brought the ball home some days earlier after joining in an impromptu game of cricket between the regiment's officers and men, assorted Government clerks and anyone who cared to play.

When the pair reached the green they faced one another and began throwing the ball to and fro. Slowly they lengthened the distance between them, still flinging the ball back and forth.

There was something odd about the boy's catching and

throwing even though he was skilful at both. At first Dilhorne threw easy balls which the lad caught, equally easily, and then suddenly they became stronger and more difficult, until he flung a very low one, slightly sideways.

The boy dived to retrieve it, and when he did so he threw his other hand triumphantly into the air to celebrate his success. His cap flew off and Jack knew that he would tell no one in Sydney what he had seen, for the boy was Hester Dilhorne!

Their laughter and shouts floating towards him, he watched the game in an agony of jealousy. It ended when Hester reached the limit of her powers, and Dilhorne, misjudging a little, threw the ball high above her head, and in trying to catch it she fell over backwards into a clump of bushes.

Dilhorne ran towards her and lifted her out, hugging and kissing her. Fortunately for Jack's sanity their game did not end as it usually did, for their time was short and they were due to dine with Will French.

They stood close for a few minutes, Dilhorne's arms around her. He kissed Hester's cheek before throwing her into the saddle, and she kissed his hand in return. They rode away rapidly, passing not far from where Jack was hidden, and the last thing he heard was Hester's voice shouting, 'Race you home!'

Jack never knew how long he sat there. He was bathed in sweat and filled with emotions which he had never before experienced. Why should that devil have such a treasure? How could he be so careless of her? He was laughing when the poor little thing fell into the bushes. He, Jack, would care for her better than that. What God was there who left him almost broken and let that swine take his pleasure around Sydney, riding his fine horses and showing off his prize?

The feelings for Hester which had swept over him on the night of the ball were intensified. His memory showed him her grace when she had run and jumped for the ball. That devil should take more care of her, not let her risk herself so.

Jack knew that he was being irrational. He hardly knew whether he desired Hester for herself, or because she was Dilhorne's wife. He only knew that since the night of the ball he could not rest easy.

Now that graceful child was to be burdened because of Dilhorne's base passions. It was not to be borne. He would put an end to him and achieve the twin aims of his life: revenge on the man who had humiliated him, and his desire to have Hester for his own. Surely with Dilhorne out of the way she might look more kindly on one who loved her so dearly.

Consumed with hate, Jack had ridden back to Sydney to begin watching Dilhorne's every movement. He had discovered that his prey regularly drove to the quarry on the same afternoon each week and he had decided that Dilhorne's journey home might provide a suitable spot for a shot from ambush.

Jack took his horse, musket and pistol. Dismounting, he lay in the shadow of a clump of small trees not far from the track along which Tom would pass. Lying in the bush, waiting for his victim, served only to increase his torment. Here he was, stranded in an alien wilderness, pursuing a man whom back home he would hardly have known, but who had become a potent symbol of the ruin into which his life had fallen.

Dilhorne's appearance brought Jack a relief almost sexual in its power. He raised his musket, sighted carefully and loosed a shot to finish off the impudent swine once and for all.

Tom's hat flew from his head. His horse reared beneath him at the sound of the shot, and with the instinct which rarely failed him, he fell from its back into the bush, to lie quite still in the hope of deceiving his attacker. With luck he would either leave the scene thinking his fell deed done, or would come over to finish what he had begun, giving Tom an opportunity to get at him.

In the silence which followed the sound of Dilhorne's horse bolting, Jack rose, seized his pistol, and debated whether to go over and finish off his victim. Even in his growing madness caution held him back.

No, he thought. Best leave him. If he's dead, well and good, if not, folly to tangle with such an artful bruiser, who would certainly be armed and might be waiting for him. There would be another day.

He could not confess the truth to himself: that his fear of Dilhorne was nearly as great as his hate.

Tom, lying prone, his right arm extended—he had plucked his pistol from his belt after his fall—was ready for his enemy as Jack had suspected. He heard the departing hoofbeats and waited for some time before rising again.

His face thoughtful, he chased after his horse which had abandoned its flight into the bush to begin peacefully grazing while his master mused on Jack Cameron and his now murderous proclivities. Tom had no doubt as to who had fired the shot and that it was no accident. He regretted that he had driven Cameron too hard in his interview with him when he had been unaware that Jack's obsession with Hester had been the final straw which had tipped him over into madness.

He also had no doubt that he must watch his back since

he was sure that Cameron was likely to attack him again once he discovered that his first attempt had failed.

Above all else, Hester must not discover what had happened for a new reason and one which was beginning to trouble him. Her health and strength, which had returned once her morning sickness had ended, had disappeared again and he wanted nothing to disturb her.

By the time he reached home there was nothing in his manner to betray that he had been the subject of a murderous attack—except that Hester, sensitive to everything to do with him, knew that something was wrong, but what, was quite another thing. Wisely, she said nothing.

Jack soon discovered that he had not so much as winged his enemy and tried to drown his disappointment in drink. There were, perhaps, safer ways of disposing of Dilhorne than killing him himself: ruining him might be a good start. He had friends in The Rocks who might do him a favour, particularly if he asked them to help him to loot the Regimental stores of liquor again—he badly needed the money which such a ploy would bring him. One way or another, he would do for the wretch.

# Chapter Thirteen

'Is anything worrying you, Tom?' Hester asked him.

They had been playing chess: the athletic activities of their early married life had stopped now that Hester's pregnancy had advanced. She had grown very large quite early on. The weight of the child seemed to be almost too much for her to carry. Even walking was difficult.

There were no more romps in the open, no excursions which took them to strange places, no driving out to the quarry, or to his place of business in Sydney where the sight of little Mrs Dilhorne on her husband's arm had become commonplace. Hester never complained about her straitened life: the stoicism which she had learned during her poverty still sustained her.

Tom turned his inventiveness to devising games and pastimes which made no physical demands on her. They played cards, he showed her magic tricks and explained how they depended on misdirection. At night she would read to him. He continued to consult her on business matters, even when she could not go out with him.

'However big you grow, Mrs Dilhorne,' Tom said firmly to her one evening, 'I am not having you dwindle into a wife.' He was quoting to her from the Congreve play which she had read to him the previous evening.

'You are my partner now and must learn the business. You may look after your child, but it must not be your whole life, for the day will come when the child has grown up and, think on, what will you do then?'

Only Tom, thought Hester, amused, could contemplate his wife, not yet due to give birth, and energetically decide what he, she and it would be doing twenty years hence.

Recently his teaching of her about his business had become more urgent. Once she had overheard him say to Joseph Smith, who had remonstrated with him for burdening his breeding wife with such matters, 'By God, man, if aught should happen to me I don't want her to be like those ignorant fools of widows who become the prey of the unscrupulous.'

Was it the prospect of an early death which was troubling him, and if so, why? Almost, as Hester watched him sitting opposite to her, mending his harness, for his hands were as skilful as his brain, she was tempted to ask him what was troubling him so. What stopped her was the thought that he would certainly tell her all in good time, for he had always done so before.

Her silence had him looking up at her.

'Tired, Mrs Dilhorne?'

Hester shook her head. 'Not more so than usual.'

Tom's intuition did not fail him. He was sure that she had detected a change in his manner since Jack had become a threat, but he was not ready to burden her with his knowledge.

Instead he murmured, 'Time for some more Gibbon, perhaps?'

Hester smiled a yes and picked up the heavy book which lay on the table by her elbow. She had begun to read to him *The Decline and Fall of the Roman Empire* and he had found that Gibbon's cynicism matched his own. They had become engrossed in the world of the Antonines where other men and women, like Tom and her, had lived on frontiers so that still others could live in comfort.

Even though Tom had been expecting another attack, it surprised him when it came. Only his finely tuned instincts saved him. He had called late at Will French's that night and was hurrying home to Hester, whom he was less and less inclined to leave alone even though he had posted an armed servant, Miller, in the hall of Villa Dilhorne to act as watchdog during his absence.

It was dark in the unpaved streets which led away from the centre of Sydney, and by night he always walked warily. It was only at the last moment that he became aware of his attackers. He never knew how many there were—possibly two or three—and it was only by great good fortune that he turned away from a blow with a cosh which might have proved fatal had he been completely under it.

Half-stunned, but with an instinctive and snarling determination to survive, he lashed out like the street-fighter he had once been, and used some of the queer tricks which he had learned from a Japanese who had settled in Sydney.

With the edge of his stiff right hand he struck the holder of the cosh in the throat so hard that he fell voiceless and unconscious to the ground. Then, his senses reeling, he put the point of his boot into the second man's groin to such effect that he gave a high-pitched scream and dropped, clutching himself, to the ground.

Tom barely conscious, fell backward against the wall of the house behind him and began to slide down it until he reached a sitting position on the ground. The third man, if three men there were, had taken to his heels on hearing the noise of some late-night revellers from Madame Phoebe's approaching them. The 73rd's finest were lurching back to the Barracks, flown with wine and singing lustily.

One of the officers saw Tom, dazed and stunned, propped up against the wall.

'By God, it's Dilhorne,' exclaimed young Parker. 'Is he drunk, do you think?'

'That'd be a wonder,' returned Pat Ramsey, bending down and meeting Tom's dulled, but still sardonic gaze.

'Not drunk, attacked,' croaked Tom. 'Help me up, Ramsey, there's a good fellow.'

'Good God, there's another of them here,' said Major Menzies, putting a disdainful toe on the ruffian whose larynx Tom had damaged.

'Should be two, at least,' mumbled Tom, swaying in Pat Ramsey's grip.

'Two!' ejaculated Pat. 'Where's t'other?'

Young Osborne found the second and Menzies examined him as well.

'He's nearly killed the pair of them,' drawled Menzies, rising. 'There's one here who'll be slow to talk again, and by the look of it his friend will be lucky if he ever pleasures another girl. What did you hit 'em with, Dilhorne? A brick?'

Parker had found the cosh and Pat had raised Tom into a sitting position on a low wall.

'They damaged his head and his left shoulder,' he reported. 'Here, Osborne, hold him up for me, will you. I want to see exactly what Dilhorne did to 'em.'

While one of the junior officers went for the watch, Pat examined Tom's victims before returning to ask, 'Just to satisfy my curiosity, Dilhorne, what exactly *did* you hit them with?'

Tom looked blearily at Pat. He was slightly concussed, one eye was closing, and bruises were beginning to appear on his face. He muttered, 'Hand—nigh broke it, and foot—' And he indicated the point of his polished military-style boot.

Osborne said helpfully, 'Let's get him to Madame Phoebe's.'

'No!' exclaimed Tom, his voice momentarily normal. 'Home. Hester will worry. Carriage round corner, I'll drive.'

'She'd worry if you drove home in this condition, my friend,' Pat said briskly, thinking that here was a splendid chance to see the inside of Villa Dilhorne. 'Parker and I will take you.'

'I'll come, too,' offered Osborne eagerly.

'No, lad, no room,' said Pat. 'But we'll tell you what was what, later.'

Privately his respect for Dilhorne, already high, had increased after seeing what he had done, half-conscious, to his enemies. That stupid ass, Jack Cameron, could count himself lucky that Dilhorne had spared him.

It was gone two in the morning before they arrived at Villa Dilhorne. Tom had given Pat his keys. He had the doors open before Miller, pistol in hand, reached them, a worried Hester, carrying a candle, close behind him. The two officers helped Tom, still suffering from pain and shock, into the hall.

Hester said sharply, 'Tom, what's wrong?' Her eyes on Stephen Parker and Pat were accusing.

Tom lifted his head.

'Hurt, not drunk,' he managed to say. 'I promised you, remember?'

The effort of speech had him putting his entire weight

on Ramsey. 'I was attacked. Good friends brought me home.'

Parker's fascinated eyes were on Hester. Her body, thickened by pregnancy, was concealed by a pink silk Chinese robe decorated with cream and yellow irises. It was loosely belted by a pale mauve sash. Her face was translucent as a result of her growing frailty, but it was delicately beautiful, and full of concern.

Once her first fright was over, she put down the candle and briskly started to organise matters. Miller was sent for further help. Pat Ramsey and Parker were asked to take Tom to his room. Both men were only too willing to find out what his bedroom was like now that they had seen the dazzling splendours of the room below.

They were particularly impressed by the screen with the running tiger on it.

Young Parker could not help regretting that he had callously rejected the rare piece of womanhood which Hester had become. Once he could have had her for the asking. He wondered, as Pat Ramsey was doing, how the brutal pirate they were assisting to his bed, and whose handiwork was lying battered in the lock-up, had managed to create such a rare treasure.

They followed Hester up the massive staircase, past the Chinese idols and through the bronze doors. Hester began to light the numerous blue and white candles, thick in their porcelain holders, which stood about the lovely room.

She was amused to see that the two officers' eyes were everywhere after they had lifted Tom on to the big divan bed. She went into the dressing-room and emerged carrying a priceless Chinese bowl: the two men stood back to allow her to wipe Tom's face, one side of which was rapidly turning purple.

Miller's arrival, after seeing to Tom's horse and carriage, left them free to leave, full of what they had seen. Hester took them into the room where the tiger rampaged. A maid brought them sandwiches and Hester poured brandy for them into Tom's priceless glasses.

After a moment's small talk she said coolly, 'Now I must ask you to tell me exactly what happened before and after you found him.'

The note of authority in her voice was such that Pat took her at her word. When he had finished she asked, 'Have you any notion of who his attackers were—or why he was attacked?'

Hester was privately of the opinion that this wretched business had something to do with Tom's recently changed manner, but she was not about to tell Pat so.

He shook his head. 'No, I can tell you nothing. The most likely supposition is that they saw a splendid opportunity to rob him, the hour being so late. The brutes were so badly hurt that I doubt whether they will be able to tell the watch anything, either.'

'He would not be kind,' she said dismissively. 'You have both been as considerate as I might have hoped. We cannot thank you enough.'

They left. Although whether it was the house or Hester which impressed them the most, neither of them could have said.

In the Mess on the following day they told their story and it was the house which they dwelt on.

'You should have seen the bedroom,' exclaimed Pat. 'Lucy Wright didn't exaggerate, she didn't even tell all. It was filled with treasures: ivory gods, Chinese vases, silks, lacquered furniture—and the bed! You've never seen anything like it. No curtains, just pillows and bolsters everywhere and it was as big as a ballroom. I swear to God it was large enough for him to have entertained all Madame Phoebe's girls at once if he'd had a mind to.'

Tom recovered quickly from the ambush. He told Hester that it must have been a botched attempt at robbery. Both of the injured men were escaped convicts who had been living in the bush around Sydney and were known to be petty thieves. The one who could speak told the magistrates that they had been after Tom's money and valuables: both Tom and Hester for their different reasons doubted this. Tom was sure that Cameron was behind it, but he had no proof.

He had other things to worry him. His wagon trains, which operated between Sydney, Paramatta and other outlying settlements, were coming constantly under attack, each one worse than the last. They were not armed, but the bandits were, and in the most recent attack one of the accompanying men had been badly injured.

Again it was supposed that escaped convicts and masterless men were responsible.

'Any idea who might be behind it?' Tom asked his wagon master, O'Neill. He had met him on the quay by the harbour.

'None, except…' He hesitated. 'No one else is suffering, only us.'

'Right. If we're the target again on the next run, I shall ride with you on the one after that. I shall be armed, with half-a-dozen reliable ruffians I know of at my back. They'll be armed, too. We can't afford a running sore of this nature to damage us.'

He said nothing more. Only time would tell whether the attacks on his wagons were merely coincidence or a sign that Jack had changed his tactics. Something else to keep from Hester, unfortunately.

\* \* \*

Governor Macquarie invited the Dilhornes to a small private dinner party. It was to be one of Hester's last outings before her baby was born. The reason for the privacy was that the Governor wished to discuss some matters with Tom in an unofficial, rather than an official, capacity.

He noted, with his usual kindly, slightly inquisitive concern for his fellow men, that all Sydney was right when it gossiped about heartless Tom Dilhorne's loving care for his heavily pregnant wife. He could not miss the occasional touching of hands, the speed with which Tom moved to effect anything which might add to her comfort, or relieve her discomfort, nor the way in which they looked at each other. It made the Governor feel old even while it pleased him.

After dinner, his wife helped Hester to her pretty withdrawing-room while her husband offered Tom brandy and cigars. Tom took a little of the first, refused the latter. He was wondering what all this was leading up to, and now thought it advisable to resume his business persona: during dinner he had been an exquisitely mannered English gentleman.

'The thing is,' began Macquarie after they had made small talk about the possibilities of exploring and settling further inland instead of being content to remain on the edge of the vast continent, 'you know how hard I've been pressing you to allow me to nominate you as a magistrate.' He paused.

Tom nodded wisely. 'But...' he said, and said no more.

Macquarie looked surprised, so Tom, for once, explained himself.

'I've learned,' he said, 'that when someone looks as confidentially at me as you've just done, and then offers me that kind of statement in that tone of voice, that there's always a but in it somewhere!'

'Well, the but in it is this,' said the Governor, laughing, 'that while I want you to be a magistrate—and I know that you'll be a good and fair one—magistrates don't usually rearrange the features of Army officers in Madame Phoebe's! I was prepared to overlook that, so my *but* refers to something else. It's this. I have gained the impression that until recently you were prepared to agree to be a magistrate, but that something has changed your mind again. Without amplifying matters further, I believe that I know and understand why that has happened.'

Tom smiled at him. 'Lots of buts there—and I know that you understand why I wish to delay being nominated, for the moment.'

The Governor nodded before murmuring, apparently inconsequentially, 'You've recovered from the attack on you, I see, but I gather that you're having other problems—or so gossip says.'

'True, so you will understand that I don't want anything to compromise my freedom of action at the moment.'

'Understood—and here's another but—but I want you to understand that when this affair has blown over satisfactorily for you, I want your word that you will agree to be a magistrate. I know that you will keep it and I am not going to allow you to wriggle your devious way out of doing as I wish. It is your Governor speaking, Mr Dilhorne, and not your friend. Otherwise I shall allow you no freedom of action while you settle your current problem as discreetly as possible.'

Tom toasted him, and gave way at last to the Governor's wishes. He could do no less. Macquarie had heard, God knew how, that Jack Cameron was behind the attacks on him and was giving him permission to settle the matter as he pleased. At the same time he was using it to blackmail him into becoming a magistrate—something which he had privately vowed never to do.

Like it or not, respectability was going to claim him for its own!

'Of course,' he said, and for once drank long and hard.

Events moved quickly after that. The week he had discussed with O'Neill passed, and in it his wagons and drays were attacked again. O'Neill, disturbed, arrived at Villa Dilhorne with the news.

'It's bad, Master Dilhorne. One wagon load lost, on the Paramatta run, and two men injured.'

'That's it, then,' said Tom. 'I'm on the next as I promised. No one is to know that I shall be with you. Send word when you're ready for me.'

'Two or three days, that's all.'

Tom rubbed his close-shaved chin reflectively. 'Make it four or five. I look a little respectable.'

When O'Neill had gone, he returned to the living-room where Hester reclined on the settle, a book in her hand.

'I've been thinking,' he told her. 'I need to spend a few days in Paramatta—business takes me there, and I don't care to leave you alone. Instead, you might like to pay a visit to Alan and Sarah while I'm away. Alan told me yesterday that he wishes to examine you at leisure, and you would have him and Sarah, to say nothing of baby John, for company.'

Hester looked at him. She knew immediately that this was something to do with what she privately thought of as Tom's trouble.

'If it will make you happy, of course I will go. I always enjoy visiting the Kerrs.'

'Then that's settled,' he said, kissing her.

He whistled as he walked out to his gig. At least he did

not need to add a deserted and vulnerable Hester to his other worries. Things might yet work themselves out.

Tom arrived at Paramatta with O'Neill, three bullock drays, two horse-drawn wagons and the half-a-dozen ruffians he had promised O'Neill earlier.

He was indistinguishable from them. He had neither washed nor shaved after he had left Hester with the Kerrs and he wore the coarse clothing of his early days in Sydney. He had passed Pat Ramsey on the road out of Sydney and Pat's cursory glance had roved unseeing over him, over his scuffed boots stretched out in front of him, his clothes and face filthy, and his battered hat pushed to the back of his greasy head.

At Paramatta they unloaded what had been ordered from Sydney and stocked up with farm produce, wooden artefacts and the lengths of the coarse cloth which the farmers' wives had woven. They waited for the evening before they set off home. Three of the ruffians were hidden under the awnings of the big drays, the other three helped with the loading, their arms concealed. Tom drove the first wagon.

He had decided on a night drive home. O'Neill was sure that they had been watched from a distance and that the highwaymen might think a night attack easier than a day one. Tom had instructed his men to hide their arms and behave in a loose, drunken fashion.

They were singing, seemingly half-drunk, when the attack came near some abandoned huts which the bushrangers had been hiding in after following the wagons from Sydney. Half-a-dozen men suddenly appeared on horseback and ordered them to get down from, and abandon, the wagons. They fired a ball over Tom's head and were obviously determined to make a real killing this time.

'Be damned to that,' Tom sang out. He then gave the

shrill yell which was a signal for the counter-attack from the men hidden in the drays, whereupon a short skirmish followed.

The thieves were not expecting such high-level resistance, and since Tom's party had the advantage of surprise this time, they made short work of overcoming their attackers. Their leader, an Emancipist named Kaye, a noted Sydney scapegrace, was taken on one side after being captured.

Tom left O'Neill to reorganise the wagons and drays which had been scattered in the attack and went into one of the huts, giving orders that Kaye should be brought in after about fifteen minutes. The delay was designed to unsettle him even more than the failed attack had done.

The wretched Kaye was thrust into the candle-lit room. On a rough deal table in the middle of the room he saw Tom Dilhorne, a cigarillo clamped between his teeth and a pistol in his hand. Dilhorne was no longer the respectable man who walked Sydney, but had the grimy raffish air and dilapidated clothing of the young ruffian who had arrived to take the town by storm.

Kaye did not immediately recognise him, so changed was he from the man he had become. His heart sank: he had forgotten how dangerous Dilhorne was.

Tom took the cigarillo from between his teeth and tried Kaye's nerves by making him wait while he ground it out on the table and then by gesturing at him with the pistol.

'What do you propose that I do with you, Kaye?'

His eyes were as hard and cruel as Kaye had ever seen them.

'Don't hand me over to the military, Master Dilhorne. I'll surely swing this time.'

'So you would. But what makes you think that I should want to?'

He gesticulated with the pistol again. 'A quick shot would rid me of a problem and save Sydney the cost of a trial.'

Lifting the pistol, he pointed it at Kaye and almost absent-mindedly sighted down the barrel. Kaye gave a great gulp.

'Don't do that, Master Dilhorne. Your life for mine would be a fair exchange.' His voice quavered on the last word.

Tom did not lower the pistol, merely looked over the top of it.

'Would it, indeed? Now what makes you say that?'

'Put that thing down, and I'll tell you.'

Tom said agreeably, 'You'll tell me with it up, or you won't be telling anyone anything.'

'It might go off accidental-like.'

'No, it wouldn't. I never do anything accidental, Kaye. Don't try my patience. I'm not quite myself tonight.'

Kaye thought that he'd never seen anyone more like himself than Tom Dilhorne sitting there, threatening to send him into eternity.

'Right then, here it is. There's a nob wants to do for you, Dilhorne, and he wants it bad. So bad he paid Fitzpatrick's lot to do you over a few weeks back. Poor Fitz made a botch of it, and won't be telling anyone anything again. So then the nob hired me to loot your wagons to do you more hurt. He'd see you dead if he could, God's truth.'

Tom put the pistol down and looked at the miserable wretch before him. His own suspicions had been confirmed. There had been nothing accidental about the attack in the street, never mind the shot which had whistled through his hat earlier.

'Go on,' he said. 'This nob must have a name. Tell me,

I'm curious. What did he pay you with? The man I'm thinking of has no money.'

'Nor he has, Master Dilhorne, but he's privy to the garrison's liquor stores these days and that's better than money.'

'So it is,' rasped Tom, 'but if you don't come out with his name I'll kill you where you stand.'

'But you know his name, don't you, Master Dilhorne? It's Captain Cameron, whose pretty face you spoiled.'

Tom picked up the pistol and pointed it at Kaye—who let out a shriek of despair at the sight—and fired it at Kaye's shoulder. Kaye fell to the ground, clutching himself.

'I told you what you wanted, Master Dilhorne. A life for a life, you agreed, and you broke your word.'

Tom threw the smoking pistol on the table as the door opened to admit O'Neill, who grinned when he saw the writhing Kaye.

'No, I didn't break my word,' remarked Tom affably. 'I offered you your life—I said nothing about your shoulder. O'Neill, see that he gets to Dr Kerr. As for you, Kaye, that should teach you not to interfere with me again.' He thrust his hand into his pocket, took out a guinea and handed it to O'Neill.

'Pay the doctor with that, and give Kaye the change.'

Once O'Neill had led Kaye out, telling him that in his opinion Master Dilhorne had grown a deal too soft these days, and that he, O'Neill, would have had Kaye's guts for garters for this and the other nights' work, Tom reloaded his pistol.

His expression when he rammed the ball home would have shocked, but not surprised, Hester. So, his suppositions had been correct. Jack was running around like a mad dog trying to kill and ruin him. Now he had several levers he might use against him. To begin with, O'Connell might like to know who was responsible for looting the Regimental stores. The question was, how could he let O'Connell know what Cameron was doing without his knowing where the information came from?

Tom laughed. Guile was sure to find a way: it always did.

After Tom had returned from Paramatta and had brought her home again from the Kerrs, Hester's fear that he was hiding something from her was as strong as ever. He said little about his time there other than to tell her some nonsense about renewing contracts with the locals—an explanation which she thought would scarcely have deceived a child!

Tom Dilhorne to spend a week renegotiating minor agreements which Joseph Smith could have dealt with in an afternoon! What did he take her for? She said nothing to him, though. Two could play at that game. Sooner or later she would discover what had really been going on.

When he had finished talking nonsense to her—she was lying on the settle and Tom was seated on the floor beside her while she stroked his head—she said almost idly, 'I trust that your business at Paramatta was successful enough to warrant your journey there.'

He glanced sharply at her but her face gave nothing away and the stroking never paused. Mrs Slyboots, he thought with some amusement, giving as little away as I do.

'Tolerable, my dear, tolerable. I have to keep O'Neill and his cohorts in a good humour—wouldn't do to think that I've lost interest in them. It's a problem with having so many irons in the fire.'

'Oh, indeed, Mr Dilhorne.'

Was her tone slightly satiric, or was he imagining it? He debated about telling her the truth, but Alan had privately warned him how frail she was, and that she needed loving care.

Instead he rose to his feet and walked across the room to pour the one glass of brandy which he allowed himself each night.

'Water, my dear?' he queried. Alan had recently advised against her drinking spirits—they might damage the child she was carrying.

Hester watched him standing sharp against the candlelight. Her stroking hand had lifted his sandy-blond hair around his head, and when he turned towards her, she caught her breath at the sight of him. The passion which she felt for him was all the stronger because of their enforced abstinence.

'You look happy, Mrs Dilhorne.'

'Oh, but I am.' She thought that he looked happy, too. The hard set of his mouth was relaxed and the humour which came so naturally to him, but was often suppressed, was given freer play these days.

He handed her the water. 'Hold your nose while you drink it, Mrs Dilhorne. I wouldn't want its strength to overpower you. It'll be hard to readjust yourself to anything so light as wine once Master Dilhorne is born.'

'You're so sure that it's a boy,' she said, smiling. 'But what if it's a girl?'

'Then I promise to love Miss Dilhorne as much as her non-existent brother.'

Hester was silent for so long that Tom asked her gently, 'What is troubling you, Hester?'

'That it is hard for you that, because I am so weak these days, we have not been man and wife for some time—'

He interrupted her. 'We are never more truly man and wife than while you are carrying my child.'

'Oh, Mr Dilhorne!' Hester was suddenly merry again. 'I cannot imagine the day when you are unable to trick me with your clever tongue.'

He reached up to take her stroking hand and kiss it.

'My dearest love, I know what you are trying to say.'

'That it is hard for you, as a man, to be so denied.'

'Hard for me!' He kissed her hand again and looked at her wonderingly. 'You say that while you lie there, helpless. Oh, Hester, what are my transient needs compared to the state to which I have brought you?'

Her face lit up. 'Why, I thought that I contributed more than a little to my state myself, Mr Dilhorne.'

'So you did, Mrs Dilhorne. But it is you who bear the consequences, I don't. The least honour which I can do you is to bear any consequences for me as patiently as you bear the child.'

He released her hand to place his own gently on her stomach. He felt the child thresh beneath it. 'Active little fellow, isn't he?'

Hester laughed. 'He, or she, nearly kicks me to pieces at times. He's as big as an elephant, but a lot more lively.' Her face twisted as the child rioted again, her stomach moving like a wave beneath his hand.

It could not be long now, Tom thought, before the child was born—Alan had warned that it might be early. 'Try to make her take a little light exercise,' he had said, 'it will go hard with her if she lies down too often.'

'Time for a stroll,' Tom said. He helped her from the settle and walked with her down the long room and back again. Driving into Sydney had stopped, the motion of the carriage distressed her—as walking did.

Whatever else, she needed his protection more than ever—and she must not learn of Cameron's villainy.

## Chapter Fourteen

Tom moved against Jack Cameron with all the speed, cunning and cold calculation which he could summon to the task. The sooner he was disposed of, the sooner he could rest easy. Once the threat to his life had receded, he could concentrate on looking after Hester, and he would no longer need to deceive her.

He was as secret as he could be while he set in motion the events which would ensnare Jack, and which would bear no trace of his own involvement. Returning from one such errand, he met Lieutenant Wright, Lucy on his arm, walking down Macquarie Street.

Tom was careful not to share with them his worries over Hester's health. He was privately and sardonically amused by the warm way in which they spoke to him—such a contrast to their manner a year before. He told them that, although house-bound, she was always pleased to receive visitors herself.

'Then I shall propose a visit at once,' exclaimed Lucy, who, in the face of Hester's remarkable transformation after her marriage to Tom, felt ashamed that Sydney's elite had done so little for her after Fred's death.

Frank's contribution to the conversation was more

downright, 'I suppose you haven't heard of Pat Ramsey's splendid news,' he offered, 'seeing that he only received it when the latest boat docked yesterday.

'He's succeeded to the family title and, more to the point, its great estates. We shall have to call him Sir Pat now—but not for long. He's wanted back home and will doubtless be resigning his commission.'

Fortune's wheel had turned in Pat's favour. Tom hoped that it would not turn in Jack's. He must have learned by now that his latest attack on his interests had failed.

Jack, indeed, was well aware of that. Kaye had never turned up for his pay in kind, nor made any attempt to contact him to explain what had gone wrong. The days passed and his impatience grew. Discreet investigations revealed that Kaye was lurking in The Rocks, his right arm in a sling.

'The result of an accident,' he told all and sundry. Jack thereupon prowled The Rocks himself, and finally cornered Kaye.

'Do I know you, sir?' whined Kaye when Jack began to question him fiercely.

'Damn you,' roared Jack whose vocabulary was limited. 'You know full well that you were doing a job for me over Dilhorne.'

'Dilhorne, is it?' Kaye's face grew long. 'I never tangle with Dilhorne. Dangerous man that. Should be careful in any dealings you have with him, Captain.'

Was it Jack's imagination or did Kaye's gaze rest on his broken nose? He flung away in anger. Useless to pursue the matter, and dangerous, too. Dilhorne had won that round and frightened Kaye off into the bargain. He had also frightened everyone else off, too.

Worse still, he had no sooner returned to the Barracks

than he found that he had more to worry about than attacking Dilhorne again. That ass Ramsey, now a baronet, damn him, told him that O'Connell wanted to see him as soon as possible.

'Messenger boy, are you…*Sir* Pat,' he sneered.

Little ever ruffled Pat, and that slid off him like water off a duck's back. He shrugged, turned on his heel and left Jack to fume his way to O'Connell's room where he found him waiting at his desk, Menzies beside him. Damn them both for canting hypocrites!

'We can do this rough,' began O'Connell, without preamble, 'or we can do it smooth. Depends on you, Cameron.'

'If I knew what you were talking about,' muttered Jack—who did.

'Don't be a fool,' O'Connell snarled at him. 'I've got proof positive that you've been robbing the liquor stores among other things. The garrison's liquor is awash around Sydney—and you are responsible.'

'I suppose it's that damned swine, Dilhorne, who's told you this.'

'Dilhorne? What's Dilhorne got to do with this? No, the Quartermaster you bribed was caught red-handed yesterday, selling it in Sydney. He's confessed and has implicated you, among others, although you're the only officer involved, thank God. It all fits, Jack, including the fact that you've been full of money lately.'

Jack's face twisted. 'What about the Government stores you siphon off to Dilhorne and others? Are you going to be broke for that, too?'

'You're light in the attic, Jack. What the Regiment disposes of to the traders here is all above board, as you well know.'

'Including the sweeteners to and from Dilhorne and the

others, I suppose. And then he has the gall to inform on me!'

'You're hipped on the man, Jack. He has nothing to do with this. I've not so much as seen him in months. What sweeteners? What evidence do you offer for such a claim? Now I've affidavits here testifying to your guilt, evidence enough to break you. But I'm not going to do that if you're sensible. Are you going to be sensible, Jack?'

'Depends on what you mean…sir.'

'I'll tell you what I mean.' O'Connell's voice was weary. 'I'm breaking the Quartermaster down to the ranks—for insubordination, not theft. That way there'll be no open scandal. He's only too grateful for not getting a flogging and a discharge. As for you, you can hand in your papers and go home on the next boat. I'm not having you running loose round Sydney.'

'Resign, you mean?'

'What else—or you can have it rough and be court-martialled. It's up to you: I don't mind which.'

'What choice is that?' Jack's face contorted. 'It's that damned Dilhorne who is responsible for this. I know it is.'

O'Connell sighed heavily. 'You don't deny anything, do you, Cameron? Let me give you some advice. Since you fought with Dilhorne, your judgement, never very steady, seems to have gone completely awry.'

'Fought with him!' Jack almost screamed. 'I never fought with him. The damned swine attacked me brutally and without warning. I know he's behind this.'

His face stern, O'Connell stood up. 'No one is behind this. You brought it upon yourself by your own stupidity, and ruined another man into the bargain. Now get out of my sight, and if you don't hand your papers in by tomorrow morning I'll have you arrested and court-martialled.

Even if you do, you'll be confined to quarters until the next ship leaves for home—taking you with it.'

Drinking himself into oblivion, Jack was well aware who had ruined him, and who was going to pay for it before he left Sydney if that were the last thing he did. There's no order which O'Connell can make which will keep me from getting at him.

Tom knew that his machinations had succeeded when he met Pat Ramsey in George Street the following afternoon. The warmth of Pat's greeting was the measure of how far he had travelled from his beginnings.

'Ah, a word with you, Dilhorne. I have the notion that you will not be surprised to learn that Jack Cameron's handed in his papers and is going home. Seems he's had enough of Sydney—at least, that's the official story.'

Tom raised negligent eyebrows. 'Has he so, Captain Ramsey? Though I suppose I ought to call you Sir Patrick now.'

'Oh, be damned to that, Dilhorne. Ramsey will do. I shall be leaving soon, and the one thing which I shall miss is the pleasure of your recent company. A pity you can't come with me.'

'A pity, indeed,' returned Tom smoothly. 'As for Cameron, Sydney will be pleased to see the back of him.'

And you as well, thought Pat, watching Tom stride away, and congratulations to you, Dilhorne, for arranging it. The Regiment will be better off without him.

The best of it is, thought Tom, that I can go to Hester with the load off my back and with no need to deceive her further: I can concentrate on looking after her.

Hester was to remember afterwards how busy that particular day was. Tom told her that he had hired a nurse to care for her until the baby came. She would arrive at the weekend.

He looked at Hester across the breakfast table. She was cheerful, but paler than ever—her eyes were dark in her wan face.

'I've a mind to stay at home with you until the nurse comes. I don't care for you to be lonely,' he said abruptly, fear gnawing at his heart.

He might have expected that she would refuse his offer. 'Oh, no, Tom. I know that you are busy today. You are arranging the business of the flour mill, are you not?'

He nodded, 'Trouble is, dear Mrs Dilhorne, there is a dinner arranged as well, and there'll be drinking afterwards, so I fear I shall be late home tonight. One thing, though, I shall not stay out late again until after the baby arrives.'

His troubles with Cameron might be over, but he would not rest easy until she had been safely confined.

'Besides,' she went on, 'I shan't be lonely today. This morning the Ladies Sewing Circle is meeting here, and Lucy is bringing Frank, Stephen Parker, Pat Ramsey and all their friends in the Regiment over this afternoon. So, you see, we are accepted at last by the Exclusives.'

Tom opened his mouth to argue with her and then remembered Pat Ramsey's friendliness the day before.

'I give in,' he said, rising and kissing her on the cheek, 'but don't tire yourself.'

The 'we' in her last little speech pleased him greatly. If there were times when he feared that Hester's love for him was merely gratitude for her salvation and not a true passion for the man, Tom Dilhorne, he took heart from such statements made so easily and without conscious thought.

'I still wish that the nurse was here already. I do not care for you to be alone.'

'Do not trouble yourself about that—I have Miller to guard me.'

At that Tom did not persist, but throughout the day his usual singlemindedness was overlaid by his memory of her, chained to the settle, so different from the Hester she had once been. The Hester who had shot at targets, had run and jumped as they threw the ball about in the garden and in the bush: he was fearful that he might never see that Hester again.

Hester had been right to tell Tom that she would not be lonely. This was particularly true when Lucy and her friends arrived. She could not help remembering, while they laughed and chattered with her, how different her life had been a year ago when she had been a lonely and ne-glected waif at Mrs Cooke's. That it had been so trans-formed was due to one man alone, and that man Tom Dilhorne, her father's ogre.

Pat Ramsey kissed her hand before they left. 'It has been a pleasure to visit you, but I fear that we may have been too much for you.'

Hester shook her head. 'No, not at all. It has been my pleasure to have you, particularly as Tom says that there is talk that the Regiment will soon be called home, and then I shall lose you all.'

The house seemed strangely silent after their departure, but she was not sorry to be alone after the bustle of the day. She lay and mused about the officers' admiration for her, despite her condition, and wondered what her life might have been like if they had looked at her like that before she had met Tom.

Which was a stupid thought, for it had taken Tom to transform her, and for the first time she thought of her mother and father without rancour or regret for their treatment of her because if they had cared for her, she would never have met him.

She would never have known the excitements and passions of living with a difficult, demanding and complex man who asked of her only—only!—that she match him and meet him on level terms. Yet at the same time when she was stricken down, as she now was, he cared for her selflessly and would have stayed with her had she not sent him on his way.

Dusk fell, and then night. Miller had taken up his station in the hall. He quartered the interior of the house to see that all was well before he did so. Hester dozed a little—and was woken by a sound.

Tom, it was Tom returning.

A smile of pleasure lifted the corner of her mouth. She dragged herself to the tantalus on a small side-table to pour him a tot of brandy and herself a glass of water. She had the brandy glass in her hand when the door opened.

But the man who entered was not Tom.

At the sight of him she dropped the brandy. The glass fell to the floor, the liquor staining the delicate Chinese rug.

'What a pity, my dear,' said Jack Cameron, his eyes devouring her. 'I could have done with that.'

He advanced into the room, his eyes glittering, one pistol in his belt, the other in his hand, pointed at her.

'Sit down, my darling,' he said. 'And if you're tempted to call to that man of yours for help, I won't hurt you, but I'll shoot him down like a dog.'

He pointed the pistol at a small table before the hearth, and dragged up a chair for Hester to sit in, bowing her into it with a deference which she thought at first was mockery—until his manner and his look convinced her that it was only too dreadfully real.

He dragged up another chair to sit opposite to her and pulled the pistol from his belt to lay it on the table while holding the other loosely in his hand. He directed it at the door.

Hester stared at him. She was astonished by her self-control. Even her voice was steady when she spoke.

'What are you doing here, Captain Cameron?'

'Oh, I like that,' he said, smiling a ghastly smile. 'It's what I would expect from a true lady like yourself. Not Guinea Jack, or the way your damned husband speaks to me.'

He paused before saying, his face twisted, 'I've come to kill him. Preferably in front of you.'

He could scarcely bear to look at her swollen body.

It was what Hester had expected from the moment that she had seen that he was armed. It was why she was so calm. He intended to kill Tom and she must prevent him from doing so: choose how, as Tom would have said. She remembered what he had once told her about magic and misdirection. Well, she would misdirect Jack—if she could.

'How did you get in?'

'I like that, too. You're cool, my dearest dear. Most women would have been in hysterics by now. Your black-guard of a husband doesn't deserve such a treasure as you, Hester.'

She knew now that he was not mocking her, that his admiration for her was real, not feigned. Hester shivered as his eyes caressed her.

'How did you get in, past Miller and the guards out-side?'

'I didn't,' he grinned, charmed by his own cleverness. 'I've been inside since mid-day. No one was looking for house-breakers then—and the house is large. I watched that damned toady, Ramsey, arrive with his hangers-on, and I watched them go. Oh, I've been patient—and all in a good cause.'

'Why do you want to kill Tom? He hurt you, I know, but you said such wicked things about us. You knew what he was like: you should have expected him to act as he did.'

'Oh, my darling,' he said, his voice unsteady. 'If he hadn't married you I might have let him live, even though he has humiliated me beyond belief and caused me to be broken—but not when he has you. I cannot bear to see such a low brute and know that you share his bed.'

'You can't mean this, Captain Cameron. You always thought me a plain piece, and took care to let me know that you did.'

'Oh, God, Hester, no! How could I have been so foolish as not to see what a pearl, what a treasure you were. You have haunted me since the ball. It has been gall and wormwood to watch you with him. And now, seeing you like this...helpless...and ill... He deserves to die for what he has done to you.'

'You are mistaken, Captain Cameron. He has done nothing to me. I want my baby as much as he does. You might as well kill me, too, if you wish to kill Tom because of the child.'

His face twisted again. 'Oh, Hester, I'll surely kill him, but I wouldn't hurt you for the world. He's corrupted you, I know, but that will pass. He ruined me, for I'm sure that it was he who informed on me to O'Connell. That fool O'Connell said that it wasn't him, but I know better. He caught Kaye at Paramatta and Kaye told.'

So—Jack Cameron had been the trouble all the time. She had been right about Paramatta as well. Oh, Tom, why didn't you tell me? Why carry all the burden yourself? But her gaze on Jack remained steady and gave nothing away.

He was not so far gone that he did not register that what he had said had touched her. He shook his head as if to clear it.

'They say he tells you everything. Quite a joke it is. Cunning Tom Dilhorne sharing everything with his lady wife. I can see that he didn't tell you about me.'

'No,' Hester agreed, 'he didn't. Are you quite sure that you want to add murder to your other crimes? It certainly won't help you.'

'No, it won't, but I shall feel better when I've shot him, and freed you from him. If I can't have you, he shan't. Then I shall be able to sleep.'

Keep him talking, said her Mentor, suddenly coming to life again after its long absence and speaking in Tom's voice. Misdirection—remember—it always works. He doesn't know that you're a crack shot. He will think that you are frightened of pistols, not used to firing them.

Hester almost nodded as the voice continued, If you can get possession of his spare pistol, remember to aim for the chest and not the head if you wish to kill him.

Yes, she told herself firmly when the voice stopped, I *do* wish to kill him if I hope to save Tom.

But I have to get his pistol first.

It lay before her on the table. It was inaccessible for the moment while he had his eyes on it. It was plain that Jack was on the edge of insanity and might even shoot her if he thought that she was about to help Tom—or made a botched attempt on him.

Hester closed her eyes. Her life wouldn't be worth much if he killed Tom, and she had the baby to consider as well. If it weren't for the baby, she would have risked herself before now.

'Thinking, Hester, my darling?'

'Yes. I was wondering how you can have descended to this. It can't really be for my sake.'

'Oh. Hester, you're wrong. I was blind, blind! If only I'd known what you were truly like, you would never have married him. I would have made you look at me, not at a felon.'

It was quite useless to try to reason with him, he was too far gone. His mad worship of her might have been amusing, remembering his original distaste for her, if it were not so dangerous. The Gods must be laughing at such a reversal—if they had not planned it for their own amusement.

Her silence made Jack angry.

'Speak to me, Hester, for he cannot be long now. Plead for him, although nothing which you could say will save him.'

'No,' she told him calmly. 'I won't.' His obsession and his rage broke uselessly against the rock of her will.

'No? Then fetch me a brandy, my darling, as you were fetching him one when I arrived. Waiting for him is thirsty work. If you were my wife, I wouldn't leave you alone at night.'

'But I'm not your wife, am I, Captain Cameron? And I never would have been—and killing Tom won't make me your wife.'

He lifted his pistol to track her on her clumsy way across the room, and held it steady on her while she poured brandy into two glasses. A noise outside alerted him.

'Do I hear the swine now?'

Hester's hands, pouring the brandy, were rock steady and the face she showed when she returned to the table was as calm and composed as though she were serving him at a tea party.

She made no reply other than to place the glasses on
the table before him. She watched him drink the liquor in
one desperate gulping swallow, reminding her painfully of
her father.

'Another?' she offered pushing her glass over to him,
and deftly moving the pistol on the table nearer to herself
after she had done so. Jack, intent on her face, missed the
small manoeuvre.

'No, *you* must drink it,' he said, pushing it back.

By now Tom's voice in the hall, dismissing Miller from
his post to his room over the mews, told them that he had
at last returned.

Hester sighed. She had hoped to make her move when
Jack was distracted by Tom's arrival, but he was still
watching her closely. Worse, her clumsy body prevented
her from making any sudden move to snatch the pistol up.
Her eyes were firmly on her enemy when the door opened
and Tom entered.

He did not at once see Jack, for the room was only half-
lit, and he and Hester were in the shadows.

'Why, my love,' he began. 'Still up, and in the dark?
You should not have waited for me…'

Until, suddenly, all his worst fears confirmed, he saw
Jack, his pistol now trained on Hester, grinning in his direction.

'What are you doing here, Cameron?'

He advanced no further, remaining quite still.

'Being entertained by your wife and waiting for you,
Dilhorne.' He waved his pistol at Tom. 'As you see, I have
come to kill you.'

'Not very wise, that, Jack. You'll swing for sure if you
do. Broke parole, did you?'

Purposefully, his eyes never leaving Jack, Tom began

to move again, close to the wall, towards the settle on which Hester had rested earlier.

'Stand still, damn you, Dilhorne. I want to see you plain before I do for you. You shouldn't have married Hester. I might have let you live if you hadn't done that.'

Tom could see quite clearly that Jack was over the dividing line which separates sanity from madness, whether temporarily, or permanently, he could not tell. He looked across at Hester who had her back to him, her eyes focused—although Tom did not know this—on the pistol in front of her, so near yet so far. She wished to do nothing which might cause Jack to shoot Tom out of hand. Give her but the one chance, though, and she would have him.

'You aren't hurt, Hester?' asked Tom, ignoring the madman.

'Not hurt, just frightened.'

Her voice was cool and unwavering.

'She's brave, Dilhorne,' said Jack admiringly. 'You don't deserve her.'

'I know that,' returned Tom, keeping his voice conversational in order not to inflame Jack. 'You won't hurt her, will you?'

'Not I,' said Jack. '*I* wouldn't have let her fall into bushes…'

Tom began to edge slowly towards the settle again. Let him once get behind it… Both Dilhornes, indeed, were calculating the odds on thwarting Jack while trying to engage him in conversation and blunt his purpose.

Almost as though he had grasped what they were doing Jack ended his cat-and-mouse game. He lifted his pistol, pointed it full at Tom and fired. Tom, divining Cameron's purpose from his rising arm, threw himself behind the settle, the bullet striking him as he disappeared from sight.

Hester, meanwhile, seized her opportunity. Jack had

half-turned away from her and the pistol on the table, his attention fixed on firing at Tom. She reached for the spare pistol, only to hear the crack of Jack's weapon and the noise of Tom's fall behind her.

She gave a heart-rending scream of anguish and despair. 'You've killed him, you've killed Tom.'

Jack dropped his extended arm, turned to her, grinning, and said, 'My pleasure, Hester, my pleasure.'

He threw the smoking pistol on to the table.

Hester, both hands clutching its mate which she had snatched up at the sound of Tom's fall, rose, kicked her chair behind her, and almost before Jack understood what was happening, she fell back two paces, crouching as Tom had taught her and as she had done so many times in play.

Using both hands she lifted the pistol before her and pointed it at Jack's chest.

Jack, who had been filled with a savage delight on seeing Dilhorne fall, now suddenly realised that death was staring at him from the barrel of his own pistol—and at point-blank range.

Face ashen, eyes glittering, Hester faced him, fell intent written on her face.

'You killed Tom, and now I'm going to kill you.'

Jack's hands flew up in an involuntary gesture. He took a long step towards her. It was plain that she meant what she said. Her crouching stance told him that she had the skill and the knowledge to fire.

'No, please, no!' he cried hoarsely.

Hester's finger tightened on the trigger. She prepared to pull it. Tom, winged, not killed, rose from behind the settle to call to her, 'No, Hester, no! Don't shoot.'

Hester pulled the trigger.

# Chapter Fifteen

The echoes of the shot rang on and on. And then there was silence.

Jack Cameron dropped his hands on finding that he was neither maimed nor dead. At the very last moment, hearing Tom's voice, Hester had deloped, firing high above Jack's head into Tom's priceless cedar-wood panelling.

Still holding the pistol, smoke curling from its barrel, her face grey, she sank back into her chair, her gaze turned towards Tom, who came from behind the settle to where she sat. They only had eyes for one another. Jack Cameron was quite forgotten.

At the sight of them, together, the hate and desire for revenge on Dilhorne which had maddened Jack for so long drained away, and with it his obsession with Hester. Oh, he could admire her courage and her beauty, but it would no longer drive him to excesses of rage and folly. He felt merely a bitter regret at being alive, for he knew that only Dilhorne's command to Hester had deflected the ball from his chest and sent it into the ceiling.

The last, worst, thing was to owe his life to the mercy of a piece of Emancipist scum.

Leaning against the wall, spent and drained, he was

overwhelmed by a sudden terrible realisation: that there was no one in the whole wide world who cared enough for him to kill for him, either in protection, or in revenge, as husband and wife had just shown that they were prepared to do for one another.

Tom sank on to his knees beside Hester, careless of whether the blood from his wounded shoulder stained her gown. He held her to him by his good arm.

Hester began to cry; great gasping sobs in which all that could be heard was his name, continually repeated.

'I thought that he had killed you,' she finally achieved.

'There's my brave girl,' he murmured. 'Hush, we're safe now.'

He began to rock her.

'I would have killed him,' she said, 'for you.'

Gradually her sobs lessened and she lay against him, exhausted.

Jack Cameron sank into the chair from which he had threatened Hester. His face, too, was ashen. His unloaded pistol lay before him, but he was incapable of reloading it, or, indeed, of performing any action.

He half-wondered what he was doing here, in this strange room on the edge of the world, watching a man and a woman who were unaware of his presence. He looked vacantly at Tom who, now that he was sure that Hester was calm again, took the pistol from her lax hand and placed it on the table beside Jack's.

'Get out,' he said to Jack, his voice almost indifferent. 'Take yourself off.'

'No,' cried Hester, rearing up. 'No, Tom! He tried to kill you. He has wounded you. You can't let him go.'

He tried to soothe her. 'My dearest love, we must be sensible. Neither of us wishes to go to court to punish this scoundrel. He's been punished enough. He hasn't killed me, and he owes me his life, for as sure as I speak, had you fired at him, and not the ceiling, he would be lying dead now.'

Hester was stubborn: the tigress at bay, defending her mate and her unborn cub.

'He should hang. I *want* him to hang. He thought that he had killed you. He was pleased. He said so.'

Tom stroked her face. 'Hush, my darling. It was my fault, too. I handled him badly. I went too far. My pride in my cleverness provoked him into action. I was trying to protect you and love made my judgement faulty. You must not do the same.'

He looked at Jack again, his face stern. 'Go now, before I change my mind. I'll send you your IOUs in the morning and you may burn them. I want no more of you. Your career is ended and I pushed you further than a man should be pushed. My wounded shoulder is a fair exchange.'

Jack's legs were like jelly. He somehow managed to stand, clinging on to the table, and to answer Tom.

'Am I to thank you for saving me?'

His sneer was weak, but there.

'No thanks,' said Tom. 'I want nothing from you, or your kind. Just go and leave me and mine alone in future. I'll say nothing of this to anyone. I want no revenge for what you have tried to do. Get back to quarters before they miss you.'

He thought that Jack was a broken man, and he was not far wrong. He turned his back on him and put his lips to Hester's hair. She was still shocked, suffering a strong reaction from what had passed.

The bitter regret which had earlier poured through Jack Cameron overwhelmed him again. His military career was over, his future was dark, and he had been spared by an ex-felon who had somehow managed to earn the sort of love which most men only dreamed of.

What woman would ever kill for him?

Neither Tom nor Hester saw him leave. Hester began to shudder again.

'It's over,' Tom said. 'He's a broken man. He's even left his pistols behind. I'll see that they're returned to him without O'Connell discovering what he tried to do.'

Gradually she quieted under his soothing and stroking hand. Tom's heart was full of love for her, and strangely, in the circumstances, thanksgiving. Not merely for being saved from death, but from what Hester's actions had revealed of her feelings for him.

'Tell me, my love, would you really have killed him? Do you care so much for me? There are times when I fear that all you feel for me is gratitude, that I deceive myself when I think that you can love me—such a brute as I am.'

'Oh, yes,' said Hester, and there was no doubt of the sincerity in her voice. 'I've loved you ever since you walked into the Board Room to interview me. You said that to me in our quarrel, and you were right. I didn't know it then, but I've thought about it since.

'You see, I didn't know what loving someone meant— or being loved for that matter. It was only after we became husband and wife that I began to understand that I had wanted you from the first moment that I saw you in that beautiful waistcoat with the peonies. I thought at first that it was fear that I felt, and then I suddenly knew that it was love—that you had become my world.

'Yes, I would have killed him. *For you, only for you.*'

Tom was silent. She was offering back to him the words which he had used in their quarrel. Head bowed, the words wrenched from him, he said to her what he had thought that he would never say to anyone.

'I don't deserve you, or your love, Hester. I'm a bad man, devious, hard and cruel. Cameron rightly winged me. I shot poor Kaye in the shoulder when he stood helpless before me. I've done other things, even more dreadful.'

'I know that,' she said, simply. 'But it doesn't matter. I love you, and that is all I know and care about. The rest is nothing. I know that you were kind to me in the beginning because it amused you. That was at first. Later, I knew that you loved me, too—as I love you. You changed me, and then you changed as well.'

She stroked his head. 'Why are we talking about this when there is your poor arm to care for? We must look after it at once.'

Tom rose to his feet reluctantly. Their moment out of time was over. His wound was not serious, but did need immediate care.

'You're as practical as ever, my love,' he said, kissing her. 'I'll tell you what to do for my shoulder, and then we'll send for Alan to look after it. He won't talk, or ask awkward questions.'

Hester fetched water and clean linen and cleaned and bound his wound. The ball had not lodged in his shoulder having, by good fortune, missed the bone. Afterwards he lay back in his great chair, drinking the brandy which she had brought him.

For once Tom was less than observant. Pain and shock working on him, disguised from him the fact that Hester, too, was in pain, and that the pain, instead of disappearing, was increasing. The effort of pushing back the heavy chair, and rising so suddenly to confront Jack with his pistol, had brought on a sharp and dreadful pain in her back. She had thought nothing of it at the time, attributing it solely to her violent movement and her ungainly bulk.

Later, when she had fetched a bowl of water to clean

up the blood on the floor and wall, the pain struck again, this time so severely that she had to lean on the big table for support. Had the pain not been in her back she would have known that the baby was beginning to come, but as it was she supposed that it was no more than one of the unpleasant symptoms of her difficult pregnancy.

Until, moving to Tom's side to check on his comfort, she experienced a pain so strong that she clutched at the arm of his chair and let out a strangled cry.

His eyes had closed, but they shot open again, and he caught at her wrist with his good hand.

'Hester? There's something wrong?'

'It's my back,' she told him in a stifled voice. 'I keep getting this dreadful pain.'

Regardless of his shoulder, Tom sprang to his feet. 'Quickly, my dear. When did these pains begin?'

She looked at him, puzzled. 'I wrenched myself when I jumped up to take Jack's pistol, and pushed the chair back so suddenly. But it can't be the baby, Mr Dilhorne. The pain is in the wrong place, and the baby's not yet due— *oh!*'

The pain attacked her with such severity that she half fell against him.

'Oh, but it is the baby, Hester. Quickly, we must get you into bed, and Alan must be sent for at once. If I weren't wounded we might have managed without him. I delivered more than one baby on the transport, and later, but this! Oh, God! We haven't even got a nurse!'

Hester had never seen Tom overwrought before. The pain of his wounded shoulder and his worry for her were taking their toll of him. Nevertheless, he even tried to lift her to carry her up the stairs, but she stopped him.

'Oh, no. I can walk without your help. You mustn't try to do too much, Tom. Think of your poor arm.'

'Damn my poor arm!'

He insisted on helping her up the stairs, holding her to him whenever the pain swept over her, which it did in ever-shortening intervals.

Even in her agony Hester could not help thinking what a comic pair they made: the wounded man and the heavily pregnant woman clumsily mounting the stairs together. Finally Tom manoeuvred her through the bronze doors and on to the bed.

'Stay there,' he told her—as though she could do anything else! 'I'll rouse Miller and send him for Alan. God grant he arrives in time.'

She heard him run downstairs, calling for Miller, Mrs Hackett and the little maid. Why not the cook? Hester thought giddily, and then all thought disappeared and she clutched at the sheet and stuffed it into her mouth.

I will not scream! I will not! The stoicism of her early years was back with her again.

When Tom returned he had put on his fine coat to conceal his bandaged shoulder and was carrying extra towels and sheets.

'Mrs Hackett's boiling water. She seems to think it's the thing. Sit up, and we'll have your clothes off, my love. You said that you wanted me with you when the baby came, and you've got your wish.'

He eased her into her night rail, never mind that his face, like hers, was livid with pain from the efforts of undressing her. He tore up a sheet, dragged one of the great chairs over and tied the ends of the rope he had made from it around one of the arms. He gave her the other end.

'Pull on that when the pains come, my darling. It will help you to bear them.'

Hester looked up at him, her eyes huge, and murmured

weakly before the pain tore at her again. 'Is there anything you cannot do, Mr Dilhorne?'

He held her hand and kissed it. 'I can't bear the pain for you, my love, or I would. It's your first child. Alan always said that they were slow so he should be here in time. Now, you're going to drink this down, Mrs Dilhorne. It'll help with the pain.'

He handed her a glass of unwatered brandy, which she drank obediently, remembering the brandy which they had drunk together on their first night of love.

Then the pain took her again and, between that and the effect of the brandy, past and present became confused so that sometimes she was alone in her room at Mrs Cooke's and sometimes she was with him in the long nights of their loving.

Time crawled by.

Tom stayed with her, wiping her sweating face, even though she scarcely knew that he was there. Once she stirred, caught at his hand and said weakly, 'You'll never know how happy you have made me, Tom.'

There was something in her tone that made it sound as though she were bidding him farewell. He shuddered at the sound. No child was worth the loss of his dearest love and for the first time he contemplated the sterile wasteland of his life if he lost her.

He clutched her hand, and bent his suffering face over it. Mrs Hackett came in with the hot water. For once there was pity on her hard old face, for there was no doubt that he was feeling Hester's suffering keenly. Later she brought him dry towels and fresh candles, and told him to rest a little while she looked after Hester.

Her pains were now coming thick and fast, a sign that the child was ready to be born, but when he propped her up, and called on Mrs Hackett to help with the delivery, nothing happened, even though Hester co-operated with him. He had seen this happen in childbirth before, and it was not a good sign. Just as he was beginning to give up hope he heard the sound of Alan's carriage on the gravel sweep before the house.

Dizzy, almost ready to lose consciousness himself, he ran down the stairs to greet Alan, who had Sarah by his side, for she often acted as his aide in childbirth.

'By God, Alan,' he said before he took him up to the bedroom. 'There's something wrong, if I'm not mistaken.'

'All fathers think that,' was Alan's quiet reply. 'Let me take a look.'

After examining Hester, though, his face was grave, and later, when the child still showed no signs of being born, he began to worry. He had soon seen that Tom was carrying an injury and, leaving Hester with Sarah, he examined his shoulder and told his friend to try to rest.

'No, I can't leave her,' he had panted.

'You can't help her even if you stay with her,' Alan told him quietly. 'I won't disguise the fact that she is very weak and I fear for both her and the child. If it comes to it, do I save the mother or the child?'

Tom turned savagely away from his friend. 'For God's sake, Alan, what a question! The mother, of course. I cannot lose Hester now. You'll never know what she was prepared to do for me tonight.'

'I can guess,' said Alan, who had heard Hester's ramblings. 'I'll do my best for them both—and for you. But the matter is out of my hands. In childbirth God disposes. If matters become desperate I promise to send for you.'

Banished from his Hester, his love, the star by which he lived, so that should she now die, his life would become meaningless, and all that he had striven for would turn to ashes, Tom sat in his chair, his head in his hands.

He had married her almost in jest, thinking that she was just one more possession which he had acquired on his way to power and domination, and now she possessed him. They were twin souls whom an unlikely fate had blessed with one another, and if she were to die now, then what was left for Tom Dilhorne?

Inside the bedroom, Alan and Sarah laboured together to save Hester, if not the baby, for it was, Alan saw quite plainly, coming down to that. Once, Sarah came out to find Tom standing in the corridor, his good shoulder propped against the wall. His face was ghastly.

'Oh, Tom, at least sit down,' she said, shocked by his appearance. 'You are making yourself ill to no purpose.'

He refused.

'No, not whilst Hester is in such agony. Oh, God, Sarah, I'm such a selfish brute and she's such a little thing. She knew how much I wanted a child. Not once in all these months of suffering has she ever complained.'

'Don't give up hope,' said Sarah earnestly. 'Alan thinks that he can save them both. Childbirth is never easy at the best of times.'

'But this is Hester, and I have never cared for anyone else—and there is nothing I can do to help her, nothing. If I could I would bear all her pain, but I can't… It will break my heart to lose her.'

He began to sob, his face in his hands, his body shaking with the violence of his grief.

Sarah had never thought to see hard Tom Dilhorne so broken. She swallowed. 'This is not like you, Tom—that I should have to ask you to be brave.'

'No, I am quite unmanned, as you see.'

He seized her by the wrist with such strength that she almost cried out. 'You must promise me that if things go wrong you will let me in. I must be with her.'

'Of course. You must trust us, Tom. If the worst comes to the worst, then we shall fetch you at once.'

The night wore on. Slowly, Hester began to fail. She had been in pain for so long and was so weak that she started to drift away on a tide of peace where neither pain, nor joy, nor any sensation could reach her.

Her inward Mentor, aroused by Jack Cameron's threats, had helped her at first, but had been silenced by her protracted agony. The claims of will and self were silent, too. Alan, looking down at her, saw what he had sometimes seen before: a look of resigned and accepting peace, and he knew what it meant. He was losing her.

Sarah, on the other side of the bed, saw it, too. Her face a mask of grief, she asked her husband, 'Shall I fetch Tom?'

'No!' exclaimed Alan violently. 'Not yet. I'll not fail them. At least I'll save Hester.'

On hearing Tom's name Hester's eyes had fluttered open, only to close again.

Alan, bent down, put his hands under Hester's armpits, lifted her into a sitting position on the bed, and placed a bolster in the small of her back.

'Hester!' he said urgently. 'Look at me.'

Her eyes opened. He willed them not to close.

'Do as I tell you. For Tom and the baby.'

Tom and the baby, her Mentor whispered, suddenly coming to life again. Think of Tom and the baby. Don't sleep. To sleep is to die. Remember, Hester, Tom and the baby. You do want to see the baby—and to see Tom with the baby, don't you?

At first Hester wanted to ignore the urgent voice. To awake, to return to life, meant pain and suffering. All that she wanted was peace—and freedom from pain. Tom would not want her to suffer.

The voice came again, louder and stronger. Think of Tom and the baby—you don't want to leave him alone, do you? Remember how much you love him.

'Yes,' she replied in a voice so weak that Alan could hardly hear her. 'I do remember. I want to see Tom again—and the baby.'

'Take Sarah's hands in yours,' said Allan, meeting her eyes which now seemed to recognise that he was there, 'and when the next pain comes, don't reject it, don't ignore it. Scream, Hester, scream as loudly as you can. Accept the pain, ride with it, and then I can help you.'

Even as he spoke the pain came again, so strong that it seemed to rise from the depth of her being. So powerful was it that Hester felt that she was being torn in two. Her scream was her first; as Alan said later, it was her stoicism which had been destroying her. The scream contained the same anguish as the one she had made when she had thought that Jack Cameron had killed Tom.

Outside, Tom put his face in his hands at the sound.

Inside, Sarah was dragged towards Hester by the strength of her grip.

Alan shouted, 'Good! And again!' seeing the next spasm strike her. 'You're nearly there. Push, Hester, push with all your strength.'

This time she pushed but did not scream, feeling a terrible relief which Alan shared with her in a different way, when a tiny, black-haired child shot into the world, to land on the bed between her legs, squalling defiance.

Alan, after handing the baby to Sarah, turned back to care for Hester, only to cry out, 'By God! There are two!'

A sandy head had appeared to signal the reason for Hester's size, her weakness and the prolonged labour.

The second child was born without difficulty. Sarah wiped Hester's sweating face again and placed the first baby on her right arm. Alan lifted the other, still wet, and also squalling loudly, on to her left.

'Two,' said Hester with wonder. The joy of the birth, successfully achieved, was filling her. Her poor bruised body and her dreadful weakness were to be accepted, not given in to, or resented, for they had brought her this prize.

'Two, you clever girl,' said Alan, 'and both boys.'

'No wonder I was like an elephant,' sighed Hester weakly. 'Two little Toms. Does he know? Oh, I must show him.'

'Alan will fetch him,' said Sarah.

'And you are not to tell him that there are two,' said Hester with a touch of her old mischief.

Alan, Sarah and Hester were to say afterwards that the only time that they ever saw Tom Dilhorne disconcerted was when Hester showed him their twin sons, saying, 'Tom and Alan.'

He stared at the two angry boys, shouting their fury at leaving the warm haven of their mother's body.

But, being Tom, he recovered quickly, as he always did.

'Compound interest, Hester, my darling. You said that you knew all about percentages when we first met.'

Finally, when Alan and Sarah gave him the two howling boys to hold for a moment, he said to the room at large, 'Dilhorne and Sons, Hester, Dilhorne and Sons.'

\*     \*     \*     \*     \*

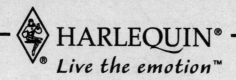

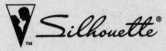

# HARLEQUIN®
## *Presents*

The world's bestselling romance series...
The series that brings you your favorite authors,
month after month:

Helen Bianchin...Emma Darcy
Lynne Graham...Penny Jordan
Miranda Lee...Sandra Marton
Anne Mather...Carole Mortimer
Susan Napier...Michelle Reid

## and many more uniquely talented authors!

Wealthy, powerful, gorgeous men...
Women who have feelings just like your own...
The stories you love, set in exotic, glamorous locations...

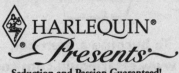

# HARLEQUIN®
## *Presents*

**Seduction and Passion Guaranteed!**

HPDIR104

**SILHOUETTE Romance**

From first love to forever, these love stories
are fairy tale romances for today's woman.

**Silhouette Desire**

Modern, passionate reads that are powerful and provocative.

**Silhouette SPECIAL EDITION**

Emotional, compelling stories that capture the intensity
of living, loving and creating a family in today's world.

**Silhouette INTIMATE MOMENTS**

A roller-coaster read that delivers romantic thrills
in a world of suspense, adventure and more.

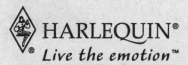